"The Klingons have responded, sir," Garrison said. "They're warning us not to interfere."

"And?" Pike prompted.

"That's it, sir. They're telling us to mind our own business . . . or else."

Now, that sounds like the Klingons, Pike thought. He didn't doubt that Garrison was accurately conveying the gist of the communication. *So now what I am supposed to do?*

"I am detecting two life-forms aboard the *Ilion,*" Spock added. "Humanoid, and growing weaker."

"Cyprian?" Pike asked, recalling the ship's alleged origin.

"Possibly," Spock replied, "but *Ilion*'s engine is approaching critical. It will explode in approximately four minutes, possibly sooner."

"Chris," Boyce said urgently, standing anxiously beside the captain's chair. "We can't let them die."

"And we're not going to," Pike said, reaching a decision. He stabbed the intercom button on his armrest. "Captain to transporter room. Lock onto both life-signs aboard the Cyprian vessel and beam them aboard . . . quickly, before it's too late."

STAR TREK®

THE ORIGINAL SERIES

CHILD OF TWO WORLDS

Greg Cox

Based upon *Star Trek*
created by Gene Roddenberry

POCKET BOOKS

New York   London   Toronto   Sydney   New Delhi

Pocket Books
An Imprint of Simon & Schuster, Inc.
1230 Avenue of the Americas
New York, NY 10020

This book is a work of fiction. Any references to historical events, real people, or real places are used fictitiously. Other names, characters, places, and events are products of the author's imagination, and any resemblance to actual events or places or persons, living or dead, is entirely coincidental.

First Pocket Books paperback edition December 2015

POCKET and colophon are registered trademarks of Simon & Schuster, Inc.

For information about special discounts for bulk purchases, please contact Simon & Schuster Special Sales at 1-866-506-1949 or business@simonandschuster.com.

The Simon & Schuster Speakers Bureau can bring authors to your live event. For more information or to book an event, contact the Simon & Schuster Speakers Bureau at 1-866-248-3049 or visit our website at www.simonspeakers.com.

Manufactured in the United States of America

10 9 8 7 6 5 4 3 2 1

ISBN 978-1-4767-8325-3
ISBN 978-1-4767-8327-7 (ebook)

Dedicated to Leonard Nimoy,
for nearly fifty years of inspiration

Prologue

"Make a wish," his mother said.

Seven candles burned atop the cake, despite the fact that neither light nor heat was required under the present circumstances. An overhanging eave provided shade from the noonday sun as Spock and his mother occupied a carved sandstone balcony overlooking the family estate on the outskirts of ShiKahr. In the distance, beyond the gates, rocky plains stretched all the way to the forbidding granite mountains looming on the horizon beneath a cloudless orange sky. The day was exceedingly warm, even by Vulcan standards. A *le-matya* howled ferociously somewhere in the hills.

"Wishes are illogical," Spock said.

The boy sat across from his mother at an elegantly wrought marble table that seemed to flow upward from the tiled floor of the balcony. He wore a lightweight white linen robe that he liked to think made him look more adult . . . and Vulcan. Wary eyes regarded the frosted chocolate cake with suspicion, as though it was a trick intended to lure him from his chosen path. His mother was an excellent cook, however, and he had to admit that the cake appeared appetizing, even with the absurd and unnecessary candles dripping wax onto the icing.

"I know," his mother replied patiently, as she often did. A silken wimple helped to shield her delicate human features from the searing Vulcan sun. A lock of auburn hair escaped the edge of the headdress and she deftly tucked it back into place. Hazel eyes gazed affectionately at her son. "It's simply a human custom."

"But it makes no sense even as superstition," he protested. "There is no internal logic or consistency. What does the blowing out of candles have to do with the granting of wishes, even if such things were possible? How is extinguishing combustion intended to produce the desired effect?"

"It's not meant to make sense," she said, attempting to explain. "Think of it as a meditative exercise, for the purpose of focusing one's attention on one's own needs and desires." She contemplated the boy, whose stoic expression gave away little of his inner feelings. "Isn't there anything you wish for, Spock, even it's not entirely logical?"

He pondered the question. It was true that he aspired to prove himself in the *kahs-wan*, the traditional survival test expected of all Vulcan youths of his age. His own time of testing would be upon him soon, but he knew that, ultimately, the outcome would be decided solely by his abilities, not any private hopes or fears. He could think of only one honest answer to his mother's query.

"I wish not to disappoint you and Father."

She reached across the table and placed her hand gently over his. "You could never disappoint me, Spock."

"Even if I do not blow out the candles?" He allowed his mother's hand to rest atop his; as human gestures of affection went, it was an easy lapse to overlook. "Or embrace similar human customs and rituals?"

This was becoming a frequent dilemma for him, and ever more so as he grew older and was expected to gain greater mastery of his shameful human emotions. Although he was determined to prove himself as Vulcan as any of his peers, none of whom had ever taken any note of his birthday, he did not wish his mother to think that he thought any less of her because of her humanity; she was merely being true to her own nature, as was only logical. He knew that his mother had baked the cake with her own hands, as she did every year, and that it would please her if he finally welcomed the gesture. Although his father was away on an important diplomatic mission, Spock could all too easily imagine Sarek watching silently in judgment, waiting sternly to see if Spock strayed from the way of his Vulcan forefathers. He saw his father sighing and shaking his head.

"Would that truly be so terrible, Spock?" his mother asked. "Enjoying a harmless human tradition?" He thought he detected a note of sadness in her voice. "Part of you is human, Spock. You will always be a child of two worlds."

"You are mistaken," he replied, as gently as he could. "I am and always will be Vulcan."

"Very well, then. If that is your choice."

She leaned forward and blew out the candles herself. Seven tiny flames flickered and died.

Spock experienced an all-too-familiar twinge of guilt, which required effort to suppress. His mother was human after all, which meant that she had feelings to hurt.

"Did . . . did you make a wish?" he asked.

She nodded. "I did."

"And may I ask what it was?"

She gave him a bittersweet smile. "I wished what all mothers wish: for you to find peace and happiness, no matter what path you choose."

He could hardly begrudge her such a selfless wish. "And long life and prosperity?"

"That too," she said.

A dry desert breeze carried the aroma of the cake to his nostrils. He thought of all the effort she had clearly put into it, and on his behalf.

"It would be illogical to let this cake go to waste," he observed. "May we eat now?"

Her smile brightened.

"Absolutely." She cut him a large slice and placed it on a plate, which she slid across the table to him. "Help yourself."

Spock allowed himself a taste, merely for his mother's sake, of course.

But he was glad that his father was not there to watch.

One

"Rigelian fever, Captain. There's no doubt about it."

Spock overheard the doctor's report from his station on the bridge of the *U.S.S Enterprise*. The young science officer listened intently while simultaneously monitoring sensor readings of the surrounding space. As the ship was presently conducting a routine survey of an uninhabited star system, no other urgent matters required his attention. He suspected that the rest of the bridge crew was also paying close attention to the conversation in the command well.

"How bad is it?" Captain Christopher Pike asked, getting straight to the point. Still in the prime of life, he was a fit Earthman of North American descent, with an athletic build, dark hair, and icy blue eyes that conveyed both keen intelligence and concern. His gold command turtleneck uniform contrasted with the blue science tunic Spock wore. A strong chin rested thoughtfully on his knuckles. "How many crew members are affected?"

"It's spreading fast," Doctor Phillip Boyce said gravely. The older man, clad in a standard blue medical jumpsuit, stood by the captain's chair at the center of the bridge. Thinning silver hair and lean, deeply lined features betrayed that he was approaching retirement age, at least by human standards. An Earth symbol was emblazoned over his heart, indicating that he had received the bulk of his medical training on his home planet. "My sickbay is filling up and more crew members are showing symptoms by the hour. I've instituted standard quarantine procedures, but I'm afraid that amounts to locking the barn door after the horse has already bolted. We could be looking at a full-fledged outbreak here."

"Damn," Pike muttered under his breath. A serious expression grew even more somber. "Can you treat it, Doctor?"

"I'm trying," Boyce said, "but this appears to be an unusually virulent new strain of the disease, which is proving resistant to conventional treatment." He shook his head ruefully. "I might as well be handing out sugar pills . . . or martinis."

Pike nodded. "What about unconventional treatments?"

"Funny you should ask," Boyce answered. "I've been scouring the medical literature—in my copious spare time, of course—and there are reports of a radical new treatment that has yielded some promising results so far. It's highly experimental, though, and has barely begun clinical trials on humans." He frowned. "I'd hate to turn our crew into guinea pigs."

Spock understood that Boyce was not speaking of a literal metamorphosis, but was merely employing a quaint human idiom. He made a mental note to review the relevant literature on this new treatment at the first opportunity. Medicine was a science, despite the doctor's occasional protestations to the contrary, and biochemistry was but one of many disciplines in which Spock prided himself on being well-versed.

"We may have no other choice, Doctor." Pike glanced toward the navigation station. "Mister Tyler, how far to the nearest Starfleet medical facility?"

Spock had already performed the necessary calculations in his head, but let Lieutenant José Tyler carry out his duties. Years of serving aboard the *Enterprise* had taught Spock that humans sometimes reacted negatively to being "shown up" by another, particularly where their own responsibilities and fields of expertise were concerned. It was an illogical and emotional response—data was data after all—but, in this instance, there appeared to be no compelling reason to answer the captain's query before Tyler did. The young Earthman was a skilled and highly capable navigator. An extra moment would make no significant difference.

"Starbase 17 is closest," Tyler reported promptly. Blond hair and boyish features made him seem even more youthful than his actual years. "But even at top speed, it will take us weeks to get there."

Four point zero eight weeks, Spock thought. *To be precise.*

"Weeks we may not have," Boyce said. "We haven't lost any crew members yet, but you know how nasty Rigelian fever can be if not treated. It can go from basic to pneumonic to septic in a matter of days, leading to shock, seizures, and eventually death."

"You don't have to paint a picture for me, Doctor," Pike said. "All right, then. What do you need to carry out this experimental new treatment, if necessary?"

"That's where it gets tricky," Boyce confessed. "The treatment requires significant quantities of a rare mineral substance called *ryetalyn,* which is not commonly found on Federation starships . . . or most anywhere else for that matter."

"So where can we get our hands on some of this . . . ryetalyn?" Pike asked, trying out the unfamiliar word. He had never heard of this mineral before, despite all his years exploring the stars.

"The devil if I know," Boyce said. "Did I mention it was rare?"

"A search of the ship's computer libraries may yield the nearest source of the mineral," Number

One suggested from her post at the helm. A dark-haired Illyrian woman whose cool composure and formidable intelligence often reminded Spock of his own people, the *Enterprise*'s first officer turned her gaze toward the science station. "Mister Spock?"

"The computer is processing the request," said Spock, who had already initiated a search of that nature. A hard-copy printout issued from the computer terminal, and Spock swiftly scanned the document. "According to past surveys of this sector, ryetalyn can be found on Cypria III, an alien colony precisely 61.09 hours from our present location."

"Good work, Mister Spock," the captain said. "So what do we know about this place?"

Spock called up a full report on the planet, and was preparing to summarize it, but Number One spoke up first, rendering his efforts redundant.

"Cypria III is a Class-M planet colonized by a humanoid species over a century ago, not long before its parent world abandoned its expansionist space program following a period of political and economic turmoil. The future Cyprians, in particular, emigrated in search of a younger and less developed world that was in a more natural state, as opposed to the heavily mechanized and industrialized culture that had overrun their homeworld. Although they maintain cultural ties to their planet of origin, the Cyprians have been largely independent for generations—and inclined to remain so. Their infrequent encounters with Starfleet have been peaceful to date, but they have expressed little interest in joining the Federation. Deeply attached to their adopted world and its rich natural bounty, they seldom venture beyond their own system and have no significant space force to speak of."

Pike regarded her with a bemused expression. "And you knew all that off the top of your head?"

"I have an eidetic memory," she reminded him. "And I endeavor to be informed on the regions of space through which we travel."

"Of course." Pike cracked a rare smile. "I expect nothing less from you, Number One."

Spock was impressed as well. Not for the first time, he reflected that the first officer would fit in well on Vulcan, perhaps even better than he did. He felt a twinge of envy, laced with a certain bitterness, but dismissed the emotion as unworthy of his Vulcan heritage and training. He could not allow his human side to distract him from his duty. The ship needed him to be at his best.

"Captain," he said. "You should be aware that Cypria III is located near territory presently claimed by the Klingon Empire." He called up a star map that appeared upon the main viewer at the front of the bridge. Dotted lines indicated areas of Klingon influence, while an illuminated yellow circle represented the Cyprian star system. "The precise borders are disputed, but, as you can see, Cypria III is less than a light-year beyond the edge of the contested region."

"Terrific," Pike muttered with what Spock recognized as sarcasm. "And what are the Cyprians' relations with the Klingons like?"

"Frosty," Number One said. "As noted before, the Cyprians value their independence. They are no more interested in becoming vassals of the Empire than they are in joining the Federation, although their uncomfortable proximity to the Klingons may be another reason they've kept the Federation at arm's length to date. Joining the Federation might be seen as a provocative act by their Klingon neighbors. Better for all concerned, perhaps, if Cypria maintains its neutrality where the Klingons and the Federation are concerned."

"A logical policy," Spock observed, appreciating the colony's position. "Positioned between two superpowers, Cypria is well-advised not to take sides."

Although the Klingons had yet to start a war with the Federation, as the Romulans had done nearly a century ago, relations between Starfleet and the Klingons had been growing steadily more confrontational over the last several years, as both parties expanded outward across the galaxy and extended their realms of influence. The Klingons, in particular, tended to be very territorial when it came to vast swaths of space. There were those who said that war was inevitable, perhaps in less than a decade, although Pike wanted to think that peace was always a possibility.

"Well," Pike said, "let's hope that neutrality doesn't extend to denying us assistance during a medical emergency, and that the Klingons feel the same way." The map on the screen gave way to a view of the stars ahead. "Mister Tyler, set a course for Cypria III, but let's stay well clear of that blurry border."

"Aye, sir," the navigator said.

"Speed, Captain?" Number One asked from the helm.

Pike glanced at Boyce, whose grim countenance conveyed a definite sense of urgency.

"Engage hyperdrive," the captain said. "Warp factor seven."

"Yes, sir." She peered into the gooseneck viewer at her station and waved her hand over the helm controls, which responded to her precise gestures. "Warp factor seven."

The *Enterprise*'s powerful warp engines activated, distorting space-time to propel the ship far beyond the speed of light. Within moments, they had left the unexplored solar system far behind and were hurling through deep space toward the Cyprian system. Spock's keen ears heard a crewman coughing hoarsely over by the engineering station. Glancing across the bridge, he saw that Ensign Hawass looked pale and feverish. The man's hands trembled as they passed over his control panel. His breathing was labored.

Alert to the crewman's distress, Pike swiftly relieved Hawass from duty and ordered him to sickbay, but it was clear that quarantine measures had indeed proved ineffective. The fever was at loose aboard the *Enterprise*, and not even the bridge was safe.

Pike frowned as he watched Hawass exit via the turbolift.

"What was that you were saying about barn doors, Doctor?"

———

"You asked to see me, Captain?"

Spock entered the briefing room to find Captain Pike reviewing a stack of status reports on the ship's systems. Pike's preference for hard-copy documents was a personal eccentricity the crew had come to indulge, despite the fact that printed reports were clearly destined for obsolescence. Spock did not fault the captain for this singular predilection; in the four years that he had served under Pike, he had never observed the captain's fondness for print to have any impact on his judgment or leadership abilities. Pike's command was exemplary.

"That's right, Mister Spock." Pike looked up from his papers and gestured toward an empty chair. "Make yourself comfortable."

Spock took a seat at the conference table. The viewscreen at the end of table currently displayed images of the colony on Cypria III from past Starfleet expeditions to the planet. A large urban metropolis indicated an advanced and thriving civilization, with technology comparable to the Federation's. Skyscrapers and maglev train tracks denoted both prosperity and progress. Lush greenery testified to the planet's flourishing ecosystem. Spock found it unsurprising that most Cyprians saw little need to leave their world, which appeared generously well-suited to humanoid life.

"Does this concern the present medical emergency?" he asked. "I've taken the liberty of familiarizing myself with—"

"I'm sure you have," Pike interrupted, "but hold that thought. We're still nearly a day away from Cypria III, so I wanted to take advantage of this lull to discuss another matter with you."

Spock had reported to the briefing room directly from the bridge, where Number One was presently in command. He wondered what this was about.

"You have my full attention, sir."

"I would be stunned to hear otherwise," Pike said, sounding amused for reasons Spock couldn't quite isolate. The human sense of humor often resisted easy analysis. "You're familiar with the *U.S.S. Intrepid*, of course."

"Naturally," Spock replied. The *Intrepid* was a *Constitution*-class starship manned by an all-Vulcan crew. It was felt by most Vulcans that a homogenous crew was the most logical choice, promoting greater efficiency and cohesion. A crew sharing the same background, culture, environmental preferences, and, of course, a commitment to logic above all else was bound to function better as a unit—or so the theory went.

Granted, it could be argued that such homogeneity ran counter to the ancient principle of IDIC, which exalted infinite diversity in infinite combinations, but most Vulcans felt that holding fast to their own time-honored customs and traditions in no way excluded respecting the ways of other species and civilizations. Vulcans had never sought to impose their own logic on others, no matter how rigorously Vulcans themselves were expected to adhere to the teachings of Surak, and regardless of how manifestly obvious it was that the Vulcan way was preferable. If there was an inherent contradiction between prizing homogeneity *and* diversity, it was one that most Vulcans managed to reconcile without too much effort.

But Spock was not like most Vulcans.

"A position as first officer has opened up aboard the *Intrepid*," Pike disclosed. "I'd be sorry to lose you, but I'd be remiss if I didn't inform you of this opportunity. It would mean a promotion for you, as

well as opportunity to be among your own people."
He chuckled softly. "I can't imagine it's always easy
for you, rubbing shoulders with us shamelessly
emotional humans day after day."

It can be challenging, Spock admitted to himself. He thought back to that earlier moment on
the bridge when he'd held his tongue regarding the
distance to Cypria III to avoid bruising Lieutenant
Tyler's ego and feelings. Accommodating and making allowances for his crewmates' volatile emotions
and frequent lapses of logic had become a routine
part of his daily existence, like the constant pull
of a heavy-gravity planet that one gradually learns
to live with, despite the perpetual strain on one's
system. It might be a relief, in that respect, to dwell
among Vulcans again. He would no longer have a
constant barrage of emotional displays chipping
away at his own hard-won self-control. He could
just be Spock, one Vulcan among many, and not *the*
Vulcan aboard the ship.

Then again, there were reasons that he had left
Vulcan and joined Starfleet in the first place . . .

"I hope that I have not given you any reason
to believe that I am dissatisfied with my posting
aboard the *Enterprise*," Spock said. "Or with my fellow crew members."

"Not at all," Pike assured him. "I'm only thinking of your own best interests here. You deserve to
know what your options are."

"Thank you, Captain."

Spock found himself oddly conflicted by this unexpected turn of events. Usually when faced with a choice, he could readily determine the logical course of action, but at this moment he truly did not know what to think. At present he was third in command aboard the *Enterprise,* after the captain and Number One; strictly from the standpoint of career advancement, the decision was obvious. Nor did he have any doubts about his ability to fulfill the duties of first officer. He deemed himself both ready and able to take on a position of greater responsibility and authority. Advancing to first officer aboard another *Constitution*-class starship was the next logical step.

And yet . . .

"You will always be a child of two worlds," his mother had once said. The words came back to him now as he contemplated the choice before him. What was preferable: to be the only Vulcan among a crew of humans, or the only half-human aboard a ship of Vulcans?

"With your permission, sir, I think it best to meditate on the matter rather than make a hasty decision. May I give you my answer shortly, perhaps after the present crisis has been resolved?"

This was a logical approach, so why did it feel like he was stalling?

"By all means, Mister Spock. Take your time.

I suspect we're going to have our hands full soon enough." He looked Spock squarely in the eye. "Just know that you have my full support whatever you decide, and you can count on a glowing recommendation should you choose to apply for the post aboard the *Intrepid*."

"Again, my thanks, Captain."

"You're welcome, Lieutenant." He sifted through the reports before him. "Let's talk again later . . . assuming any of us survive this damn fever, that is."

The control console on the table chimed urgently, signaling a transmission from the bridge. Spock routed the signal to the viewscreen, where Number One's image promptly appeared. The familiar steel-gray confines of the bridge could be spied in the background.

"Pike here," the captain said crisply. "What is it, Number One?"

"A complication, sir. We've received what appears to be a distress signal . . . from Klingon space."

Spock raised an eyebrow. Calling such news a complication was an understatement, to say the least. Pike rose immediately to his feet, worry written on his face.

"We're on our way, Number One. Pike out."

Spock hurried after the captain.

Two

Pike marched briskly onto the bridge, followed closely by Spock, who had ridden up in the turbolift with him. "Captain on the bridge," Number One announced as she surrendered the captain's chair to him, returning to her regular post at the helm controls. Pike took his seat while Spock reported to the science station. Pike noted that Boyce had beaten them to the bridge, no doubt responding to the emergency as well. He hoped the doctor's services would not be required.

"All right," Pike said. "Fill me in."

"Aye, sir," Chief Petty Officer Garrison reported from the communications station. A stolid, brown-haired Starfleet veteran, he had come up through the ranks to attain his current position. Pike knew him to be steady and reliable, even in a crisis. "The signal is coming from a Cyprian trading vessel, the *Ilion*, en route from a star system presently under the control of the Klingons. Details are sketchy, but the nature of the signal indicates that the ship is in serious jeopardy."

"Have you communicated directly with the *Ilion*'s captain or crew?" Pike asked.

"No, sir. I've tried hailing them, but no response yet. Only an automated emergency beacon, repeating over and over."

"Understood," Pike said. "Keep trying, Mister Garrison."

"Aye, Captain."

Just for a moment, Pike flashed back to the bogus "distress signal" that had lured the *Enterprise* to Talos IV not very long ago, but he quickly pushed those troubling memories aside. He had more pressing matters to deal with now.

Two of them, in fact.

First the fever, now this, he thought. *Even in deep space, it never rains but it pours.*

"A Cyprian trader?" He glanced at Number One. "I thought you said the Cyprians never left their home planet?"

"I said 'seldom,' Captain," she reminded him. "And most Cyprians don't. This trader is obviously an exception."

So it appears, Pike thought, wishing that the adventurous trader had stayed home. "Time to intercept?"

"Roughly five hours, sir," Tyler answered, as though he'd anticipated the captain's query. "But it means detouring from our present course to Cypria III . . . and bringing us within spitting distance of the Klingon border."

Damn, Pike thought. Even without the Klingons to factor in, the timing of this emergency could not be worse. Boyce needed his ryetalyn to begin treating the crew and every delay gave the fever more time to spread throughout the ship, yet they could hardly ignore a ship in distress. That went against his every instinct as a captain and Starfleet officer.

"Duly noted, Mister Tyler, but our duty is clear. Plot an intercept course with the *Ilion.*" He glanced over at the comm station. "Mister Garrison, signal the *Ilion* that we're on our way."

"Aye, sir," the enlisted man said.

Boyce joined Pike in the command well. Pike noted that the doctor looked rather older and more haggard than usual, as though he was already worn out from dealing with the flood of fever patients into his sickbay. Boyce leaned wearily against the sturdy dark gray safety rail circling the command area. He didn't say anything, but Pike knew Boyce had to be distressed by this unexpected turn of events. White knuckles gripped the handle of a portable medkit, while the doctor's jaw tightened. He seemed to be biting back a complaint.

"Sorry, Doctor," Pike said, "but I'm afraid you're going to have to wait a little longer for that ryetalyn."

"So it seems," Boyce muttered unhappily. "Mind you, I can't fault you for responding to an SOS—I'd probably do the same if I was in your shoes—but this is time we can ill afford to lose. I'm doing what I can to slow the progress of the fever but, at the rate things are going, people are going to be dying by the end of the week. I'm trying to put out a forest fire without water."

Number One spoke up from the helm. "Captain, a suggestion. Why don't I take a shuttle to Cypria III to obtain the ryetalyn while the *Enterprise* continues on to assist the *Ilion*. We can rendezvous later, after you have dealt with whatever emergency has befallen the Cyprian vessel."

"You know, that's not a bad idea," Boyce said to Pike. "Time is of the essence if we're to avoid becoming a plague ship, so the sooner we get that ryetalyn, the better. If nothing else, Number One can make contact with the Cyprians and get the ball rolling, so that the ryetalyn will be processed and ready for us when we're done with this rescue mission."

Assuming the Cyprians are cooperative, Pike thought, *which isn't necessarily a sure thing.*

But that was a bridge they'd have to cross if they came to it. At present, Number One's suggestion sounded like their best bet for getting the ryetalyn in a timely fashion.

"Let's do it," he decided, glancing at Boyce. "What about you, Doctor? Do you have to accompany her to the colony?"

Boyce shook his head. "I can be more useful

here, dealing with my patients in sickbay. Plus, you may need me on hand to deal with any casualties from the *Ilion*." He turned toward the helm. "I can brief Number One on what I need to carry out the treatment."

"Just inform me of what you require, Doctor," she said, rising from her seat. A thought creased her brow. "I do have one concern. Is there any danger of spreading the infection to Cypria III? I would not want my landing party to become a vector for disease."

"That shouldn't be an issue," Boyce assured her. "The Cyprians are humanoid, but not human. By all accounts, they're immune to Rigelian fever. Nevertheless, we should take the reasonable precaution of screening you and the rest of your party to make sure that none of you are infected yet."

Pike agreed. "See to it, Doctor."

"I am certain you will find me quite free of contagion," Number One stated confidently. "My immune system is, as you know, exceptional."

Pike believed it. "Number One" was not just her rank. It was a description that had fit her perfectly even before she was named first in her class at Starfleet Academy four years in a row. The Illyrians were a people who aspired to excellence, physically and mentally, and the *Enterprise*'s first officer was a prodigy even by the standards of her own perfectionist kind, who practiced a form of selective breeding just short of genetic manipulation. She had always been "Number One" at everything: studies, athletics, you name it. Her superior intelligence and rigorous self-discipline could be, frankly, a bit intimidating at times, but Pike knew he was lucky to have her as his executive officer. He trusted her implicitly. If anybody could get that ryetalyn in time, she could.

"Just the same," he said, "get yourself and your team checked out before you go."

"Of course, Captain," she agreed readily. "A prudent precaution." She turned over the helm to Lieutenant Sita Mohindas, who was standing by to relieve her. "Well, Doctor, shall we get to it? Time is short, after all."

Pike trusted Number One to pick out her own team, including a couple of security officers. The Cyprians were supposed to be friendly enough, but it always paid to be cautious when visiting an alien world. He'd been brutally reminded of that on Rigel VII, at the cost of three lives. The deaths of those crew members still weighed heavily on him.

"Good luck, Number One, and be careful."

"I always am, sir." A hint of a smile lifted the corners of her lips. "Give my apologies to the Klingons, should you encounter them."

"Here's hoping that won't be necessary," Pike replied.

The turbolift carried her and Boyce away, and

Pike hit the intercom button on his armrest. "Captain to hangar deck. Prepare *Kepler* for immediate departure."

The *Kepler* was one of the *Enterprise*'s two shuttlecrafts. He wanted the shuttle ready to launch as soon as Boyce gave the landing party the thumbs-up, before the *Enterprise*'s detour took them too far off their course for Cypria III. The shuttles were capable of warp speed, but, given the ticking clock in sickbay, every light-year counted.

He turned his attention back to the crisis at hand. "Mister Garrison, any word from the *Ilion* on the nature of their emergency?"

"Negative, sir," the man reported. "Sorry, Captain."

Pike frowned. As captain he was responsible for the lives and safety of more than two hundred crew members serving under his command, and he didn't like putting them at risk with so little information to go on. *I'd feel a damn sight better about answering that SOS,* he thought, *if I had a better idea of what was waiting for us down the road—practically in the Klingons' backyard.*

An epidemic was bad enough. He didn't want to butt heads with the Empire, too.

Three

"Captain!" Garrison called out. "The *Ilion* is being pursued by the Klingons!"

Pike sat up straight in his chair. Hours had passed since the *Kepler* had left for Cypria III in search of the ryetalyn. The *Enterprise*, racing at top speed, had made good time responding to the *Ilion*'s distress signal, but just what sort of conflict were they flying into here?

"Give me more, Mister Garrison," Pike ordered. "What are you picking up?"

"I'm intercepting messages from the Klingons to the *Ilion*, sir. They're demanding that the *Ilion* lower its shields and surrender."

Surrender? Pike thought. *That doesn't sound like the Klingons.*

"Any response from the *Ilion*?"

"No, Captain." Garrison fiddled with his earpiece. "Only the same urgent distress signal."

Just our luck, Pike thought. He had hoped that they could affect a rescue and get in and out of this region quickly, without encountering any Klingons, but apparently that wasn't in the cards. The *Enterprise* was already on the fringes of the disputed space claimed by the Empire. He would have to tread carefully here to avoid provoking an armed confrontation—or starting a war.

"Visual?" he asked.

"Coming within range, Captain," Spock reported from the science station. He passed his hand over the controls. "Increasing magnification now."

The *Ilion* appeared on the viewer, small and blurry at first, but rapidly sharpening into focus. Only slightly larger than a Starfleet shuttlecraft, it resembled a rust-colored egg with short stubby wings above its glowing cobalt nacelles. Its smooth, streamlined contours, well-suited to flying through planetary atmospheres as well as deep space, matched the profile for Cyprian spacecraft found in the *Enterprise*'s computer libraries, although some of the outer fittings appeared to have been refurbished from other vessels. A second-hand hydrogen intake unit looked distinctly Regulan in origin, while the meteoroid sensor showed evidence of Tellarite design. Hull panels of varying hue, texture, and newness, as well as other replacement parts and signs of general wear and tear, suggested that the rugged little vessel had been around the block a few times and seen better days, even before it ran afoul of some irate Klingons.

And those Klingons had obviously gotten a

few licks in already, despite the *Ilion*'s evasive maneuvers. Fresh scorch marks blackened the wings, telling Pike that the Klingons had attempted to disable the *Ilion*'s compact warp nacelles. Vapors vented from hairline fractures in the hull, while the ship's overtaxed shields were flickering visibly, on the verge of failing completely. Flashing traceries of bright blue Cherenkov radiation revealed a worryingly patchy deflector grid around the embattled ship, enough to keep its passengers from being snagged by Klingon transporter beams, perhaps, but not enough to withstand a concentrated attack. The *Ilion* zigzagged toward the *Enterprise*, veering erratically from port to starboard and up and down, in a last-ditch attempt to evade another hit from the Klingons. It rolled and banked as though piloted by a lunatic—or someone with nothing left to lose.

Clearly that distress signal had been no false alarm.

"Whoa," Lieutenant Mohindas exclaimed at helm. A slim, dark-haired woman who hailed from the Delhi city-state, she was an excellent pilot and all-around officer. "What do you think they did to upset the Klingons?"

"Breathe?" Tyler suggested, sitting beside her at the nav controls. "Since when do Klingons need a reason to go on the warpath?"

Pike noted the crew members' remarks. Under ordinary circumstances, he would caution Tyler against stereotyping an entire alien species, but this time he let it pass. The Klingons *were* quick to anger—and nobody you wanted to run up against in a dark corner of space. If there was a way to get along peacefully with the Empire, the Federation sure hadn't found it yet.

He regarded the wounded ship on the viewer. The closer it got, even more damage caught Pike's eye. Cracks threatened the structural integrity of the *Ilion*'s tinted forward viewing port. Sparks sprayed from the laboring nacelles, flaring brightly before being snuffed out by the vacuum. Charred bits of plating went flying off into space, along with clouds of ash and smoke. It became harder to tell if the ship's erratic course was an evasive maneuver or simply a loss of navigational control. *Ilion*'s shields were shredding faster than solar sails in an ion storm. From the looks of things, the *Enterprise* had arrived just in time.

But to do what?

"The Klingon vessel is coming into view," Spock reported, peering into the gooseneck monitor at his station. "It appears to be a D-5 battle cruiser."

An image on the viewer confirmed Spock's readings. Pike's jaw tightened at the daunting sight of the immense vessel chasing after the *Ilion*. Its bulbous command pod thrust aggressively ahead of its massive engineering hull, which consisted of two downward-pointing wings. A deceptively fragile-looking neck connected the prow of the ship to the aft section, while Pike's gaze was drawn to the disruptor cannons tucked beneath its wings and the photon torpedo launcher mounted in the bottom half of the command hull, below the bridge. The battle cruiser was a formidable warship, comparable in size and strength to the *Enterprise*, at least according to Starfleet Intelligence. Pike was in no hurry to test the accuracy of that assessment.

"Raise shields," he ordered. "Full strength."

Unlike the *Enterprise*, the *Ilion* was clearly no match for the battle cruiser. Pike was impressed that it was still in one piece. Granted, it was keeping one step ahead of the Klingons now, relying on its speed and evasiveness to stay intact, but the battle cruiser had enough firepower to blast it to atoms with just one shot. How had it managed to last this long?

"Interesting," Spock observed, as though wondering the same thing. "The Klingons appear intent on capturing the *Ilion* rather than destroying it."

Disruptor fire, bright as emeralds against the darkness of the void, sprayed from the battle cruiser's weapons ports. Bolts of destructive energy passed above and around the *Ilion*, missing the endangered vessel by mere kilometers. A close call, Pike noted, but maybe not as close as one might expect? The Klingons were a warrior race. They weren't known for sloppy marksmanship.

Warning shots? From Klingons?

"Hail the Klingon vessel!" Pike ordered. "Find out what's going on here!"

"Aye, sir!" Garrison replied, even as the tense situation played out on the viewscreen before Pike's eyes. The *Ilion* had apparently led the Klingons on a merry chase, but it was obviously on its last legs. Its tattered shields looked flimsier than an Orion dancing girl's veils. They flickered erratically.

"Captain," Spock said sharply. "Sensors indicate that the *Ilion* is in extreme distress. Its shields are buckling, its structural integrity is severely compromised, life-support is failing, and their overtaxed warp engine is approaching a catastrophic breach." He kept his gaze glued to the readouts on his monitor. "I suspect that the ship's pilot has exceeded all recommended safety parameters . . . with dire but predictable results."

Pike got the picture. "They pushed *Ilion* too hard for too long, trying to get away from the Klingons, and now the ship's coming apart."

"Precisely, Captain," Spock said. "Add that to the damage already inflicted on the ship by the Klingons, and *Ilion*'s destruction is a near certainty. Only minutes remain to it."

So much for being captured instead of destroyed, Pike thought. It was as though whoever was flying *Iion* would rather die than be taken alive.

"The Klingons have responded, sir," Garrison said. "They're warning us not to interfere."

"And?" Pike prompted.

"That's it, sir. They're telling us to mind our own business . . . or else."

Now, that sounds like the Klingons, Pike thought. He didn't doubt that Garrison was accurately conveying the gist of the communication. *So now what I am supposed to do?*

"I am detecting two life-forms aboard the *Ilion*," Spock added. "Humanoid, and growing weaker."

"Cyprian?" Pike asked, recalling the ship's alleged origin.

"Possibly," Spock replied, "but *Ilion*'s engine is approaching critical. It will explode in approximately four minutes, possibly sooner."

"Chris," Boyce said urgently, standing anxiously beside the captain's chair. "We can't let them die."

"And we're not going to," Pike said, reaching a decision. He stabbed the intercom button on his armrest. "Captain to transporter room. Lock onto both life signs aboard the Cyprian vessel and beam them aboard . . . quickly, before it's too late."

Transporter Chief Pitcairn's gruff voice replied at once. "*Yes, sir.*"

"Lower shields, Mister Tyler," Pike ordered. "Just long enough to beam any survivors aboard."

Spock turned away from his monitor. "Is that wise, Captain? The Klingons—"

"Will hopefully think twice before firing upon a Starfleet vessel," Pike said. "At least long enough for us to transport *Ilion*'s crew and passengers to safety."

It was a gamble, but Pike didn't see any choice. They couldn't beam anyone aboard without lowering their shields, and those people aboard the *Ilion* were doomed if they didn't try. With any luck, the *Enterprise* wasn't yet within firing range of the oncoming battle cruiser, but it was hard to tell with any degree of certainty. Even a century-plus after Broken Bow, there was still a lot Starfleet didn't know about the Klingons and their capacities.

"The Klingons are still ordering us to back off," Garrison said. "And they don't sound happy."

So what else is new, Pike thought. "Tell them we're on a mission of mercy."

"Not sure 'mercy' is in their vocabulary," Tyler said. "I hear the Klingons don't take prisoners."

"And yet they seem determined to capture *Ilion* and its passengers." Spock arched an eyebrow. "Curious."

My thoughts exactly, Pike reflected. More than ever, he wanted to know whose lives they were trying to save—and why the Klingons apparently wanted them alive.

"Spock, get down to the transporter room, on the double." Pike wanted to head there himself, to find out whom exactly they were beaming aboard, but he could hardly leave the bridge while they were staring down a Klingon battle cruiser. With

Number One away, Spock was currently second-in-command aboard the ship, so Pike delegated the job to him. "Doctor, you had better join him. You may be needed."

"Try and stop me," Boyce said. Medkit in hand, he hurried toward the turbolift. "Come on, Spock. Time's a-wasting."

"You need not remind me, Doctor." Spock turned the science station over to Ensign Weisz, a short, wiry youth with curly black hair and, according to Spock, a notable aptitude for computers—for a human, that was. Spock moved briskly, intercepting Boyce at the rear of the bridge. "I'm quite aware of the urgency."

The turbolift had barely departed, taking the two men with it, when the *Ilion* died a fiery death on-screen. A blinding flash lit up the viewer as the *Ilion*'s overheated engine gave way. Pike blinked and raised a hand to shield his eyes from the glare before the screen automatically dimmed the image to compensate. A shock wave from the explosion rattled the bridge. Yeoman Colt, who had been approaching the command well with the latest round of status reports, gasped and grabbed on to the safety rail to keep her balance. Her data slate clattered onto the hard metal deck.

"Sorry, Captain," she blurted. "That was quite a bump."

Pike barely noticed the slim young redhead's

stumble. Leaning forward in his chair, gripping the armrests, he peered intently at the screen. Blue spots danced before his vision, but he could make out the *Ilion*'s fate easily enough. Nothing remained of the ill-fated Cyprian vessel but a cloud of plasma and particulate debris. The ship had been all but vaporized.

But what about her passengers?

He hit the intercom again. "Transporter room! Did you get them?"

———

A shock wave rocked the turbolift. Clearly, Spock deduced, the *Ilion* was no more.

Rushing into the transporter room alongside Boyce, he was surprised to find the transporter platform empty. Although he and Boyce had wasted no time arriving there, he had still expected to find the survivors of the *Ilion* already beamed aboard, provided that Chief Pitcairn and his assistant had managed to lock onto the endangered individuals in time.

He quickly surveyed the situation. Pitcairn, a beefy Earthman with closely cropped brown hair, was manning the primary control console, while to his right, Technician Sam Yamata operated the auxiliary controls. Transporting individuals in the form of energy patterns was not a task to be taken lightly; currently Starfleet protocols built a certain degree of redundancy into the process for safety's sake. No one desired a replay of the tragic DeLambre incident. One such disaster was enough.

Both men were clearly struggling at the controls. Beads of perspiration dotted Pitcairn's furrowed brow. Yamata peered intently at his sensor readings through a pair of archaic black-rimmed glasses. Spock recalled that the man possessed a significant allergy to Retinax and other conventional treatments for myopia. Both men looked as taut as the strings on a Vulcan lyre.

"What's the matter?" Boyce asked anxiously, clutching his medkit. "Why haven't you beamed them aboard yet?"

"The Klingons have locked onto them too," Pitcairn said, never looking away from his controls. His big hands worked the levers with remarkable deftness. "We've got a tug-of-war going on here."

Spock instantly grasped the severity of the situation. The targeted individuals could not long exist in an energized state before their patterns were irrevocably degraded. He briefly considered ceding the *Ilion*'s survivors to the Klingons, if only to save them from being lost forever, but was reluctant to do so before making every effort to bring them aboard the *Enterprise* instead. He doubted that he would be doing the survivors any favors by letting the Klingons "rescue" them. Indeed, the unknown individuals might well prefer to have their atoms painlessly dispersed into space compared to what they could expect at the brutal hands of the Empire.

"What is your honest assessment, Transporter Chief?" Spock asked. "Can you successfully wrest the patterns from the Klingons?"

"I'm giving it my best shot," Pitcairn said. "We locked onto the subjects first, and were closer to the Cyprian ship to boot, but the Klingons are working overtime to hijack the matter stream from us. It's all we can do to keep the patterns intact without losing them."

Yamata squinted at his readings. "The scanners are still picking up two distinct patterns, but they're practically suspended between us and the Klingons." Worry tinged his voice. "I've never known a transport to take this long before . . ."

"Allow me, Technician." Spock crossed to the room to the control podium, choosing to deal directly with the crisis. "I believe I can be of assistance here."

Yamata stepped aside, surrendering the console to Spock without protest. If anything, he looked relieved and grateful for Spock's intervention, although the technician's feelings were the least of Spock's concerns at the moment. A rapid inspection of the scanner readings confirmed that both the matter streams were in danger of being torn apart by the conflicting forces being exerted on them. In a worst-case scenario, it was entirely possible—and growing increasingly probable—that the streams would be split between the two ships, so that each transporter station received only a portion of the individuals in transit.

"Divert power from engineering to the annular confinement beams," Spock instructed Pitcairn while recalibrating the quantum resolution protocols. A recent treatise from the Vulcan Science Academy, regarding oppositional wave form functions and their practical application with respect to phased subatomic decoupling, suggested an innovative approach that might yield positive results in this instance. "I am attempting to enhance our lock on the patterns . . . and disrupt the Klingons' hold on the subjects."

The trick was to bring the confinement beam into synch with the quantum wave amplitude of the phased matter, resulting in a heightened state of subatomic entanglement while simultaneously pulling it out of alignment with the Klingons' beam: in essence, tightening the *Enterprise*'s grip on the matter stream while making it too "slippery" for the Klingons to hold on to.

Assuming the technique achieved the desired result.

"Enhancing pattern lock now," Spock stated, subtly adjusting the quark manipulation fields. "Wave functions building on our end. Destructive interference flattening the Klingon beam."

Status indicators on the control panel verified his assessment.

"That did the trick," Pitcairn grunted, "but we still ought to bring them aboard one at a time, just to be safe. Those patterns have been in transit too long. I want to devote all available power and processing to each individual as they materialize, even if that means storing the second pattern in the buffer a few moments longer."

"Understood." Spock found it fortunate that there were only two survivors to be rescued. A larger party would not have allowed them time enough to rematerialize each humanoid individually. "Proceed."

"Here goes nothing." Pitcairn pushed the levers all the way up, attempting to bring aboard the first subject, while Spock carefully monitored the second pattern as it was retrieved by the *Enterprise*'s exterior emitter arrays. The molecular imaging scanner suggested that both patterns were still viable, but Spock kept a close eye on the Heisenberg compensators to ensure that neither matter stream underwent any significant fluctuations. Doppler shift factors were also calculated and monitored. Pitcairn lifted his gaze toward the elevated transporter platform directly before them. "Coming through now."

A glittering column of energy formed above the platform, suspended between a glowing pad and the phase transition coil hanging directly above it. The telltale whine of a transporter beam reached Spock's ears. Despite his carefully cultivated Vulcan reserve, he experienced a surge of relief as the beam coalesced into a female figure that, at first glance, indeed appeared to be Cyprian in origin.

Short blond hair, shaved almost down to the scalp, revealed the flared, scalloped ears typical of her people. She was tall and lean and clad in rugged, well-worn civilian attire consisting of a faded vest, shirt, trousers, and boots. Soot stained her apparel and tanned, weathered face, making it difficult to determine her age, although Spock estimated that she was possibly in her early thirties by Cyprian standards. A smoky odor clung to her, accompanying the fresh scorch marks on her clothing. A pistol of some variety rested in a holster at her hip, although she appeared in no shape to pose a threat.

Multiple injuries were immediately evident. Dark orange blood dripped from a scalp wound, while second-degree radiation burns marred her face and neck, as well as the back of one hand. Her hair and eyebrows were singed. She gasped for breath, reminding Spock that her ship had been losing life-support in its final moments. She tottered unsteadily upon her feet while clutching her side and grimacing in pain. More blood trickled from the corner of her lips, raising the alarming prospect of internal bleeding. Spock feared that the troubled transport process may have added to or exacerbated her injuries. At the very least, the trauma may have been sufficient to induce shock. She clearly belonged in sickbay. It was fortunate that Doctor Boyce was on hand to render assistance.

"Wha—?" she panted. "Where—?"

Her wide eyes captured Spock's attention. The right was normal enough, aside from its striking silver iris, but the left had been replaced by a translucent crystal orb embedded in the socket. Holographic readouts flickered inside the orb, which was presumably a prosthetic of sorts. She glanced around her in alarm, taking in her new setting—or perhaps searching for the rest of her party.

"Wait. Where is . . . ?"

Gasping, she staggered forward a few steps before collapsing. She tumbled off the platform onto the deck below. She landed hard, ending up sprawled at the base of the steps leading up to the platform. An agonized moan escaped her lips.

"Hold on there!" Boyce said, already rushing to her side. He knelt beside the fallen woman, while Yamata hurried to assist him. "It's all right," Boyce assured the woman. "You're safe now. I'm a doctor.

"Never mind me!" she said fervently, her voice hoarse from smoke inhalation. She grabbed on to the front of Boyce's blue coverall to pull herself halfway up to a sitting position. Desperation was evident in her face, body language, and tone. A distraught silver eye pleaded with the doctor. Her voice trailed off as she gradually lost consciousness. "Please, you have to help us! Don't let them take her back..."

Spock arched an eyebrow. *Her?*

That question would have to wait, he realized, until they had beamed aboard the second survivor. Time was not in their favor here; despite his best efforts, they could not hold the other pattern in the buffer much longer. It was imperative that they complete the transport immediately. Spock only hoped that it had not been too long already and that their guest would materialize whole and undamaged, as opposed to missing any critical parts of their anatomy.

"With all deliberate speed, Mister Pitcairn," he urged.

"Autosequencer engaged," the transporter chief replied. "Resetting the primary energizing coil." He slid the control levers back up the board while muttering under his breath. "Take that, you grabby Klingon sons of bitches."

A second pillar of coruscating light appeared on the transporter platform, only meters away from where Boyce and Yamata tended to the unconscious Cyprian. The doctor looked up from his patient, understandably concerned as to the condition of the new arrival. Spock also watched intently as the shimmering matter stream resolved into . . .

An angry Klingon.

"Dishonorable curs!" she snarled, displaying the sharpened canines of a born carnivore. Her scorched attire was of typical Klingon fashion, consisting of tight-fitting golden chain mail over a knee-length black leather dress fashioned barbarically from the hides of animals. A blood-red gemstone gleamed from a pendant at her throat. Studded wrist bands adorned her arms, while high black boots protected her feet and lower legs. Raised scars ridged her brow and a mane of wild black hair fell past her shoulders. Dark eyes, accented by horizontal stripes of black and blue eye shadow, flashed with unchecked fury from a youthful face. "How dare you abduct a daughter of the Empire?"

Her furious gaze lighted on Boyce's patient and she lunged at the injured Cyprian. Yamata tried to tackle her, but she elbowed him in the face, then sent him sprawling backward with a roundhouse kick to his gut. He landed hard upon the deck, groaning and clutching a bleeding nose. Barely giving him a second look, she turned back toward the defenseless Cyprian. She bared her teeth and growled.

"Keep back!" Boyce sprang to his feet, placing himself between the Klingon and the obvious target of her wrath. He held up his hands to block her. "This woman is injured."

"Only injured?" the Klingon growled. "Good! That means I get to kill her myself!"

"Not a chance!" Boyce refused to budge. "You're not getting near my patient as long as I—"

She seized him by the throat, choking him. Boyce struggled to free himself from her grip, but she was clearly stronger than the elderly physician. Strangled gasps conveyed his distress.

"Out of my way, old man! My quarrel is not with—"

Spock's fingers clamped down on the junction of her neck and shoulder. He had never attempted a nerve pinch on a Klingon before, but it proved as effective on their hostile visitor as it had on myriad other humanoids. The stranger went limp, her own fingers losing their grip on Boyce's throat as she slid insensate to the deck, landing in a heap not far from her intended victim. Closed lids hid her previously hate-crazed eyes. She breathed softly, dreaming of whatever Klingons hunted in their sleep. It was, in fact, the most peaceful Spock had ever seen a Klingon.

"Thanks, Spock!" Boyce massaged his bruised throat. He peered down at the subdued Klingon. "But what kind of all-fired mess have we waded into?"

"An excellent question, Doctor." Spock remained

on guard as he knelt to inspect the Klingon, wary to the possibility that she might be dissembling. Taking no chances, he swiftly verified that she was both unconscious and, oddly, unarmed. "She has no weapons on her person. Highly unusual for a Klingon."

"I'll consider myself lucky, then," Boyce commented, before taking a closer look at his attacker. "Well, at least she seems to be in better condition than our other visitor." He employed a medical scanner to inspect the Klingon for hidden injuries. His eyes widened in surprise as he inspected the results. "What the devil?"

Spock took note of Boyce's reaction. "What is it, Doctor?"

"This is no Klingon." Boyce stared in shock at her. "This woman is Cyprian!"

"The Klingons are hailing us, Captain."

The imposing battle cruiser loomed ominously on the viewer, making Pike glad that the *Enterprise*'s shields were back in place. Readouts on the bridge confirmed that two humanoids had been beamed aboard the ship, although he was still waiting for a direct report from the transporter room regarding the status of the new arrivals. The atomized remains of the *Ilion* were already dispersing into the empty space between the *Enterprise* and the battle cruiser.

Pike had to wonder how the Klingons would react to losing their prey.

Not well, he guessed.

"Put them through," he ordered Garrison. "Let's hear what they have to say."

Pike sat up straight in his chair and assumed his steeliest expression. If there was one thing he knew about Klingons, it was that they respected strength and despised weakness. It was vital that he faced them as an equal from the start.

Garrison nodded. "Aye, sir."

The battle cruiser vanished from the screen, supplanted by a close-up of a scowling Klingon soldier, whose grizzled countenance conveyed both experience and authority. A bald pate capped his skull, but gray infiltrated his bushy black beard and eyebrows. Ridges on his forehead indicated that he'd escaped the genetic disorder that had given many of his contemporaries more human features. The golden sash stretched diagonally across his chest bore medals and insignia befitting a general. The sash matched the metallic gold vest he wore over his black military uniform. His head and shoulders filled the screen, offering only a glimpse of the battle cruiser's bridge, which was suffused with a ruddy, incarnadine light.

"*Identify yourself!*" the Klingon demanded.

Ordinarily, Pike would be happy to do so, particularly as he was a newcomer to these parts, but he wasn't about to let the Klingons get the upper hand right from the get-go. He needed to push back a bit, if only to win their respect.

"You first," he countered.

"This is our territory," the Klingon general growled. *"You are the trespassers here."*

"Maybe, maybe not," Pike said. "As I understand it, there's some ambiguity as to where the actual border lies."

The Klingon bristled. *"Are you challenging our claims to this region?"*

"Not in the least," Pike insisted. Standing one's ground was one thing; allowing this encounter to escalate into a full-blown border dispute was something else altogether. "We have no territorial ambitions here. As we alerted you before, we're here on a mission of mercy, nothing more."

"Mercy?" The Klingon uttered the word with obvious disdain. *"Is that what you call this?"*

Pike saw an opportunity to probe for more information. "What would you call it?"

"The brazen kidnapping of a Klingon national from an outpost under my command!"

Kidnapping?

Okay, I didn't see that coming, Pike thought. He felt like he was boxing in the dark, not knowing what was at stake or even who the good guys were. He decided to throw the Klingon an olive branch, if only to buy time to get his facts straight.

"This is Captain Christopher Pike of the *United Space Ship Enterprise.* I assure you, General, that I know nothing about any kidnapping, but I am perfectly willing to discuss this matter with you, once I check on the condition of the survivors. Bear with me for just a moment."

He signaled Garrison to mute the audio component of the transmission, while he got on the intercom again.

"Transporter room, report!"

Spock's voice emerged from the speaker. *"My apologies for the delay, Captain. There were complications that demanded our immediate attention."*

Pike didn't like the sound of that. "What sort of complications?"

Spock's report was admirably concise as he informed Pike of the tumultuous arrival of the survivors—and Boyce's surprising discovery regarding the kidnapped "Klingon."

"She's a Cyprian?" Pike echoed. "Are you sure of that?"

"Absolutely," Boyce said, breaking into the conversation. *"I've double- and triple-checked the readings. Appearances aside, this woman is no more Klingon than you or me."*

Pike tried to make sense of it. A Cyprian abducting a Klingon who was actually a Cyprian?

"I'll take your word for it, Doctor. Look after both our guests. Pike out."

He contemplated the viewer, where the unnamed Klingon was fuming visibly. Spittle sprayed from the general's lips as he barked silently at the screen. He shook his fist.

"The Klingon commander is getting impatient," Garrison reported unnecessarily.

"I don't doubt it," Pike said. "Let's not keep him waiting any longer."

The general's voice boomed from the screen. "*—or risk the wrath of the Klingon Empire!*"

"Pardon the interruption, General." Pike ignored the tail end of the ultimatum. "I'm afraid I didn't catch your name."

The Klingon grunted in exasperation. "*You are addressing General Krunn of the Klingon Empire, presently in command of the Imperial Battle Cruiser* Fek'lhr, *and I demand the immediate return of my stolen kinsman, as well as custody of her perfidious abductor. Surrender them at once, if you care for the safety of your ship and crew.*"

Pike overlooked the threat for the time being. "I've been informed that we have indeed rescued two survivors from the *Ilion*, but their identities have yet to be determined. Perhaps you can assist us in this regard?"

"*Their identities are no mystery to us,*" Krunn said. "*The Klingon is Merata, a daughter of the Empire. The Cyprian is the so-called 'trader' who abused our renowned hospitality by stealing Merata away*" like a thief in the night. Return them both or suffer the consequences!"

"Not so fast." Pike was not about to make a decision regarding the survivors before he got the full story. Who exactly had kidnapped whom here? "Both parties are currently under the care of our ship's surgeon. There will be time enough to sort things out once we've attended to their medical needs."

"*Medical?*" Krunn asked sharply. "*Is Merata harmed?*" Pike thought he detected a note of genuine concern in the general's voice before his belligerent attitude returned with a vengeance. "*If Klingon blood has been spilt—*"

Pike held up a hand to forestall any further threats. "My understanding is that the woman you call Merata has not suffered any serious injuries," he said, neglecting to mention a certain Vulcan nerve pinch. According to Spock, she had been fit enough to start a brawl in the transporter room and nearly choke the life out of Boyce. "But we're taking every reasonable precaution to ensure the continued health of both our guests."

Including not turning them over to any irate Klingons just on their say-so.

"*We do not 'call' her Merata,*" Krunn protested. "*That is her name, and she belongs here with her own people, not on a Starfleet vessel.*" He spit out the word "Starfleet" as though it tasted bad in his mouth. *"And not alongside the vile Cyprian bandit who kidnapped her!"*

Pike debated pointing out that this Merata person was apparently Cyprian, not Klingon, but decided to hold that card in reserve until he had a better idea of what was actually going on here. What if Krunn was unaware of Merata's true origins? Exposing that secret might just make a volatile situation even more explosive. If Merata was, for instance, a Cyprian spy, she might not appreciate having her cover blown, and Pike could readily imagine other tumultuous scenarios as well. All that was clear at this point was that they had stuck their noses into a very murky situation. Pike almost wished that the *Enterprise* had not picked up that fateful distress signal in the first place, but then, he recalled, two lives would have surely been lost when the *Ilion* combusted. Saving those lives justified any present risk or uncertainty.

"That remains to be verified," Pike stated. "You'll forgive me if I investigate this matter more thoroughly before taking any further action regarding the final disposition of the individuals in question."

"This is none of your concern, human!"

"I respectfully disagree," Pike said. "We saved their lives, which makes them our responsibility, at least for the present."

It was an old principle, common to many civilizations and cultures through the galaxy. Pike hoped it would carry some weight with Krunn.

No such luck.

"*And our honor demands that you turn them over immediately!*" Krunn raged. "*Look to your own lives, humans, which are growing shorter by the moment!*"

"Captain!" Weisz reported from the science station. "The Klingons are charging their disruptor cannons."

Pike maintained a poker face for the Klingon's benefit, even as his nerves were stretched tighter than a drum. How far was Krunn willing to take this? Would he risk war with the Federation just to rescue one "Klingon" of uncertain provenance? *And how far will I go,* Pike wondered, *to protect two strangers, one of whom may be a criminal?*

This wasn't just about the survivors of the *Ilion* anymore. Pike's ship and crew were in jeopardy. He could feel the tension increasing aboard the bridge. The very atmosphere felt heavier somehow.

"Hold on a second," Pike said. "Let's talk."

"*I grow weary of mere words,*" Krunn said. "*Make your choice, human. Return what belongs to us, and you may live to see another day.*"

"The name is Pike," the captain said. "And you should know that I don't take well to threats. We don't want a fight, but we'll defend ourselves if necessary. And that's not likely to end well for either of us."

Krunn laughed harshly. "*You think I fear combat?*"

"No, but I'm hoping you're wise enough to

choose your battles . . . and not risk war over a possible misunderstanding."

*"There is no misunderstanding! You are holding
one of our own against her will!"*

That might be so, Pike conceded. From what
Spock said, Merata had been none too happy when
beamed aboard the *Enterprise*, but her fury had
mostly been directed at the other Cyprian. Neither
he nor his people had been able to truly interview
her yet.

"I have yet to hear that from her own lips," Pike
said honestly. "Until then, I suggest you hold your
fire . . . for everyone's sake."

"Do not presume to stay my hand," Krunn said.
"A Klingon does not make idle threats."

"Captain, they're firing their disruptors!" Tyler
announced. "Here it comes!"

There was no time to alert the rest of the ship.
The disruptor beams slammed into the *Enterprise*'s
shields, rattling the bridge. Emergency alarms
went off, competing with echoes of the blast, and a
blinding green flash drove Krunn's menacing visage from the viewscreen. Pike blinked and averted
his eyes from the glare, which quickly faded, leaving nothing but snow and static upon the screen.
He braced himself for another salvo while calling
out orders.

"All decks, condition red!" he said over the
intercom. "Bridge crew, report!"

"Shields down six percent," Tyler said, "but holding."

"Damage reports coming in," Garrison added. "Nothing serious. No major casualties reported yet."

Could be worse, Pike thought, wondering why Krunn hadn't launched a second attack or deployed his torpedoes yet. For all his bluster, the general was showing uncharacteristic restraint for a Klingon, just as he'd seemingly gone to great lengths to avoid destroying the *Ilion* while Merata was still aboard the Cyprian ship. It appeared Krunn was equally reluctant to attack the *Enterprise* for fear of harming their puzzling new guest.

On the screen, a flurry of visual snow resolved back into Krunn. A burst of static heralded the return of his harsh, guttural voice.

"I trust I made my point, Pike. That is just a taste of what you can expect if you persist in your present course." He scowled at Pike across the gulf of space. *"Make your inquiries, but do not try our patience. The matter is far from concluded. We will not rest until our daughter is restored to us . . . and her captor faces Klingon justice."*

The transmission cut off abruptly. Krunn's baneful visage vanished from the screen, which once again showed the *Fek'lhr* facing off against the *Enterprise.* If anything, the battle cruiser appeared even closer than before, as though deliberately invading the *Enterprise*'s personal space.

"The Klingons' disruptor beams are powering down, sir," Weisz reported. "Torpedo launcher inactive."

"Whew." Tyler let out a sigh of relief. "Looks like you called their bluff, Captain."

"For now," Pike cautioned.

The battle cruiser wasn't going anywhere. The only thing holding them back, Pike assumed, was Krunn's apparent unwillingness to risk harming Merata, who wasn't even really a Klingon. An unusually cautious attitude for a Klingon commander; in Pike's experience, the war-like aliens placed little value on individual lives.

Which begs the question, Pike thought. *Just who is she, anyway?*

Four

Sickbay was already packed with victims of Rigelian fever. Extra beds had been installed in the main examination room, which had been declared a quarantine zone, while the rec rooms, gymnasium, and bowling alley had been drafted into service to handle the overflow of incoming patients. Sterile field generators fought to contain the spread of the disease, but many of the nurses, orderlies, and lab technicians were wearing protective gloves and masks as an extra precaution. Doctor Boyce and his staff scurried to tend to the flood of fever victims, many of whom were already flat on their backs. Pike hadn't seen anything like it since that pandemic on Urtomar IV a few years back.

Most of the patients were still in stage one of the infection, suffering severe flu-like symptoms, including chills, fatigue, and rising temperatures. Pike saw them shivering beneath insulated blankets even as nurses applied cold compresses to their brows. Even more disturbing was the handful of patients who were already advancing into stage two; as the infection spread into the lungs, they coughed and wheezed and gasped for breath. Handheld respirators brought some relief, but Pike knew that was only a stopgap solution, treating the symptoms rather than disease. He didn't immediately see anyone suffering from stage three yet, thank goodness, but, unless they got their hands on some ryetalyn, that was only a matter of time.

"The crisis is escalating at a worrisome rate," Spock observed, having entered sickbay alongside Pike. "Beyond the direct threat to the crew, the ship's operations will inevitably be compromised if too many personnel fall ill."

Pike glanced at his science officer. Spock appeared unmoved by the suffering before them, but the captain chalked that up to the man's Vulcan reserve. For himself, Pike wished that he had time to visit with the sick. Unfortunately, he had the Klingons to deal with, not to mention a couple of unexpected new passengers.

"Sorry for the interruption, Doctor," Pike said, approaching Boyce. "But I understand one of your other patients has regained consciousness?"

Boyce nodded. "She's just starting to come to." He handed a patient's chart over to a nurse, along with some brief instructions, before turning back toward Pike. "This way."

He escorted Pike and Spock toward the surgical recovery ward, just off the main examination room, while briefing the captain on the status of the injured Cyprian, who was being kept isolated from the quarantine zone. Cyprians were supposed to be immune to the fever, but Pike agreed with the doctor's decision to keep an alien of unknown intention apart from the other patients. Sick crew members and overworked nurses didn't need a stranger in their midst.

"You need to go easy on her, Chris," the doctor said. "She's in pretty bad shape. Radiation burns, broken ribs, a few punctured organs, aggravated by a bad case of transporter shock. I had to perform emergency surgery to staunch the internal bleeding." He frowned at the memory. "That close call on the *Ilion* really did a number on her. She's lucky to be alive."

"But she's talking?" Pike asked.

"Says her name is Soleste Mursh," the doctor informed him, "and that *Ilion* was her ship, but that's about all I've gotten out of her. She insists on speaking to you."

"Fine with me," Pike said. "I'm eager to hear her side of the story."

"I confess to a certain curiosity myself," Spock divulged, "regarding both our guests."

Pike glanced around sickbay. "And the other woman? Merata?"

"Doctor Boyce found no serious injuries to her

person," Spock reported, "so I took the liberty of having her confined to the brig."

"The brig?"

Krunn's not going to like that, Pike thought.

"Given her violent behavior and prior attacks on members of the crew, it seemed a reasonable precaution," Spock said. "As you humans say, better safe than sorry."

Pike noted, not for the first time, that Spock spoke of humans as though he was not half-human himself. Despite being born of a human mother and a Vulcan father, Spock had been raised on Vulcan as a Vulcan and clearly identified as such. He made every effort to distance himself from his human roots, aside from signing aboard a starship crewed almost entirely by his mother's people. Pike had never seriously discussed the issue with Spock, who seemed to value his privacy, but the young science officer's very presence on the *Enterprise* was something of a paradox, or so Pike occasionally thought.

"Good call," Pike said. "So how come she came through that fracas unscathed while your other patient took such a beating?"

"Dumb luck?" Boyce guessed. "Possibly she was confined to a different part of the ship, or didn't get struck as hard or as head-on by a disruptor impact or an explosion onboard. Maybe she landed on her butt instead of her head or missed being winged by a flying piece of debris." He threw up his hands.

"Who knows? You know how it goes, Chris. One man walks away from a shuttle crash, while his co-pilot doesn't. It's a crap shoot sometimes."

"A crap shoot?" Spock asked.

"Random chance," Pike translated, not too surprised to find out that Vulcans didn't gamble. *I wonder if Klingons believe in luck.*

The captain made a mental note to check on Merata after he interviewed her alleged kidnapper, whom he found waiting in the recovery ward. Due to the shortage of beds, she was still tucked into one of the surgical biobeds beneath an insulated metallic sheet. Pike took note of her singed hair and eyebrows, as well as the artificial crystal eye in one socket, before glancing up at the life-signs monitor mounted over the head of the bed. He was no doctor, but her vitals appeared stable, if weak, just as Boyce had reported. *She's been through a lot,* he gathered, *but better off here than in the hands of the Klingons.*

"Hello," he greeted her. "I'm Captain Pike. You wanted to talk to me?"

She tried to sit up, but the effort obviously hurt her. She bit down on her lip to keep the pain inside. Boyce hurried over to assist her.

"Take it easy there." He helped her up into a sitting position. "You've been through surgery. No sudden movements, all right?"

"Never mind me," she said, grimacing, before fixing her gaze on Pike. "My sister? Is she safe?"

Pike was taken by surprise. "Merata is your sister?"

"That's not her name!" Anger flared upon the patient's face, blazing through the pain and weakness. "Her name is Elzura. Elzura Mursh. And she was stolen from us nearly a decade ago!" She leaned forward and grabbed Pike's arm. "Please tell me you didn't let the Klingons take her again, not after I've searched for her for so long!"

"The individual in question is still safely aboard the *Enterprise*," Pike assured her, "but I'm slightly in the dark here. Why don't you start from the beginning?"

"The beginning," she said bitterly. "Would that be before or after those Klingon savages tore apart my family?" Her tone and expression darkened as she recounted her tale. "It was about ten years ago, as we reckon time on Cypria. The Klingons had embarked on a campaign of terror and harassment, trying to drive our colony from 'their' territory. Oh, they never formally declared war on Cypria, and the Empire always played dumb regarding the attacks, but we all knew who was behind the raids, the sneak attacks on our factories and farms and outlying facilities. The marauders barely tried to conceal their identities, lest we fail to get the message . . ."

Pike could believe it. The Klingons were an aggressive species, and they didn't always rely on outright conquest to expand their Empire and influence. Sabotage, assassinations, forced alliances, and propped-up puppet governments were among the weapons in their arsenal, along with plenty of ferocious warriors eager for blood and glory. He could easily see the Klingons trying to make life very uncomfortable for the Cyprian colonists.

"My father ran a mining facility on our primary moon," she continued. "He was there, looking after little Elzy, when the raiders attacked without warning or provocation. He was killed by the Klingons along with everyone else, their bodies left to rot, but my sister's remains were not found among the dead. Recovered security footage showed one of the marauders carrying her off, even though she fought back as hard as she could." A note of pride entered her voice. "You should have seen her, Captain, standing up to the Klingons, refusing to surrender. But she was only seven years old. She never stood a chance against those monsters!"

Pike's imagination painted a vivid picture of a brave little girl up against a party of hostile Klingons, who were intent on slaughtering everyone in sight. It occurred to him that the Klingons might have been equally impressed by the child's courage and spirit. Perhaps that was why they'd spared her? Perhaps even adopted her?

"I'm very sorry, Captain Mursh," he said, sympathizing with the woman's tragic story. Pike had no siblings that he knew of, but he'd lost his mother and stepfather back on Elysium years ago. "It must have been hard for you, losing your father . . . and your sister."

"Thank you, Captain," she said, "and please call me Soleste. I'm no captain of any great spacefaring vessel. More like a homeless tracker, searching for the sister taken from me so long ago."

Pike contemplated her artificial eye. He wondered if she'd lost the real one in the raid on the mining facility, or perhaps later in her travels. "If you don't mind me asking, how did you survive the Klingons' attack?"

"I was away at college at the time. School was out, however, and I was *supposed* to be back home with my family, visiting over the break, but I'd self-ishly chosen to hit the beaches with my friends instead." Emotion cracked her voice. "I should have been there, fighting beside my father, protecting Elzy, not partying the night away while my family was under attack. I could have done something!"

Boyce placed a hand gently on her shoulder. "Chances are, you would have just died along with the others. You can't blame yourself."

"Easier said than done." She stared bleakly into the past. "Everyone told me that she was as good as dead. That we should mourn her and move on, that we should just *forget* about her, but what kind of person abandons her own flesh and blood? I *had* to find her and bring her home, no matter how long it took!"

It was impossible to miss the sheer intensity in her voice. Soleste Mursh was clearly a driven woman and apparently had been for many years. Pike wondered how much she'd sacrificed on her decade-long quest. Her future? Her prospects? Maybe even an eye?

"Ten years I searched for her, rooting through every filthy Klingon hellhole between here and Qo'nos, posing as a dealer in kevas and trillium. Ten years of false leads and wild-goose chases and not a few double-crosses." Her finger traced the outline of her missing eye. "Until I finally found her on D'Orox, an obscure military outpost light-years from here . . . only to discover that she had become one of them! That she actually thought she was a Klingon!"

Pike was starting to get the picture. "So you abducted her."

"I *rescued* her," Soleste insisted. "I saved her and was taking her home at last, until that battle cruiser caught up with us. I tried to get away, pushing *Ilion* to its limits, but . . ." She looked Pike in the eyes. "You have my gratitude, Captain. If not for you and your crew, neither my sister nor I would have ever seen Cypria again. Your heroism will not be forgotten, by me or my people."

Pike couldn't help thinking that this might help

when it came to obtaining the ryetalyn from the Cyprians. *They owe us one.*

But what about the Klingons?

"I'm afraid it may be more complicated than that," he said. "From what I hear, your sister didn't act like she wanted to be rescued."

"She doesn't know any better. She was just a little girl when those barbarians stole her. They've had a decade to brainwash her, to make her forget who she is and where she came from." Bitterness dripped from her voice. "Would you believe she didn't even recognize me? Her own sister?"

"She certainly gave no indication," Spock confirmed, "that she was aware of your kinship when she attempted to murder you in the transporter room."

Soleste winced at the memory. Spock's bedside manner left something to be desired, Pike reflected. *No surprise there.*

"I had to stun her to get her off the planet," Soleste admitted, "and keep her restrained while we attempted our escape. But it will be different once we're back on Cypria and reunited with what's left of our family and her true people. We can help her remember who she really is and where she belongs. Our family will be whole again."

Possibly, Pike thought, although he suspected that it might be a less than rosy homecoming, in more ways than one. How would the folks on

Cypria react to the fierce "Klingon" warrior in the brig, and vice versa? "You have more family on Cypria?"

"Yes. My mother and my little brother. They were also away the night of the attack. Lucky for us, I suppose, although it never really felt that way . . ."

Pike recalled that the *Kepler* was still en route to the Cyprian system. At last report, Number One and her party were making good time, although they were still several hours away from reaching their destination.

"Please, Captain, let me take Elzy home. I'm begging you!"

Her nails dug into his arm with surprising strength. He gently disengaged them.

"I'll take it under consideration," he promised. "After I talk to your sister."

The corridors felt unusually deserted as the three men made their way to the brig, which was located a deck below, in one of the most heavily protected sections of the ship. They passed the occasional crew member going about their duties, but the halls were nowhere near as bustling as Pike was used to. The spread of the fever was already taking its toll on the crew's readiness, with growing numbers sick in bed or unable to report to their posts, while those uninfected were wisely avoiding public spaces unless required to by duty. Ordinarily, it was not uncommon to see off-duty personnel roaming the halls in casual attire, pursuing various leisure-time activities, but not today. Pike guessed that any available rec rooms, gardens, and galleys were ghost towns. They caught an empty turbolift while Pike conferred with Spock and Boyce.

"Are we certain that Merata is actually Elzura Mursh?" he asked. "And that Soleste isn't mistaken or fooling herself? She's clearly obsessed with finding her stolen sister, so we can't rule out the possibility that she's merely convinced herself that our prisoner is Elzy, whom she hasn't actually laid eyes on for a decade or so."

"It *has* been ten years," Spock agreed, "and Elzura was only a child when last seen. If she is still alive, she would be much changed by now, particularly if she has been raised and groomed by Klingons."

"Well, I can run a DNA comparison to verify any familial ties," Boyce said, "but Merata is definitely Cyprian. Her teeth have been filed to points, her eye color has been cosmetically changed, she's had an ear job, and the scarring on her forehead is clearly intended to emulate Klingon brow ridges, but I'm guessing that Merata and Elzy are one and the same."

"I need more than guesses, Doctor," Pike said, more brusquely than he intended. "I need to know for certain."

If Boyce was bothered by the captain's tone, he didn't show it; it took a lot to ruffle the well-seasoned doctor. "Understood. I'll get right on that DNA test."

"Thanks," Pike said, softening his voice. "Sorry. I didn't mean to bark at you there."

The older man shrugged. "You've been dealing with Klingons. It's bound to rub off on you."

"Are you suggesting, Doctor," Spock asked, "that the Klingons' bellicose attitudes are contagious?"

"Let's hope not," Pike said. "Especially where our prisoner is concerned."

The turbolift dropped them off on the next deck and they marched rapidly to the brig, where they found a single security officer stationed outside a force-shielded cell. Pike noted with concern that the guard looked a bit under the weather. He was pale and trembling slightly. His eyes were watery.

"You all right, Ensign?" Pike asked.

"I'm fine, sir," the guard insisted. "Just a slight headache, sir. That's all."

Pike doubted that. "Call for another guard, and report to sickbay once your relief arrives."

"Really, sir, I can manage—"

"You heard the captain," Boyce interrupted. "I want to get you checked out, although you may have to take a number."

The guard knew better than to argue with the captain *and* the ship's doctor. "Aye, aye, sir."

Pike and Boyce exchanged worried glances as they walked past the guard to the nearest detention cell, where, on the opposite side of an invisible force field, a young Klingon woman paced restlessly back and forth like a caged animal. Her dark eyes widened at the sight of Spock. Rage contorted her face.

"You! Vulcan!"

She lunged at Spock, only to be repelled by an electrostatic charge. Energy crackled and flashed at the impact, the shock of which knocked her backward but did nothing to douse her fury.

"Cowards! Reprobates! Do you fear to face me without a wall between us? Release me at once, and I may spare your miserable lives!" She glared at Spock. "Do not think you will catch me unawares again, Vulcan. You will pay dearly for placing your unclean hand upon a true daughter of the Empire. Heed my words: I will not be so delicate when I have my own hands upon your throat. You will choke to death on your own sickly green blood!"

Spock took her threats in stride. "Fascinating," he observed. "A typically Klingon response."

"I *am* a Klingon, you cold-blooded Vulcan *petaQ*." She swept her gaze over Pike and Boyce before sneering at Spock once more. "What are you doing on a human vessel, anyway? Do they keep you as a pet . . . or a spare computer?" She let out a derisive laugh. "The whole galaxy knows that your people lost control of the Earthers more than a century ago and now watch impotently as your former charges eclipse your fallen glory!"

"That's enough." Pike stepped forward. "If you have any trouble with my people, you can take it up with me."

She grudgingly acknowledged him. "And you are?"

"Captain Christopher Pike of the *U.S.S. Enterprise* . . . and your host for the present." He indicated the force field between them. "My apologies for confining you to our brig, but your actions in the transporter room forced our hand."

"Spare me your sniveling excuses! You are wise to fear me!"

She threw herself at the force field again, as though hoping that sheer fury would be enough to overcome it, or perhaps simply as a show of defiance. She howled in frustration as the shield stubbornly resisted her efforts. She pounded her fists against the invisible barrier.

Much like I did in that cage on Talos IV, Pike thought. He couldn't blame Merata for being upset over her captivity. He hadn't taken it much better himself.

"I understand that you were beamed aboard the *Enterprise* against your will," Pike said, "and under adverse circumstances. I can arrange to provide you with more comfortable quarters if you agree not to cause any more disturbances."

She snorted at the very idea. "Save your breath, human. I want nothing from you but your blood. I will not trade my vengeance for mere comfort. I am Klingon!"

So you say, Pike thought, *but the facts tell a different story.*

He took a moment to take a closer look at the prisoner. At first glance, she certainly appeared Klingon enough, but if you looked closely you could possibly see the Cyprian behind the bared teeth, leather garb, and guttural curses. The ridges on her forehead, for instance, were indeed scar tissue and not bone, while her earlobes, which were largely obscured by her wild black mane, could have been surgically trimmed down to Klingon proportions. Different species aged at different rates, which made assessing the ages of aliens a tricky proposition, but she struck him as young, maybe even adolescent, which made her the right age to be Elzura. And was it just his imagination or could he detect a distinct resemblance to Soleste Mursh, perhaps along the nose and jaw?

"You keep insisting you're Klingon," he said, "but that's not entirely so, is it? According to our doctor, you're actually of Cyprian descent."

She reeled backward as though Pike had just slapped her across the face, then glared at him with utter loathing. If looks could kill, he would have been vaporized in an instant. Pike wondered if he'd made a mistake in confronting her with the truth. He seemed to have hit a nerve.

"My heart is Klingon! My honor is Klingon!" She fingered the jeweled pendant hanging from her neck. A blood-red gem, inscribed with a Klingon symbol, reflected the harsh lighting of her cell. "Test my courage, my warrior's spirit! Meet me in combat if you dare. Subject me to your most brutal tortures. I'll prove to you that I am a true daughter of Kahless . . . by eating your heart while it's still beating in the palm of my hand!"

Boyce's hand went instinctively to his bruised throat. "Good heavens."

"An interesting case study in nurture over nature," Spock observed. "Despite her actual biology, she appears almost more Klingon than an actual Klingon."

Glancing at his science officer, Pike wondered if Spock could relate. Did he feel obliged to act even more Vulcan than most Vulcans because of his half-human blood?

"You don't need to prove anything to us," Pike said. He decided to table the subject of her Cyprian roots for the moment, since that was apparently a hot button for her. He wanted to get through to her, so they could have a fruitful discussion, not provoke any further outbursts. Any discussion of her actual ancestry could wait until she'd had a chance to calm down, if Klingons—or even "Klingons"—

ever calmed down. "We're just trying to understand you and your situation."

He considered pointing out that the *Enterprise* had saved her life, but recalled that Klingons were not known for their gratitude. If anything, they were said to resent any suggestion that they required assistance, especially from "weaker" species. Starfleet had learned that early on, back during Jonathan Archer's historic voyages.

"The only thing you need to understand is that I do not belong here, not in this cage and not on your ship." She spit at the force field, which sparked briefly in response. "If you do not intend to release me, or kill me, then stop wasting my time."

Pike tried another tack. "I understand you're called Merata."

"That is correct." Her chin lifted proudly. "Heir to a noble house. When my father comes for me, you shall all regret insulting me in this manner. He will show you no mercy, not even in the manner of your deaths."

"Your father?" A horrible suspicion struck him with the force of a disruptor blast. "Wait a second, who exactly is your father?"

"General Krunn," she declared. "A mighty warrior of the Empire!"

Boyce traded looks with Pike. "Oh, brother."

Tell me about it, Pike thought. He kicked himself for not putting the pieces together before now.

No wonder Krunn was determined to get Merata back while taking pains not to put her at risk. She wasn't just "a daughter of the Empire." She was *his* daughter.

His *adopted* daughter.

A messy situation had just gotten a whole lot messier. It seemed Soleste's long-lost sister was Krunn's daughter—and they both wanted her back.

"Hah!" she mocked them. "Well you should tremble at my father's name. I am Merata, daughter of Krunn, and woe to any who tempt our wrath!"

Terrific, Pike thought.

He hoped Number One was having an easier time of it.

Five

"How long are they going to keep us cooped up here?" Lieutenant Giusio asked.

"An excellent question," Number One replied. "But I'm afraid that remains to be seen."

Since touching down on Cypria III, the landing party had been held in quarantine in a wood-paneled decontamination chamber at the spaceport outside the planet's capital city of Sapprus, while the cautious Cyprians subjected the *Kepler*'s crew to a time-consuming battery of scans and tests. A sterile blue radiance, reminiscent of that employed in the decon chambers of older Starfleet vessels, suffused the chamber, which was about the size of the *Enterprise*'s main transporter room. Padded benches made the wait somewhat easier for Number One and her team, which consisted of two security officers, whose sidearms had already been surrendered to the local authorities, and a nurse on loan from sickbay. Subdued music, playing softly from concealed speakers, was no doubt intended to soothe the nerves of those in isolation. Although impatient to get on with her mission and secure the ryetalyn, Number One reflected that matters could be worse.

At least we were not obliged to strip down and slather ourselves with decon jelly, she thought, *unlike previous generations of Starfleet personnel.*

She could live with that.

"Attention, visitors," a voice announced from the same unseen speaker. *"You have been found clean of infection. Thank you for your patience . . . and welcome to Cypria III."*

"About time," Nurse Olson muttered. Along with the rest of the party, he rose from a bench and tugged his blue-gray field jacket into place. "Feels like we've been cooling our heels forever."

"Their planet, their rules," Number One reminded him. "We're here as guests and supplicants, requesting assistance. Everyone, mind your manners."

"Yes, sir," Olson replied. "Just eager to get down to business, that's all."

Number One sympathized. "As are we all."

A doorway opened automatically, and they exited the chamber to find a welcoming party waiting for them in a reception area beyond. As with the decontamination chamber, the décor emphasized polished wooden panels and tiles in various shades of brown. Transparent skylights provided plenty of natural sunshine. Lush tropical flowers blossomed from potted plants. The Cyprians' aesthetic clearly tended toward the organic, at least in this region of the planet. Number One found it a pleasant change from the stark gray interior of the *Enterprise.*

The Cyprians themselves were a handsome people, whose appearance matched the descriptions in the Starfleet database. Only their scalloped ears distinguished them from humans or Illyrians, although this was more visible on the women, who wore their hair short, perhaps to show off the flare of their ears. By contrast, the men sported long hair roughly the same length as Number One's own dark tresses. Both genders favored brightly colored loose linen clothing, predominately in hues of green and orange and purple. Elaborately trimmed and embroidered vests served as status symbols, Number One understood; the more ornate and expensive the vest, the more notable the individual. The men wore tunics and knee-length shorts, while most of the women seemed to prefer skirts of assorted lengths. Number One recalled that Starfleet was contemplating giving female officers the option of wearing skirts instead of trousers while on duty.

She wasn't entirely sure what she thought of that.

"Ah, our honored guests!" a booming voice greeted them. It belonged to a stout Cyprian male whose long blond hair compensated for his receding hairline. A ruddy complexion and gleaming white teeth stood out among his beaming features as he came forward to meet the landing party, accompanied by what was perhaps his entourage. The rich fabric and intricate designs on his tangerine vest denoted his importance and authority. "We've been looking forward to meeting you."

Number One recognized the man as the democratically elected prime minister of the planet. According to her research, he was said to be a born politician, but not overly isolationist in his views. She hoped that he would prove easy enough to deal with.

"We needn't have kept you waiting," Number One replied, unable to resist lodging a minor protest. "Our ship's surgeon verified that our landing party was free of infection prior to our departure from the *Enterprise* many hours ago. Furthermore, it's my understanding that your people are happily immune to the ravages of Rigelian fever."

"Perhaps," he conceded, "but who knows what other exotic bugs you might have picked up in your travels? Better safe than sorry, as I believe you humans say. And what sort of public official would I be if I didn't take every precaution to ensure the health and safety of my constituents . . . especially during an election year?"

Number One let the matter drop. The *Enterprise* was still at least a day away from Cypria III. Despite the frustrating delay, there was still sufficient time to obtain the ryetalyn before the ship arrived to rendezvous with the *Kepler*. Perhaps she could even begin the process of refining the ryetalyn to meet Doctor Boyce's specifications.

"We greatly appreciate your hospitality," she said diplomatically, "as well as all your very reasonable precautions."

Arriving at Cypria had not been as easy as simply landing at the spaceport. *Kepler* had needed to pass through an impressive array of orbital defenses to reach the planet's surface. The shuttlecraft's sensors had detected substantial laser cannons mounted on both natural and artificial satellites, as well as around the perimeter of the major cities and population centers. There were also indications of large underground shelters.

Given the Cyprians' proximity to the Klingons, Number One couldn't blame them.

"Atron Flescu at your service." He took Number One's hand and shook it vigorously before turning to introduce the rest of the welcoming party by their duties. "And this is my chief of staff, my press secretary, my personal holographer, and various senior aides and advisors. I'd list them all by name, but I'll give you a chance to get your bearings before barraging you with a lot of new names and faces. I'm certain we'll have plenty of time to get to know each other better during your stay on our lovely planet."

"I have an excellent head for names," Number

One stated, ironically enough, "but my own can be taxing for those not raised on my native Illyria. It may be easier for you to address me as Number One, as my crewmates do." She introduced the rest of the landing party. "Lieutenants Giusio and Jones, as well as Nurse Olson, a member of our ship's medical staff. On behalf of the *U.S.S. Enterprise*, and Starfleet in general, I want to thank you for kindly offering to assist us with our present situation."

She had already been in contact, via subspace radio, with the authorities on Cypria and made them aware of the *Enterprise*'s need for suitable quantities of ryetalyn. Her understanding so far was that the Cyprians were inclined to cooperate. She anticipated no difficulties, but knew better than to take success for granted. As Captain Pike liked to say, "Hope for the best, expect the worst." She would not consider her mission accomplished until the ryetalyn was safely aboard the *Enterprise* and the outbreak of fever brought under control.

"Of course, of course!" Flescu replied. "Cyprians are a generous people. We're always ready to lend a helping hand to those in need. He glanced over at his designated "holographer," who appeared to be observing the meeting from the sidelines. "Make sure you're getting my good side."

"Always," the woman promised. A glowing crystal visor concealed her eyes. Number One assumed the visor functioned as a recording device of some sort, capturing the encounter for posterity—or perhaps simply for the prime minister's reelection campaign. "Just pretend I'm not here."

Number One found that easier said than done, but accepted that the Cyprians had their own way of doing things. And certainly the landing party had nothing to hide. Putting up with the holographer struck her as a small price to pay if it meant getting the ryetalyn.

"Perhaps if we can continue on to the capital?" she suggested, hoping to hurry matters along. "I have heard that it is a very impressive and attractive city."

"Absolutely! I'm sure you and your people are anxious to stretch your legs and get a little fresh air after your long journey and necessary confinement." Flescu beckoned for them to follow. "Come this way, please."

He led them out of the reception area onto an elevated outdoor platform, where Number One got her first impressions of Cypria III. The heat and humidity hit her first. Compared to the temperature-controlled environment of the spaceport, the climate outside was hot and sweltering. Sapprus was located in the equatorial region of the planet's eastern hemisphere, and the tropical atmosphere reminded Number One of Newer Mumbai or Dorado Prime. A heavy floral fragrance wafted on the warm afternoon breezes. She felt overdressed in her standard field jacket and uniform.

"Whew," Lieutenant Jones exclaimed. She wiped her brow. "Feels like I'm back in Atlanta."

Sapprus rose in the distance, less than three kilometers away. Gleaming in the sunlight, it was a city of towering skyscrapers and elevated railways. Number One assumed that the polished wooden facades of the buildings were just that, concealing sturdier metallic supports. Or perhaps the buildings were indeed constructed of wood and merely reinforced and strengthened by artificial means? In any event, the city proudly displayed the abundance of the planet's verdant forests. She could well understand why the original colonists had chosen to settle here.

"My apologies for the heat," Flescu said. "We quite like it ourselves, but perhaps you prefer a more temperate environment?"

Number One had hiked Vulcan's Forge in her youth. She figured she could endure a little humidity. "We're simply happy to visit your world."

A maglev train car waited at the platform. Along with ornamental trimming, the car also boasted an embossed government seal that resembled the twining, curlicue designs on the prime minister's vest. He gestured toward it proudly.

"My personal tram," he said. "Nothing but the best for our distinguished guests."

Number One contemplated the vehicle and the monorail track stretching toward the city. "We're honored by the privilege, but would not a site-to-site transport be more efficient?"

"Perhaps," Flescu answered, "but a short, scenic ride will give you a better opportunity to take in the beauty of our lovely capital."

"That's very thoughtful of you, but our mission *is* of some urgency." She tried to speed matters up without appearing too impatient or ill-mannered. "Perhaps there will time for sightseeing later?"

"It's an express train," he insisted. "It won't take long at all."

She conceded to the inevitable. "Very well. Shall we be on our way?"

They boarded the tram, which proved mercifully climate-controlled as well as luxuriously furnished. Number One sat across from Flescu in a plush booth divided by a varnished wood table on which drinks and refreshments were laid. Her security officers took care to scope out the interior of the car before finding seats for themselves and Nurse Olson. Number One noted that the prime minister had his own security detail, which could be recognized by their dark burgundy uniforms and caps. They remained discreetly in the background, keeping watch while not calling undue attention to their presence. They were armed, she observed, with both batons and compact laser pistols. She wondered what had become of the landing party's confiscated weapons and whether they would be returned to them later.

"We should be under way momentarily," Flescu said. "Do enjoy the view and help yourself to some refreshments. The egg nuts are particularly tasty this time of year."

True to his word, the tram lurched to life and began cruising toward the city. Taking advantage of a window seat, Number One watched with deliberate patience as the city proper came into view. Flowers and greenery were plentiful, showcased in landscaped parks, plazas, and gardens. Fountains and manmade waterfalls sparkled in the sunlight, adding to the impression of a modern civilization enjoying the benefits of a more than habitable Class-M planet occupying the most hospitable orbit in its solar system. A clear azure sky added to the attractive scenery.

Evidence of the upcoming election was also readily apparent. Number One spotted numerous holographic posters and billboards urging Cyprians to vote for Flescu, as well as a lesser number promoting other candidates. She suspected that Flescu's holographer, who was continuing to assiduously document the landing party's arrival, was taking pains to keep those *other* billboards out of her shots. Number One's own native world of Illyria was more of a meritocracy than a democracy, with officials selected through careful testing and aptitude exams, but Number One understood how politics worked. You couldn't truly understand the Federation—or even Starfleet—without some grasp of the concept.

"Your timing is excellent," Flescu commented. "You're missing the rainy season."

"How fortuitous," she replied politely. "I could claim to have done so on purpose, but, as you know, necessity dictated the timing of our visit." She attempted to steer the discussion toward the matter at hand and retrieved a microtape from one of her jacket's inner pockets. "Our ship's surgeon has prepared a detailed list of our requirements. Quantities, isotopes, levels of purity, and so on. A refined powder would be preferable, but we can apparently make do with untreated ore or crystals."

Flescu handed the tape off to one of his aides. "I'm certain we can accommodate your specifications, but you understand, of course, that ryetalyn is quite rare—and valuable—in this sector of the galaxy." A calculating look entered his eyes. "I assume we will be compensated at some point, by either Starfleet or the Federation?"

"Naturally," she said, having anticipated that this issue might arise. In its journeys, the *Enterprise* had occasion to deal with cultures practicing a wide variety of economic systems and its crew often found

themselves required to employ assorted forms
of currency and credits. She had no doubt that
Starfleet would authorize whatever expenditures
were required to quell the outbreak aboard the *Enterprise,* but hoped that she wouldn't have to waste
too much time and energy haggling over the price.
She was a Starfleet officer, not an Orion trader. "I'm
sure suitable compensation can be arranged, on top
of Starfleet's sincere gratitude."

"Which is of no small value in its own right,"
Flescu granted. "It never hurts to be owed a favor
by a powerful neighbor." He chuckled briefly before glancing over at the holographer recording his
every word. "Not that cost is any issue, of course,
where sentient lives are at stake. But I would be
remiss in my duties if I wasn't fiscally responsible
when it comes to our vital natural resources."

"I quite understand." Number One allowed the
prime minister to play to the camera. "You need to
look out for your people's interests."

"Exactly so!" Flescu beamed sunnily. "I knew we
would see eye to eye."

Number One trusted that the holographer
would be retired at some point, perhaps when it
came down to working out the unexciting logistics
of preparing the ryetalyn for delivery to the *Enterprise,* but for now she would have to go along with
the political posturing and hope that Flescu eventually had all the footage he needed for his reelection

campaign. Then, maybe, she could finally get on with her actual mission.

"So I understand that the *Enterprise* is en route to Cypria as well," Flescu said. "I'm told there was an emergency involving a Cyprian vessel?"

Number One nodded. She had informed the Cyprians of the *Enterprise*'s detour during *Kepler*'s approach to the planet while first explaining the purpose of her mission.

"That is correct. The *Enterprise* responded to a distress signal from a Cyprian spacecraft, the *Ilion*. The ship could not be saved, but I'm happy to report that there were no fatalities. The survivors are now safely aboard the *Enterprise* and are being looked after by Captain Pike and his crew."

Number One chose her words carefully. The captain had briefed her regarding the outcome of the rescue mission and the thorny issues that had arisen since. She was reluctant to volunteer too much information at this juncture, but the *Ilion* was a Cyprian vessel after all. She could hardly keep them in the dark regarding the fate of one of their own ships and its passengers.

"Well, I suppose we can be thankful no one was killed and that the *Enterprise* was able to rescue the survivors." Flescu turned to one of his aides. "What do we know about this ship, the *Ilion*?"

The aide consulted a handheld device. "A small trading vessel currently registered to a Soleste Mursh."

Number One was impressed at how quickly the aide retrieved the information. The Cyprians' computer networks could apparently give Starfleet's data libraries a run for their money.

"Mursh . . . Mursh," Flescu murmured. "Where do I know that name from?"

As before, the aide soon had the information at his fingertips. "The Mursh family was among the victims of a Klingon raid ten years ago. The father killed, a child apparently abducted. Soleste Mursh is the eldest child." The aide squinted at the device. "She's offered a standing reward for any information leading to the recovery of her missing sister, Elzura, for several years now. She's apparently quite intent on finding the lost girl."

"Of course." Flescu snapped his fingers. "The attack on the lunar mining facility. A terrible tragedy, for both the family and all of Cypria. It was appalling incidents like that which made it clear we needed to bolster our planetary defenses so that such a grievous atrocity could never happen again." He presented a resolute profile to the holographer. "I'm proud to say that we have no suffered no such raids under my watch."

Number One wondered if she should mention that the *Ilion* was destroyed while attempting to outrun a Klingon battle cruiser. *Perhaps not at this moment.*

"You said there were survivors," Flescu recalled. "Plural. Who else beside the Mursh woman?"

Number One hesitated, but saw no way to duck the matter. The Cyprians deserved the truth, which would surely come out once the *Enterprise* returned Soleste Mursh to her people. It would not do for them to discover that the landing party had withheld crucial information from them, not if the *Enterprise* was still counting on Cypria's help with regards to the ryetalyn.

"A second Cyprian woman was rescued," she divulged. "There is reason to believe that she may, in fact, be Elzura Mursh."

Flescu's eyes lit up. He turned eagerly toward his staff. "Did you hear that? Find the rest of the family and get them here right away." He rubbed his hands in anticipation. "We need to arrange a proper homecoming!"

His entourage scurried to carry out his orders, filling the tram with a hubbub of muted voices speaking into assorted communications devices. Number One suppressed a frown; the prime minister clearly saw political gain in the possible return of Elzura to her homeworld, but the Illyrian worried that he did not have all the facts and that this distraction might get in the way of her mission. First and foremost, she needed to remain focused on the ryetalyn.

"You should be aware," she said, "that there are complications."

Something in her tone got his attention. He regarded her warily, his broad smile growing more forced.

"What sort of complications?"

Six

"Let me get this straight," Pike said. "The Cyprians are now refusing to provide us with the ryetalyn?"

"Not until 'Little Elzy' is returned to them," Number One confirmed. Her somber visage occupied the viewscreen in the briefing room. *"There's some concern that you might choose to 'appease' the Klingons by giving Elzura back to them."* Regret tinged her voice. *"I'm sorry, Captain. Perhaps I should not have fully informed the prime minister of the particulars of this matter."*

"It was going to coming out eventually," Pike assured her, not wanting his first officer to blame herself for a situation that had turned sticky the moment he'd chosen to beam the *Ilion*'s passengers aboard. "Outside of keeping Soleste Mursh in solitary confinement, and cut off from her own people, I'm not sure how we were going to keep the whole Elzura/Merata mess under wraps. And lying to the Cyprians at the same time that we're asking for their help hardly sounds like a shrewd diplomatic move to me." He sighed. "We're just going to have to play the hand we've been dealt."

Spock gave him a puzzled look. The young officer was seated at the conference table along with Pike and Doctor Boyce, while Yeoman Colt was also present to take notes on the meeting. As this was primarily a medical and diplomatic matter, Chief Engineer Barry was not in attendance. Spock voiced his confusion. "Hand, Captain?"

Pike guessed that Vulcans weren't into card games.

"A human idiom, Mister Spock. Remind me to explain it to you later." He turned his attention back to Number One. "I don't suppose you can convince the Cyprians to treat the ryetalyn as a separate issue?"

The fever was spreading like wildfire through the ship, testing sickbay's ability to keep up with it. At last count, at least a quarter of the crew was showing signs of infection, amounting to some fifty men and women in the early stages of the disease. Many were still trying to keep working at their posts, but they were fighting a losing battle. Even the ones that were still on their feet were hardly at peak performance.

"*I'm doing my best,*" Number One said, "*but passions are running high regarding this issue, and there's a political dimension as well. Prime Minister Flescu is running for reelection, and my impression is that he wants very much to be the leader who wel-*"

comes the long-lost child home, not the man who let the Klingons take her back."

"Terrific," Pike said. "As if an irate Klingon general and his bloodthirsty 'daughter' aren't difficult enough, now we have to deal with politics, too?"

That cage on Talos IV was starting to seem positively cozy by comparison.

"I'm afraid so, Captain," Number One reported. *"Trust me, I don't like it any better than you do. Frankly, things are starting to get a little tense here."*

"Understood," Pike said. "Watch yourself, Number One, and keep me posted. *Enterprise* out."

The screen went blank as he cut short the transmission. He looked away from the viewer to address Spock and Boyce.

"All right, gentlemen, let's take stock of our situation. We have a deadly fever raging through the ship, a Klingon battle cruiser on our tail, and an ill-tempered hot potato in our brig. And now, according to Number One, the Cyprians are refusing to help out unless we turn over Merata or Elzura or whatever we want to call her. Thoughts?"

"For what it's worth," Boyce said, leading off, "I can confirm that Elzura Mursh and Merata are indeed one and the same. I ran that DNA comparison you asked for, and Merata is definitely related to Soleste, beyond any reasonable margin for error."

"Well, that settles that," Pike said, "but we're still left with a big problem. Both the Cyprians and the

Klingons want her back, and neither side is going to be happy until they get her. With us stuck in the middle."

"Excuse me, sir," Colt said, speaking up, "but shouldn't that be her decision?"

Pike didn't mind her adding her own two cents to the discussion. Despite some initial awkwardness when she'd first taken over as his yeoman, replacing an old friend lost on Rigel VII, Colt had proven to have a good head on her shoulders. He was glad she felt comfortable enough to speak her mind.

"Unfortunately, it's not that simple," he replied. "Beyond the potentially dire consequences of antagonizing the Klingons *or* the Cyprians, we have to remember that Elzura was abducted against her will as a child, no matter what she's been raised to believe since. Who knows how that's affected her?" He looked over at Boyce. "I don't suppose you had a chance to do a full psychological analysis while she was choking you?"

"Hardly," the doctor said with a snort. "But you raise a valid concern. There's a psychological phenomenon identified on Earth centuries ago, Stockholm syndrome, that suggests that, under certain circumstances, a hostage can come to sympathize and even identify with her captors. Given that Elzy was only seven years old when she was carried off, she might not be thinking clearly, nor looking out for her own best interests."

"There is also the fact," Spock observed, "that under Cyprian law Elzura is legally a minor and her family can rightfully claim custody of her."

"I'm not sure Merata would agree," Pike said, "let alone General Krunn."

The *Fek'lhr* had stuck to the *Enterprise* like glue, even as the Federation starship had resumed course for Cypria III. At present, the battle cruiser was staying just beyond weapons range, but Pike wasn't sure how long they could expect Krunn to show restraint; the Klingon commander was unlikely to give up until he had his "daughter" back, while the Cyprians were bound to object to a Klingon warship tailing the *Enterprise* all the way into their territory. This whole situation was a powder keg just waiting for somebody to strike a match.

Of all times for so many of my crew to be flat on their backs, Pike thought.

Boyce eyed him with concern. "What are you going to do, Chris?"

"Good question, Doctor." Pike rubbed the bridge of his nose, feeling a headache coming on. "We're still several hours from Cypria III. Perhaps Number One can still talk the Cyprians into compromising, at least where the ryetalyn is concerned."

"I wouldn't count on that," Boyce said. "No offense, Mister Spock, but in my experience, emotion usually trumps logic, especially when it comes to family and politics."

"No offense taken, Doctor," Spock replied evenly. "I fear I cannot dispute your assessment. More's the pity."

Pike wondered what it was like for Spock to explore a universe that so seldom lived up to Vulcan standards of logic and discipline. From what Pike had seen of sentient life throughout the quadrant, Vulcans were practically unique in their commitment to logic over emotion. Then again, Spock *did* have a foot in both camps, not unlike Merata. They were both the products of two wildly different cultures and races. And Spock seemed to deny his human heritage almost as vigorously as Merata rejected her Cyprian roots.

"I suppose helping ourselves to some ryetalyn without the Cyprians' permission is out of the question?" Boyce suggested hesitantly. "Just asking."

Pike understood that the doctor was only thinking of his patients and the overall health of the crew. "I appreciate your position, Doctor, but even if we wanted to just go in and grab some, the planet's formidable defenses would make that a very dicey proposition. Nor do I believe that Number One and her team are in any position to steal some." Four crew members holed up in a government building could hardly function as a covert strike team. "Beyond that, Starfleet is not in the business of raiding independent worlds, not even uncooperative ones."

"I know, I know." Boyce sighed wearily. "It's just that this is a matter of life and death, Chris, for more good men and women than I want to count. In the long term, this blasted fever is as dangerous as any space battle." He glanced at the exit. "In fact, I should really be getting back to my sickbay, if that's all right with you."

"You're dismissed, Doctor." Pike looked around the table. "You, too, Yeoman."

Boyce and Colt rose from their seats and headed out into the corridor, while Spock remained seated at the table. "You wish me to remain, Captain?"

"That's correct, Mister Spock. I need a few more minutes of your time."

Spock regarded him attentively. "If this is about the opening on the *Intrepid,* I confess that I have been preoccupied with more pressing matters—"

Pike brushed that aside with a wave of his hand. "No. That can wait. This is about Merata."

Spock gave him a puzzled look. "Merata?"

"For better or for worse, that young woman is the center of this storm. Somebody needs to get through to her, get her side of the story, so we can figure out where she really belongs."

"But is that what matters here?" Spock asked. "With all due respect to her personal well-being and autonomy, there are significantly larger is-sues at stake: the lives of the crew, the risk of war with the Klingons, the Federation's relations with

Cypria III, and perhaps even the safety of the landing party. It may well be that, in this instance, the
needs of the many outweigh what is best for one
particular individual."

"Perhaps," Pike said, seeing his point, "and it
may come down to that, but all we've gotten from
her so far is threats and violence and angry outbursts. If I'm going to play Solomon with regards to
her future, I'd like to have a better idea of whose fate
is in my hands."

This time Spock caught the reference. "As I recall, Solomon solved his dilemma by threatening to
slice the disputed child in two. That option strikes
me as inadvisable in our present circumstances."

Pike assumed that was a joke.

"I'm inclined to agree, which is why I'm delegating you the task of getting to know this girl and
finding out who she really is, Merata or Elzura or
none of the above. We need to find a way to get past
her hostility and understand her."

A hint of a frown appeared on Spock's stoic
countenance. "I hope you are not suggesting a
mind-meld, Captain."

Pike shook his head. Mind-melds were still
mysterious to him, but he understood that such a
telepathic merging was a profoundly intimate and
even dangerous procedure. He was not about to ask
that of Spock—or Merata—unless it was a matter of
life and death.

And maybe not even then.

"Just *talk* to her, Spock. Try to forge a connection."

"If you think that best, sir, but I have to ask: Why me? Surely there are others aboard the ship better suited to the task. I am a science officer, not a counselor or psychologist, and need I remind you that Vulcans are hardly known for our sociability?"

"And yet your father is a diplomat, isn't he?"

Spock stiffened. "I am not my father."

Pike thought he detected a slight edge to Spock's voice. It was subtle, but it was there. Pike wondered if maybe there was some bad blood between Spock and his father, and if this had anything to do with Spock's half-human nature.

"Maybe not, but you're all I have right now."

Spock continued to resist the assignment. "Perhaps Doctor Boyce . . . ?"

"The doctor has his hands full in sickbay," Pike said. "Number One is stuck on Cypria III, in the middle of a potentially volatile situation, and I've got a ship full of angry Klingons to keep my eyes on. I'm sorry, Spock, but *somebody* has to deal with Merata, and I'm afraid you've drawn the short straw."

"I understand, Captain." Spock sounded resigned to the task, but still somewhat skeptical about his prospects. "I will endeavor to carry out your orders, but . . . she *is* a Klingon, sir, in all but genetics. It is doubtful that anyone, let alone a Vulcan, will be able to establish a productive dialogue with her."

"You may be surprised, Spock." Pike didn't want to get too personal, but he couldn't help thinking that Spock's own dual heritage might ultimately help him relate to their controversial guest. "Call it a hunch, but I'm hoping that maybe, just maybe, you and Merata will be able to find some common ground after all."

Spock arched an eyebrow. "If you say so, sir."

Seven

"Lives are at stake, Prime Minister. Every hour we delay puts the crew of the *Enterprise* in greater jeopardy."

Number One argued with a life-sized holographic transmission of Flescu in the VIP suite of her temporary lodgings in Sapprus. She and the rest of the landing party had been put up in Envoy House, a downtown residence reserved for visiting dignitaries. The five-story wooden building overlooked a spacious plaza, and its balconies offered excellent views of the city, but Number One was presently focused on the three-dimensional figure "standing" before her in the suite's richly furnished living area. A projector in the ceiling made it seem as though the recalcitrant politician was actually present and not simply speaking to her from his own offices across town. The resolution quality was impressive; aside from the occasional flicker, the hologram appeared almost tangible.

"I sympathize with your predicament," Flescu said, "but my hands are tied. Ever since the news leaked that Elzura had been rescued from the Klingons, all of Cypria has been united in its conviction that she be brought home at last and not returned to the brigands who brutally stole her in the first place. I have no choice but to reflect the will of my people."

Especially during an election season, Number One thought.

Unfortunately, he was not exaggerating. Cypria III had a thriving global media industry and the saga of Little Elzy had been headline news for over a day now, with public opinion running strongly against any cooperation with the *Enterprise* until the long-lost child was delivered back to her planet of origin. The situation was volatile enough that Number One had already instructed the landing party to remain safely inside Envoy House and resist the temptation to explore the city. She did not wish to risk any angry confrontations with the locals.

"About that leak," she asked, "how is it that this became public knowledge?"

Flescu threw up his hands. "Who knows? Frankly, I suspect my political opponents are behind this. They would like nothing better than for me to look weak and impotent when it comes to dealing with your Starfleet, and unable to defend an innocent Cyprian family against the Klingons. But if your captain could just do the right thing and bring Elzura back to where she belongs, then this whole crisis would evaporate. I'd look like a hero, you'd get your ryetalyn . . . everyone wins."

"What of the Klingons?" she asked. "They are no less determined to take Merata back and are unlikely to give her up without a fight. Are you prepared to risk a Klingon attack for the sake of one young woman who doesn't even want to return to Cypria?"

"You underestimate our defenses," Flescu bragged. "I think we can repel a single battle cruiser."

"And if the Klingons return in force? What then?"

"Cypria will never bow to Klingon threats or intimidation." He lifted his chin defiantly. "Let them come."

She tried to reason with him. "So you would endanger the lives of millions for one lost child?"

"Don't be naïve," he chided her. "She's not just an individual anymore. She's a symbol now, of Cyprian independence and the security of every Cyprian family. And facts and figures are no match for a symbol where politics are concerned."

She feared he was correct in that regard. "You know your business, I suppose, but my primary concern is the health of my crew. It would be tragic if suffering men and women continue to sicken while we haggle over a . . . symbol."

"Which is why you and your captain need to come to your senses and be practical about this.

Time is on our side, Number One," he said smugly. "We've waited a decade to get Elzura back. How long can you afford to wait for our ryetalyn?"

Not long, she admitted privately. "That is . . . uncertain."

"Why don't I give you some time to think about it?" Flescu said. "Enjoy the rest of your day."

The hologram vanished in a blink, leaving her staring at empty air.

"Well, that was unproductive," she muttered.

———

"You again, Vulcan? I thought I made it clear that the very sight of you disgusts me!"

Merata remained confined to the brig, trapped behind the transparent force field. Her contempt was of little concern to Spock, save that it did not bode well for the success of his assignment. Watching the prisoner roam restlessly about her cell, he feared that the captain had been overly optimistic concerning his odds of getting through to her. Merata did not seem inclined to open up to any of her captors, least of all him. And they had hardly gotten off to an auspicious start in the transporter room, when he had been forced to incapacitate her. Klingons were known for holding grudges.

"I apologize if my appearance is unpleasing," he said. "I regret that there is little that I can do in that regard."

"You can remove your foul self from my presence, you cold-blooded Vulcan coward." She sneered at him through the force field. "How did you placid, spineless worms ever work up the nerve to venture beyond your own wretched sandpit of a planet, anyway?"

Spock did not feel obliged to defend his people or his world. Instead he pushed on in an attempt to fulfill the captain's orders, despite his own doubts as to the usefulness of the endeavor.

"My name is Spock." He surveyed the stark accommodations of the brig. An uneaten meal, composed of barely cooked animal flesh, bleeding red, sat ignored in one corner. "Is there anything I can provide to make your present confinement more amenable?" A rank odor penetrated the invisible barrier. "Perhaps a change of attire?"

"I will dress as a Klingon or not at all!" She smoothed the layer of golden chain mail over her dress. The crimson pendant at her throat bore a symbol that Spock now recognized as the mark of her adopted house, as seen also on General Krunn's baldric. She regarded his Starfleet uniform with disdain. "You don't even look like soldiers."

"That is because we prefer to be explorers." He indicated his own blue tunic. "And scientists."

She turned up her nose at his explanation. "Bah! Klingons do not idly observe the universe. We seize it by force of arms!"

That was not entirely correct. No advanced technological civilization could arise or endure without scientists, but it was Spock's understanding that scientific research was perhaps undervalued by Klingon society, which placed a greater premium on martial prowess and accomplishments. In that way, they were the polar opposites of his own people, who prized pure scientific research and regarded force as, at best, a necessary evil. Certainly, his father considered the Vulcan Science Academy far worthier than Starfleet, at least as far as Spock was concerned

"In any event," he persisted, "I am certain that proper Klingon attire can be fabricated to suit you."

"I want no favors from you, Vulcan. Only to be returned to my people."

A touch of frustration tested his emotional control. He was not convinced that attempting to communicate with Merata was a judicious use of his time or talents. Conversing with her was like scanning an unstable neutron star—all you got was static and random bursts of radiation. It was an exercise in futility.

"Releasing you is not presently within my abilities. Are you certain there is nothing else you require at this time?"

"Are you deaf, Vulcan? I want nothing . . ." She started to reject his efforts at hospitality once more, then paused to reconsider. A bloodthirsty grin lifted her lips, and she cracked her knuckles ominously. "What of the perfidious she-*targ* who waylaid me? Can you grant me five moments alone with her?"

"Your sister, you mean?"

Merata froze as though caught in a stasis beam. Her jaw dropped and, for the first time, her stubborn defiance faltered. She stared at Spock in shock. Her voice, when it emerged, was barely more than a croak.

"S-sister?"

Fascinating, Spock thought. Had he finally found the chink in Merata's faux Klingon armor? He recalled Doctor Boyce's observation that family issues often exerted an irresistible pull on the emotions. It was an insight that Spock, if he was truly honest with himself, could personally attest to. His own feelings toward his parents were . . . complicated. And he had not laid eyes on his own brother for over a decade.

"Soleste Mursh, the other survivor of the *Ilion*, is your elder sister."

"You're lying!" she erupted. "I have no sister!"

"The DNA evidence is conclusive." He recalled the way she had lunged at Soleste in the transporter room. "I take it you did not recognize her before?"

"I . . . I thought there was something familiar about her," Merata said haltingly, before her temper flared again. "The lying witch lured me aboard her pathetic vessel on the false pretext of showing me her wares, and I foolishly lowered my guard, thinking her no threat. When I regained consciousness, I was bound and disarmed aboard that Cyprian garbage scow, which was under fire from my father's warship." She blinked in confusion. "But . . . my sister? No, this is a trick. You are trying to deceive me, Vulcan!"

"But if she is not your sister," he countered, "why would she go to such lengths, risking her ship and her life, to rescue you?"

"I needed no rescue!" She angrily seized a plate from her meal tray and flung it against the force field, which bounced it harmlessly back into her cell. Meat and vegetables splattered onto the floor. "I am the daughter of Krunn. I was where I belonged!"

"*Adopted* daughter," Spock stressed. He had not even flinched when she'd thrown the plate. "You must surely be aware that you are not biologically Klingon, despite your various cosmetic modifications."

"I am Klingon in every way that matters!" She traced the ridges on her brow with a finger. "See these scars? I carved them myself . . . with my own blade!"

Curious, Spock thought. He would not have guessed that she had mutilated herself, particularly considering that the majority of the Klingons in this sector had no cranial ridges. It appeared that she was indeed determined to present herself as more

Klingon than even the typical Klingon, perhaps to compensate for her shameful Cyprian roots?

Spock knew the feeling.

Perhaps this was the common ground of which the captain spoke?

It was a troubling thought. As a rule, Spock guarded his privacy. Sharing confidences did not come easily to him, in part because this might expose the all-too-human feelings he strove to deny, but it seemed that he might not have any choice in this instance, not if he hoped to carry out the captain's orders to the best of his abilities. He could hardly expect Merata to open up and acknowledge her complicated identity and past unless he was willing to do the same . . . to a degree.

"It cannot have been easy," he said, attempting to empathize with Merata's position, "being the Cyprian daughter of a Klingon general. I . . . understand . . . why you might wish to reject your Cyprian heritage."

"Spare me your sympathy, Vulcan. You know nothing of what you speak."

He noted that she did not deny that her situation had been a difficult one, only that he could not comprehend what it had been like for her. He took a deep breath, bracing himself for what he had to say next. Given a choice, he would have rather wrestled a rabid *sehlat* than speak openly of personal matters, but he had his orders.

"My father is the head of a very old and honorable Vulcan house," he divulged, "but my mother is a human . . . from Earth."

Her eyes widened in surprise. She stepped closer to the force field, so that only the thin barrier separated them, and peered at him suspiciously.

"You look Vulcan to me."

"Thank you," he said sincerely. "But I assure you that, although raised as a Vulcan, I am half-human."

He was tempted to point out that he was, at least from a biological standpoint, more human than she was Klingon, but feared that she would react badly to that observation. At the same time, he was acutely aware of the gold-shirted security officer posted on guard a few meters away. Lieutenant Willard did not appear to be eavesdropping on the conversation, but Spock lowered his voice nonetheless.

Merata tilted her head, scrutinizing him from another angle.

"Did you take a knife to your ears," she asked, "to make yourself look fully Vulcan?"

Her own ears had obviously been cropped. Doctor Boyce had indicated earlier that it had been done professionally, presumably by a skilled Klingon surgeon working at Krunn's request. Or had that surgeon merely repaired Merata's own crude efforts to make herself look more Klingon?

"That was not necessary," Spock said. "However, I might have considered it, had it been so."

His reply was an honest one. Growing up on Vulcan as a child of mixed ancestry had been challenging, to say the least. The jeers of the other Vulcan children still echoed at the back of his mind sometimes. He could only imagine how much more difficult it might have been if he had been born with more human features. He might well have considered cosmetic alterations, even at the expense of his mother's feelings. Certainly he had always made every other effort to appear as Vulcan as possible.

Had Merata encountered similar taunts and bullying while being raised as a Klingon? If so, it was a testament to her strength and endurance that she had survived at all. Vulcan bullies were bad enough; their Klingon counterparts would surely be many times more brutal. Spock acquired a newfound respect for the ferocious young woman before him.

"And is your blood green or red?" she asked with a smirk. "Alas, I never had a chance to find out."

"Green, like my father's. Just as your blood must be the same color as your sister's."

"My so-called sister!" she insisted, although her objection sounded slightly more perfunctory than before, as though uncertainty had begun to sap her outrage. She fell uncharacteristically silent and still for a moment before speaking again. "What did you say her name was?"

Spock guessed that she was only feigning ig-

norance. She had been seven years old when abducted. He was not entirely conversant with the
developmental patterns of Cyprian offspring, but,
by most humanoid standards, she would have been
old enough to retain *some* memory of her original
family. Or so he assumed.

"Soleste," he said to jog her memory. "And you
were once known as Elzura."

"My name is Merata!"

Spittle sprayed from her lips as she furiously
asserted her Klingon identity. She bared her teeth
and glared murderously at Spock, who feared for a
moment that he had pressed her too hard and too
quickly. He made a mental note to refrain from employing her Cyprian name for the time being.

"Very well, *Merata*," he conceded. "But indulge
my curiosity. How much do you remember of your
early childhood on Cypria III, before you were 'adopted' by the Klingons?"

"That is none of your concern, Vulcan." She
stalked away from the barrier and resumed her
pacing. "I grow weary of this meaningless babble.
Answer me truly: How long do you intend to hold
me against my will?"

"That remains to be determined," he answered.
"Although, once again, more hospitable accommodations can be provided for you. We would prefer
to treat you as a guest during your stay aboard this
ship."

She snorted in derision.

"A guest who is not free to leave is still a prisoner."

He could not fault her logic. "A reasonable conclusion, I admit."

"Then we have nothing more to discuss." She turned her back on Spock. "Leave me."

Spock appraised the situation. Time was of the essence, and the captain was in need of a better understanding of their guest, but he concluded that it might be unwise to attempt to interrogate Merata any further at this juncture, when she presumably needed time to process the startling information he had shared with her. To his surprise, a degree of progress had been achieved in establishing a dialogue with Merata, so he did not want to sacrifice those gains by "pushing his luck," as the captain might put it. A strategic retreat was often the most logical course of action.

"As you wish," he assented. "We can resume our discussion at some other time. Please inform the guard if you wish to speak with me in the interim."

He turned to leave and had almost exited the brig when a voice called out from the cell.

"Vulcan."

He pivoted to address her. "Yes?"

Merata stood at the very edge of the barrier. Her eyes met his across the length of the brig.

"That woman. *Soleste*." She pronounced the name

with obvious distaste. "How serious are her injuries. Will she live?"

Her voice was flat, betraying neither concern for her sister's welfare nor an unquenched desire for vengeance against her abductor. Spock wondered once more how much she recalled of her early years and her family.

"Doctor Boyce is an excellent physician. He is confident that she will make a full recovery."

Merata's face was rigid and inscrutable, almost Vulcan in its absence of emotion.

"I see."

Spock took the risk of going a step further. "If you wish, I can arrange a meeting, provided you consent to certain reasonable security measures."

She ignored the offer.

"Go away, Vulcan. You've said enough for today."

That appeared to be the case.

Eight

"Approaching Cypria III, Captain."

"Thank you, Mister Tyler," Pike said to the navigator. He noted with concern that Tyler looked less than his usual ebullient self. The young officer appeared tired and hungover, as though he'd just returned from an overly eventful shore leave on Ishtar Station. Pike hoped to heaven Tyler wasn't coming down with something Rigelian. "Slow to impulse."

"Aye, sir," Mohindas replied from the helm.

The *Enterprise* dropped out of warp, and Pike watched as the planet came into view on the screen before him. Cypria III looked much like Earth, complete with polar icecaps, a handful of continents separated by vast oceans, and patches of wispy white clouds drifting through its atmosphere, occasionally obscuring the rotating planet below, which appeared more than hospitable to most conventional forms of life. Cypria III looked like a world worth settling—and possibly fighting for.

"We're being hailed by the planet," Garrison

reported. "They're requesting that we enter an orbit outside the area patrolled by their defense satellites."

Pike nodded, unsurprised. He had no intention of attempting to seize the ryetalyn by force, but apparently the Cyprians did not entirely trust him to show such restraint. Under the circumstances, he could hardly blame them, even as he resented them withholding the much-needed cure.

He glanced around the bridge, noting the toll the spreading fever was already taking on the ship's operations. The bridge was still fully staffed, but only barely, without the usual complement of auxiliary crew members to supplement each station, while many of the posts were currently being worked by junior officers and NCOs with less experience than Pike might have preferred. He was tempted to call Spock back to the bridge, but decided against it. According to Spock, the science officer was, against all odds, starting to establish some sort of rapport with Merata. Pike figured that was more important than chaining Spock to the science station. Ensign Weisz could keep working that post for the time being, or at least until he came down with the fever, too.

"Comply with their request, helmsman," he instructed Mohindas, before turning toward the science station. "What's the story with our Klingon friends?"

Weisz peered into his gooseneck monitor. "They're

still shadowing us, Captain. Not quite within weapons range, but close enough as to make little difference."

"Maintain minimal shields," Pike ordered. He disliked the extra energy expenditure involved; standard policy was only to raise shields in the event of a genuine emergency, but he didn't want to tempt the Klingons into launching a sneak attack in an attempt to recover Merata. "And keep a close eye on them."

"Will do, sir," Weisz said. "I can't imagine doing otherwise."

Pike visualized the *Fek'lhr* hanging in space somewhere behind them. He hadn't really expected Krunn to turn back at the border of the Cyprian system, but it was still worrisome that the Klingons had followed them all the way here, practically into orbit around Cypria III. He could only assume that the Cyprians' defense forces had detected the battle cruiser's approach and were already on high alert. More than ever, Pike felt like he was sitting on top of an overloading laser pistol that could explode at the slightest provocation.

Cypria III came closer to view. He could make out at least three moons now and a couple of artificial defense satellites. The *Enterprise* entered into a stationary orbit above the planet's eastern hemisphere and Pike's gaze was drawn to the equator, where the landing party was presently located.

Night was creeping across a lush green continent glimpsed through drifting wisps of cloud cover. Sapprus, the capital city, was not visible from this distance, but Pike knew it was there.

"Get me Number One," he instructed Garrison, "but employ maximum encryption. We don't want anyone listening in, least of all the Klingons."

"Understood," the petty officer said. "Hailing landing party now."

It was vitally important that Krunn not find out about the fever raging aboard the *Enterprise*, which the Klingons would correctly see as a weakness to exploit. He glanced around the bridge again, just to make certain that there were no obviously sick or infected crew members in view, and spotted a shaky-looking technician replacing some burned-out control circuits over by the navigation sub-systems. Pike could hear the man wheezing as he forced himself to keep working. He sounded like a leaky air-pressure manifold.

"Dorgan. Go get some coffee. You look like you could use a break."

It said something about how sick Dorgan was that he didn't put up a fight. "If you say so, Captain." He walked stiffly to the turbolift, as though every muscle ached. "I'll be right back."

"Take your time." Pike waited until the man was safely out of sight before checking with Garrison. "Have you made contact with the landing party?"

"Affirmative, sir," Garrison replied. "Opening frequency now. Full encryption protocols in place."

Number One appeared upon the viewscreen. She looked tired, Pike thought. He couldn't remember how late it was in Sapprus right now. He hoped he hadn't woken her.

"*Welcome to Cypria III, Captain,*" she greeted him. "*Is this transmission secure?*"

Clearly she had also grasped the importance of not advertising the outbreak aboard the *Enterprise.* It probably wouldn't even do for the Cyprians to realize just how dire the situation was becoming. That might simply increase their determination to use the ryetalyn as a bargaining chip to force him to turn over Merata to them. He glanced at Garrison, who nodded back at him.

"You can speak freely, Number One," the captain assured her. "Any progress to report?"

"*I wish,*" she sighed wearily. "*You may have come all this way for nothing, Captain.*"

Not necessarily, Pike thought. They would have needed to return Soleste Mursh to her home planet in any event. "The Cyprians are still playing hardball about the ryetalyn?"

"*I'm afraid the matter of Elzura is rapidly becoming a planetary obsession, Captain, fanned by the Cyprian media and various political factions. There have already been public demonstrations and marches demanding Elzy's immediate return to Cypria.*" She sounded as though she was already tired of debating the issue with her hosts. "*The ryetalyn may be our top priority, but the Cyprian people are much more concerned with what becomes of Elzura.*"

Pike found her report troubling. He recalled a similar controversy on New Hiraji several years back, over the custody of some refugee children with family on both sides of a bitter planetary conflict. Neither side had wanted "their" children raised by the enemy, resulting in unrest, inflamed rhetoric, and, ultimately, a tragic escalation in hostilities. Pike could see this situation with Elzura turning ugly fast.

"What about the safety of you and the landing party? Do you need to return to the *Enterprise*?"

If push came to shove, would the Cyprians even allow the *Kepler* to depart with the landing party? Nobody had said anything about holding Number One and her team hostage in exchange for Merata, but Pike had to consider that possibility. Would they be able to get close enough to the planet to beam them up instead?

"*I appreciate your concern, Captain,*" Number One replied, "*but I dislike leaving a job unfinished. I have another meeting with the prime minister scheduled for tomorrow. I am not optimistic that he will change his mind, but . . . we need that ryetalyn, sir.*"

"No argument there," Pike said. "Would it help if I met with the prime minister face-to-face?"

He was reluctant to leave the ship under the present circumstances. The last thing he wanted was to be stuck down on the planet if the *Enterprise* got caught in the middle of a shooting war between the Klingons and the Cyprians, but if a personal meeting could possibly end the stalemate . . .

"*You belong on the ship, sir,*" Number One said. "*With all due respect to your personal charisma, your presence would not change the politics here on the ground, nor douse the passions this controversy has ignited. But there is one thing I can ask of you.*"

Pike was both relieved and disappointed to hear that his beaming down to the planet would not make any difference. "What's that, Number One?"

"*The remainder of the Mursh family—the mother and the younger brother—are en route to the capital. They want to visit the* Enterprise *to meet with our guests.*"

Pike could see that. If he had one relation in sickbay and another newly rescued from the Klingons, he'd want to see them, too.

"What's your take on this, Number One?"

"*It strikes me as a reasonable request, sir. And it may buy us some goodwill with the Cyprians. A gesture of good faith as it were, showing honest respect and compassion for the family involved.*"

"I agree," Pike said. "Instruct the Cyprians to make the necessary arrangements. Tell them we're happy to welcome the Murshes aboard."

If nothing else, Soleste would doubtless be happy to be reunited with her family. He just hoped the family's arrival wouldn't complicate an already volatile situation. How exactly would Merata react to meeting her biological family again, after all these years? That was bound to be awkward at best.

"I'll inform the Cyprians immediately," Number One said. *"And how are matters aboard the* Enterprise, *if I may ask?"*

"Just as you'd expect," he replied carefully. Encryption or no encryption, he wasn't taking any chances. The last thing they needed was for the Klingons to find out about the outbreak aboard the ship.

Especially since he was starting to feel a bit feverish himself

———

"I trust your new accommodations are to your liking?"

Spock had finally convinced Merata to accept better lodgings, exchanging the brig for confinement in one of the ship's guest quarters a short time ago. The key to overcoming her resistance had been to offer her a greater degree of privacy rather than comfort; the latter was a decadent human luxury, the former could be viewed as a sign of respect.

As the *Enterprise* was primarily an exploratory vessel, not a pleasure cruiser, the modest stateroom was only slightly less spartan than her cell in the brig. Intended for the occasional passenger, it was furnished with a single-sized bed (which could also double as a sofa), a personal viewer unit mounted in a sturdy triangular housing in the center of the room, a desk, a couple of chairs, and a computer terminal, the last of which had been disabled to prevent Merata from attempting to signal the *Fek'lhr* or gaining access to any of the ship's vital systems. Curved metal walls were relieved only by a few shelves and storage compartments. A sealed door cut her off from the corridor outside. Food slots offered her access to the ship's galley. A small supply of recreational reading, translated into Klingon by the ship's computer library, had also been provided. Spock wanted to think that Merata would take advantage of her confinement to acquire a greater familiarity with Federation history and literature, but suspected that was wishful thinking.

"It will suffice," she decreed, casting a scornful gaze over the quarters, "until my father reclaims me over your bloody remains. Should you survive, expect no mercy because of this meager courtesy."

Spock had not anticipated anything in the way of gratitude from Merata. It was enough that she had not yet attempted to kill him, despite the absence of a force field between them. He judged that significant progress in itself, even as he kept one hand on the grip of his laser pistol to discourage any sudden attacks. He stood by the doorway, watching with a reasonable degree of caution as she inspected the compact stateroom. The weapon waited at his side, not aimed at her, but ready to be employed with sufficient speed if needed. In addition, a security guard was posted outside the door to ensure that she remained confined to quarters.

"I am pleased that it meets with your approval," he said. "The temperature and gravity can be adjusted to suit your preferences."

She turned to face him, her arms crossed defiantly atop her chest.

"What pleases you does not concern me, Vulcan. To what do I owe the dubious honor of this visit?" She offered him one of her customary sneers. "Or should I call you 'half-breed' or 'mongrel' instead? Is that why you are here, to entertain me with sad tales of your polluted bloodline and your embarrassing human mother?" She snickered coldly. "What sort of female willingly mates with a cold, unfeeling Vulcan? I'd sooner wed a Denebian slime devil."

Spock declined to be baited. He had heard worse things said of his mother back on Vulcan, but knew that Amanda required no defending. His mother's character and integrity were beyond reproach.

"I merely wished to inform you that your sister has asked to see you."

Her smirk gave way to a frown.

"And what makes you think that I have any interest in seeing her?"

Spock noted that she no longer attempted to deny her kinship to Soleste. This, too, he took as promising.

"Curiosity?" he suggested. "It has been many years since you last met as sisters, discounting your tumultuous reunion on D'Orox. Are you not at least intrigued by the prospect of seeing her again?"

"Why should I be?" She affected an indifferent tone. "That was another life, long past and all but forgotten. We are no longer who we once were. What have we to say to each other now?"

"That you cannot know until you try." He appealed to her warrior's pride. "Are you afraid to encounter her again?"

"You question my courage? A risky strategy, Vulcan."

"There are many types of courage," he replied. "Courage in battle is one. The courage to face one's past, and one's true self, is another." He saw her face begin to flush with anger and hastened to qualify his remarks. "I am in no position to judge your own brand of valor. Only you know what is truly in your heart. But your sister is injured and poses no threat to you. She is no longer your opponent."

"No, just my kidnapper," Merata said harshly. "If not for her, I would still be back in the Empire and not held captive on this accursed vessel."

Spock refrained from pointing out that, if not for the Klingons, she would not have been abducted and raised as a Klingon in the first place.

"That is correct," he conceded. "But, while I do not pretend to be well-versed in Klingon ways, it was always my understanding that the Empire took family honor and obligations very seriously. Would a true Klingon turn her back on her kin?"

"But she is not Klingon!"

"No, but she *is* your sister by blood." He looked her squarely in the eye. "Does not that count for something?"

Merata had no ready answer. Growling in frustration, she shook her fists in the air and stomped around the small chamber for a few moments before coming to a stop directly in front of him. Spock waited patiently for her to regain her composure while keeping a firm grip on his laser pistol. He hoped that removing her from the brig had not been a faulty decision on his part.

"What would you do, Vulcan?" she challenged him. "If you were in my place?"

Was Merata genuinely soliciting his advice? Spock believed this to be the case, despite her characteristically aggressive tone and body language. Her possibly sincere query placed him in the unwelcome position of having to relate to her in a highly personal manner once more—and opening a door he would have preferred to have left shut.

"I have a brother," he confessed. "A half-brother, to be precise, on my father's side. He chose to reject his Vulcan heritage and follow a different path. I have neither seen nor heard of him for more than a decade. I cannot even be certain that he is still alive."

The forbidden topic felt strange upon Spock's tongue and triggered memories he had done his best to bury. As a boy, Spock had idolized his half-brother's fierce intellect, but after Sybok renounced logic to explore the forbidden realm of unchecked emotion, Sybok had been more than simply banished from Vulcan. It was as though he had ceased to exist. He had vanished from Spock's life, never to be spoken of again.

"And have you searched for him?" Merata asked. "This renegade brother of yours?"

"As your sister searched tirelessly for you?" Spock shook his head. "No, I have not. Nor have I ever breathed a word of him to another . . . until this very moment."

"And am I to feel flattered by this confidence?" She examined him warily, searching his face for clues to his intentions. "Is this some subtle ploy to win my trust and trick me into forgetting that I am your prisoner?"

Spock deflected the accusation. "You asked me what I would do in your case," he reminded her. "I am simply drawing upon my own experience."

"And?" she pressed him. "What *would* you do, Vulcan, if you crossed paths with your absent brother once again?"

An unlikely prospect, Spock reflected. The galaxy was a vast expanse, replete with worlds both known and unknown. Sybok could be almost anywhere, assuming he still lived. It defied probability that they would ever meet again.

But if they did . . . ?

"I do not know," he admitted. "But I like to think that I would not hesitate to hear him out."

"Easy for you to say, Vulcan. Your brother did not steal you from your home like an Orion slave trader!"

"She may have felt she had no choice, under the circumstances." He maintained a neutral tone and expression. "In the end, it is your decision."

She glowered at him unhappily. Her fists were clenched at her sides.

"That is little help to me, Vulcan." She nodded at the pistol at his side. "Best hold on to your weapon, if you know what is good for you."

He fully intended to do so.

Nine

"You test my patience, Pike! Hand over my daughter— and the criminal who abducted her—before I unleash the might of the Empire against you!"

Krunn's bellicose visage filled the viewscreen. His harsh tone made Pike's head hurt even more than it already did, but the captain refused to be bullied. Although feeling suspiciously tired and achy, Pike rose from his chair to stand defiantly on his own two feet. His head throbbed dully, the pain bouncing back and forth between his temples while taking frequent rest stops behind his eyes. His throat was scratchy.

"I told you before," he said. "No decision has been made regarding the ultimate disposition of either of our guests. It appears the situation is more complicated than you originally led us to believe."

In fact, Pike had already decided that under no circumstances was he going to turn Soleste Mursh over to what passed for Klingon justice. Merata/ Elzura, on the other hand, posed a more troubling dilemma.

"*There is nothing complicated about it!*" Krunn insisted. "*My daughter is being held captive aboard your ship and you are harboring her kidnapper!*"

"The Cyprians disagree," Pike said, neglecting to mention that the Cyprians also had the *Enterprise* over a barrel with respect to the ryetalyn. "As far as they're concerned, your people abducted Elzura Mursh in the first place, and her sister was merely rescuing a child stolen from her family many years ago."

Krunn offered no apologies. "*The spoils of war. If they had wished to keep what was theirs, they should have fought harder to defend it. Would they have preferred that we left the girl for dead?*"

"That doesn't change the fact that your 'daughter' was born a Cyprian," Pike said.

"*The past is the past,*" Krunn said. "*Merata is a Klingon now, and a daughter of my house.*" He held up his hand to display a faded, crescent-shaped scar between his thumb and forefinger. "*You see this mark? Merata did this to me with her teeth when she was just a child.*" Paternal pride could be heard in his voice, as though he was bragging about a baby's first word or step. "*Tell me that she does not have the soul of a Klingon!*"

Pike could believe it. From what he'd witnessed, Merata certainly had a fiery temperament. Small wonder that she seemed to have thrived as a Klingon.

"I appreciate that you care for your daughter," he replied, "but the Cyprians have a legitimate claim to her as well, as does her biological family."

"*'Legitimate'?*" Krunn bristled. "*So you* do *intend to turn her over to them!*"

"I didn't say that." Pike was not going to let Krunn put words in his mouth. "Trust me, the Cyprians are just as frustrated by this stalemate as you are."

"*Do not lie to me, human! Why come all this way if you do not intend to deliver Merata into the hands of her former kin?*"

"We were coming here anyway," Pike said honestly. "We have other business on Cypria III."

Krunn eyed him suspiciously. "*What kind of business?*"

"That's none of your affair," Pike said. "To be honest, this issue with Merata is an inconvenient distraction."

The pounding in his head, which was growing stronger the longer he stood, was a cruel reminder that there was more at stake than one interplanetary custody battle. He ought to be dealing with the fever sickening his crew right now, not playing referee between the Klingons and Cyprians. A febrile chill passed through him, and he did his best not to shiver visibly.

"*Then why not rid yourself of this 'distraction' by returning my daughter?*"

"Because I have a responsibility to listen to both sides of the story," Pike answered. "Perhaps we can work out some kind of compromise?"

"*Klingons do not compromise!*" Krunn's face grimaced in disgust. "*We accept only victory or death!*"

So I gather, Pike thought. To be honest, he was surprised that Krunn had shown as much patience and restraint as he had. Was it merely that he remained reluctant to endanger Merata by launching a substantial attack on the *Enterprise*? Or was he to some degree hesitant to risk an all-out war with the Federation?

"That attitude is not going to help us here," Pike retorted. "You may have to add the word to your vocabulary if we're to arrive at a satisfactory outcome for all concerned."

Krunn glared at Pike much as Merata had done earlier.

"*Hear me, Pike. We are watching you closely. Any attempt to transfer Merata to the planet's surface will be met with immediate reprisals. Do you understand me?*"

"Perfectly." Pike knew he couldn't let that threat go unchallenged. "Just understand that we are monitoring the *Fek'lhr* as well and will not tolerate any moves against this ship." He felt a cough coming on and swallowed it with effort. His throat had graduated from scratchy to sore. "And I suspect that the Cyprians feel the same."

Krunn examined Pike across thousands of kilometers of space. Pike kept a brave front, although his legs were starting to feel a little rubbery and his head was throbbing like the devil. He would have killed to sit down for a moment, but could not afford to show even a hint of weakness. He hid the pain in his eyes behind a steely gaze.

"*Bold words, Captain,*" the Klingon said finally. "*I wonder if you have the spine to back them up.*"

"Try me," Pike said.

The transmission was cut off abruptly. Pike tensed. Could this be the prelude to an attack?

"Sensor readings," he asked sharply. "What is *Fek'lhr*'s weapons status?"

Weisz looked up from his monitor at the science station. "They do not appear to be charging their disruptor banks, sir, or prepping their torpedo tubes."

Pike dropped back into his seat with as much assurance as he could muster. That Krunn was still holding his fire was a relief, but also somewhat worrisome. In his experience, Klingons seldom put off a fight for long. By their lights, today was always a good day to die, not tomorrow.

So what was Krunn waiting for?

"Captain!" Garrison called out from the communications station. "I'm picking up some unscrambled transmissions to and from the Klingon ship." He shot Pike an urgent look. "The incoming messages are from Klingon space, sir."

Pike spun his chair around. "What are they saying, Mister Garrison?"

"Hold on, sir. Just give me a moment to clean up the translation."

"On the double, Mist—" A ragged cough choked off his order. He placed a fist before his mouth in hopes of muffling the cough, only to find Yeoman Colt standing by his chair. Distracted, he hadn't even noticed her approach.

"Excuse me, Captain," she said casually. "I thought you might like a hot cup of tea."

He glanced up at her as she handed him the cup. She kept her expression cool and professional, as though this minor service was of no importance, but he had to wonder: Had she figured out already that he'd contracted the fever?

Was it that obvious?

He sipped the tea, which proved just what the doctor ordered, soothing his irritated throat. "Thank you, Yeoman. That was very . . . thoughtful of you."

Not to mention observant.

"Just doing my job, Captain," she replied. A flicker of anxiety showed in her eyes. "No matter what."

She does *know I'm sick,* he realized. *And it's only a matter of time before the rest of the crew catches on, if they haven't already.*

"Translation complete, Captain," Garrison reported. "I think you need to hear this."

"Pipe it through," Pike ordered, his voice sounding slightly less hoarse than before. "Let's hear what the Klingons are saying."

A deep, guttural voice echoed across the bridge:

"Attention, Fek'lhr! *We have received your message and reinforcements are on their way. Imperial Battle Cruisers* Ch'Tang *and* BortaS *will rendezvous with you in approximately twenty-six hours. Let your enemies tremble in fear.* Qapla'!"

"Oh, boy," Tyler commented. "The more the merrier."

Pike scowled. "Are we certain these transmissions are for real, Mister Garrison, and not just a subspace echo trick?"

"Absolutely, sir." The communications officer muted the playback. "I'm confirming communications between all three vessels." He scratched his head. "It's like they're not even trying to scramble their signals."

"They're not," Pike realized. "Krunn wants us to know he's expecting reinforcements, just to pressure us into surrendering Merata all the sooner."

No wonder Krunn was biding his time. In slightly more than a day, he'd have the *Enterprise* outnumbered three to one, by which time Pike knew his fever would be worse. The tea helped a little, for the moment, but wasn't going to be enough to keep the infection from spreading to his lungs and beyond. He was getting weaker while the Klingons were gathering strength.

Time was on Krunn's side, in more ways than one.

Ten

The demonstrations were getting larger and louder.

For the second night in a row, thousands of Cyprians had filled the large plaza across from the front entrance to Envoy House. A candlelight vigil had swelled into a literal mob scene despite the oppressive heat and humidity, while a hovering holographic billboard rotated above the crowd, depicting a ten-year-old image of Elzura Mursh as an impish-looking child hugging a stuffed toy lizard. Several times larger than life, the hacked billboard, which had previously displayed an ad for Prime Minister Flescu's reelection campaign, reminded Number One of the monumental floating idols of Ludlow's Planet. Along with the rest of the landing party, the worried Starfleet officer viewed the demonstration from the questionable safety of a penthouse balcony. The strident chants of the protestors could be heard from even five stories up.

"BRING ELZY HOME! BRING ELZY HOME! BRING ELZY HOME!"

Number One contemplated the giant holographic Elzy looming over the scene. Prime Minister Flescu was right about one thing. Little Elzy had definitely become a symbol of sorts, even if, judging from Captain Pike's description, the actual woman now bore little resemblance to the adorable moppet of years gone by. *Kepler* had departed *Enterprise* before the Mursh sisters had been beamed aboard, but Number One gathered that the actual Elzura was more Klingon than not. She wondered how the crowd would react if they saw Merata instead of Little Elzy. Would they still think they could "rescue" her from the Klingons?

Probably, Number One thought. *They might even become more intent on saving her.*

A makeshift podium had been erected in the plaza so that various speakers could exhort the crowd. Cheers and a smattering of applause rose as a new participant took the stage. Static crackled and the image upon the large floating billboard shifted, the dated portrait of Elzura replaced by the stern features of a middle-aged Cyprian woman with short blond hair, scalloped ears, and intense bronze eyes. Number One recognized the woman as Council Member Letya Brovi, the prime minister's chief opponent in the upcoming election. Her amplified voice rang out over the crowd.

"Friends! Fellow Cyprians! Thank you all for coming out tonight. I cannot tell you how much it touches my heart to see this spontaneous outpouring for the Mursh family during this crucial time. Know that I fully share your resolve that Little Elzy be brought home at last. We cannot and will not allow the Klingons to take her back. We cannot and will not let a Cyprian child continue to be raised as a Klingon!"

The crowd shouted and yelled in agreement. Signs and banners, many bearing the same now-iconic image of Little Elzy, waved above the assemblage. Brovi waited for the tumult to die down before continuing her speech.

"It seems we're all in agreement, then," she said with a chuckle, before adopting a more ominous tone. "But what about our esteemed prime minister? He *says* he wants to bring Elzy home, but why is she still being held aboard the *Enterprise*, with a Klingon battle cruiser lurking nearby to carry her away at the first opportunity? He *says* he's negotiating with the human captain, Pike, but what is there to negotiate?" She turned her gaze toward Envoy House as she worked up the crowd. "Why does Starfleet have any say over the future of a Cyprian child, of a Cyprian family? Maybe Atron Flescu lacks the will to stand up to Starfleet—and the Klingons—but what about the rest of us? Elzura Mursh has already lost her childhood to the Klingons. Are we going to let them take her future, too?"

"NO!" the mob roared. "BRING ELZY HOME!"

"Don't tell me," Brovi said. She threw an accusing finger at Envoy House, the provocative action mirrored and magnified by her huge holographic simulacrum. "Flescu's Starfleet friends are right over there, enjoying our hospitality even as their captain keeps Elzy from us. Tell *them* what we want, what all of Cypria wants!"

En masse, the crowd turned toward the residence. Thousands of angry faces glared up at the building, as though staring directly at the landing party on the balcony. The chanting resumed, even louder than before, and now directed straight at Number One and her team.

"BRING ELZY HOME! BRING ELZY HOME! BRING ELZY HOME!"

Up on the balcony, which was adorned with potted ferns and other greenery, Lieutenant Giusio scowled at the irate mob below as he leaned on the carved wooden railing. A Starfleet veteran, he was a large man with grizzled features and a laconic manner. "Gotta admit," he said, "I kinda wish we could get our weapons back."

Number One shared his concern. Cyprian security forces, recognizable by their blood-red uniforms and helmets, had set up a protective barricade in front of Envoy House, just in case, but the guards were severely outnumbered and their allegiances uncertain. *Can we truly count on Cyprian guards to defend us against their own people?*

Envoy House was comfortable, but she found

herself pining for the cramped confines of the *Kepler*, which was still parked at the spaceport, many kilometers away. She could wish that the shuttle-craft was closer at hand.

"At least they left us our communicators," Lieutenant Jones observed. An incorrigible optimist, the able-bodied young officer had a tendency to look for silver linings in even the most dire of circumstances. Number One hoped this would not be tested on this mission. "That's something, I guess."

"The prime minister has guaranteed our safety," Number One stated in order to maintain morale.

"For what that's worth," Nurse Olson groused. A lanky redhead with a slight Jovian accent, he backed away from the railing. "Even the staff here are giving us dirty looks. I went looking for some cream for my coffee this morning, and I swear one of the kitchen workers glared at me as though I'd asked to dissect her firstborn child." He wiped the sweat from his brow. "I'm half afraid to eat the meals for fear that somebody has spit in them."

"Scan them with a tricorder first," Giusio suggested. "That's what I'd do."

Olson looked puzzle. "For saliva?"

"No. Poison."

"That's enough," Number One said, although part of her worried that maybe Giusio had a point. She wanted to think that was simply paranoia talking, but, as she'd told the captain, passions were running high at this point, even more so than the sweltering temperature. She was sweating herself, in more ways than one. "Let's go inside and get away from the heat."

A sliding glass door closed behind them as they abandoned the balcony for the main living area of the VIP suite. The cooler environment came as relief, but the glass was not enough to drown out the ceaseless chanting outside.

"BRING ELZY HOME! BRING ELZY HOME! BRING ELZY HOME!"

Number One suspected that she would not be getting much sleep tonight.

Eleven

"The Cyprian shuttlecraft is approaching from the planet, Captain."

"Thank you, Mister Garrison," Pike said. "Onscreen."

The shuttle, which was ferrying the Mursh family to the *Enterprise*, appeared on the bridge's viewscreen. The ovate craft was of similar design as the *Ilion*, but in much better condition than Soleste Mursh's well-traveled, ramshackle trading vessel. *Climber One* was a diplomatic courier and looked it. A gleaming hull, crafted to resemble paneled wood, was polished to a spotless sheen. Elegant green trim, fashioned in the image of leafy green vines, adorned the craft's curving contours and wings. Golden running lights glowed like sunlight. Pike had to admire the Cyprians' sense of aesthetics. *Climber One* made a Starfleet shuttle look boxy and utilitarian in comparison. He hoped it was a smooth ride as well.

Here they come, he thought. *The rest of the family.* Beaming them aboard would have been faster

and easier, but the Cyprians had objected to the
Enterprise coming within transporter range of the
planet's surface, insisting that it occupy a higher
orbit instead; apparently they still didn't trust Pike
not to raid them for the ryetalyn. Pike had com-
plied with their stipulations, but couldn't help wishing that the approaching shuttle was bearing a load
of processed ryetalyn as well. At last report, at least
a third of the crew was down with the fever, with no
sign of the outbreak abating.

Maybe this gesture would help soften the Cyprians' embargo on the cure?

Pike watched the shuttle draw nearer. "Status of
the *Fek'lhr*?" he asked.

"Unchanged," Weisz reported. "Guess they're
still waiting for those reinforcements."

Pike was only too aware that two more Klingon
battle cruisers were en route to the Cyprian system
and expected to arrive with hours. *All the more reason to do this now,* he thought.

"Acknowledged," Pike said. "Lower shields."

In theory, the Cyprians were providing cover for
the *Enterprise* with their satellite-based laser cannons, but Pike wasn't about to leave his ship vulnerable to a Klingon attack for any longer than it took
Climber One to make it safely into the *Enterprise*'s
hangar deck. Tempting Krunn with an unshielded
target was just asking for trouble.

"Aye, sir," Weisz said.

"Inform the shuttle that they're clear for landing," Pike instructed Garrison. He rose to his feet and a sudden wave of dizziness reminded him that his fever had not gone away. For a second, the bridge seemed to spin around him as though caught in a gravitational eddy. Nausea beckoned, and he clamped his jaws shut. His headache went from dull to razor-sharp. It like felt like somebody was mining for lithium inside his skull—with a pickaxe.

Colt, who had been keeping close at hand, took a step toward him, just in case he needed assistance. "Captain?" she asked in a low voice.

"I'm fine," he lied, waiting for the bridge to stop spinning. He took a deep breath to steady himself. The pounding in his head ratcheted down a notch so that it was merely miserable. His throat felt like he'd gargled super-heated plasma. "Just a bit stiff from riding my chair too long."

"Of course," she replied, playing along. She stepped back, but remained near enough to grab him if he lost balance. Chestnut eyes watched him with barely concealed concern. "Shall I accompany you to the hangar deck, Captain?"

Pike resisted the temptation to look around to see if the entire bridge crew was watching him. Not for the first time he regretted that Number One—and her exemplary immune system—was unavailable to take over if necessary. There was a worrisome tightness in his chest, making breathing more difficult. His lungs felt congested. His eyes felt like throbbing nuggets of pain.

"Thank you, Yeoman, but that won't be necessary. Mister Spock will be also be present to greet our guests, so that's probably an adequate reception committee. Feel free to take a break."

He looked over Colt. As far as he could tell, she was not yet showing any signs of having been infected with the fever.

Thank goodness for small favors, he thought.

Gritting his teeth against the pain and strain of being up and about, he made his way from the command circle to the turbolift. "Mister Tyler, you have the conn."

"Aye, sir," the navigator said, coughing. "Excuse me, sir."

Pike winced inside.

That clinches it. Tyler has it, too.

The *Enterprise* was turning into one big sickbay.

———

The tricorder hummed as Olson scanned the meal laid out on the table. He squinted at the readings on the device.

"Looks clean to me," the nurse pronounced. "Dig in."

Sunlight entered the suite through a large plate-glass window as the landing party gathered in the dining area for lunch. The meal, which had been delivered via a food slot from the kitchen on the ground floor of Envoy House, consisted of an assortment of local meats, fruits, nuts, and vegetables, along with pitchers of fermented fruit juice and a foamy, black variant on coffee that Number One found adequate at best. The lush variety of the menu testified to the planet's enviable biodiversity, particularly here at the equator. Plates, cups, and utensils had also been provided. Number One considering hanging on to a few of the sharper knives, just in case. Despite the Cyprians' hospitality so far, it might be best to put aside a few weapons for self-defense, in the not entirely unlikely event that a volatile situation grew uglier still.

"No Cyprian saliva?" Jones teased Olson.

"Not that I can detect." Olson put down the tricorder. "Although that's not exactly what the tricorder is designed to scan for."

Giusio helped himself to a slice of purple huskfruit and dipped it into a bowl of spicy yellow sauce. "Good enough for me," he said. "Unless you'd prefer the emergency rations back on the *Kepler*."

"That would not be my first preference," Number One admitted. She had once been forced to survive an entire month on emergency rations while stranded on a heavy-gravity planet in the Jemal system. "And let's be grateful that the Cyprians do not prefer live food like—"

The window exploded inward as a metallic object crashed through it into the suite. Number One dived for cover, shielding her eyes against a spray of clear flying granules, as the rest of the landing party did likewise. A rain of particles pelted the dining area. Adrenaline jump-started her reflexes even as her Starfleet training kicked into gear. Lifting her head, she looked for whatever had shattered the window.

"The missile!" she called out. "Where is it?"

Giusio scrambled to his feet. Bits of broken glass clung to his uniform. Blood dripped from a scratch on his cheek. "Over there!" he shouted, pointing toward the main living area. "Watch out, it might be armed!"

That possibility had already occurred to her. Looking where he indicated, she spotted the object in question: a metallic silver disk, roughly the size of a large dinner plate, which had come to rest against a wall on the far side of the suite. Colored lights blinked along the rim of the disk, and a flashing yellow crystal was embedded at its center. Its internal mechanisms buzzed and clicked.

"Clear out!" she ordered. "Evacuate the building!"

"But, Commander—" Jones began.

"That's an order, Lieutenant!"

She sprang to her feet and raced for the blinking disk. Snatching it from the floor, she dashed toward the broken window, then remembered the crowded plaza outside. Hordes of demonstrators, still demanding the return of Elzy Mursh, occupied the plaza day in and day out. The sound of their chanting invaded the violated suite, along with the hot, muggy atmosphere. Number One could not in good conscience fling the possibly explosive device out of the suite into the streets below. She looked around desperately for some way to dispose of the missile, but saw only the elegant wooden furnishings of the penthouse suite, now littered with tiny cubes of shattered window. A spiral staircase led to a rooftop garden, but who knew how powerful any explosive might be or whether she could get it up to the roof in time. She couldn't even disintegrate the suspect object without a laser pistol.

I'm sorry, Captain, she thought. *This one is on me. Don't blame yourself.*

The central crystal stopped flashing and Number One feared her time was up. She instinctively dropped the disk and backed away. Glancing around, she saw to her dismay that her team had refused to abandon her and remained at her side. She didn't know whether to be deeply moved or to report for them for insubordination.

"I ordered you to leave," she said.

"What's that, Commander?" Giusio said, cupping a meaty hand over his ear. "I can't hear you over all that chanting."

But instead of detonating, the disk projected a holographic simulacrum of Little Elzy, who stared at them with sad, mournful eyes. Clutching her stuffed lizard, she frowned and shook a tiny finger at the landing party. A childish voice emanated from the disturbingly lifelike hologram.

"Bring me home, please!"

Number One remained tense, still unconvinced that the message was not a prelude to an explosion. "The tricorder!" she demanded. "Give it to me!"

Olson lobbed the device to her. She was simultaneously impressed and annoyed that he had chosen to stay put as well. Security officers were expected to put themselves in jeopardy as needed, but the nurse was going above and beyond the call of duty. Doctor Boyce would be proud of him.

She caught the tricorder with one hand and immediately scanned the disk, holding her breath until she determined that the device did indeed appear to be nothing more than a mobile holographic projector unit, possibly launched from somewhere nearby. No explosive or other hazardous materials registered on the sensors.

"Relax," she told the others. "It seems somebody was just trying to send us a message."

For now, she thought.

———

"Are you well, Captain?"

Spock inspected Pike as the captain joined him in the reception area outside the hangar deck. He noticed at once that Pike was clearly ill, although the captain was making an admirable effort to conceal the effects of the fever. Spock's acute hearing could scarcely miss the congestion in the captain's lungs and the rasp to his voice. The captain's face and body language also displayed subtle signs of distress and exhaustion.

"Well enough," Pike said, "for the time being."

Spock was by now very familiar with the characteristic progression of Rigelian fever. By his estimate, the captain had entered stage two of the disease, which meant the infection was now attacking his respiratory system. "If you require me to take command . . ."

"I'll let you know, Mister Spock."

Spock let the matter drop for now. In truth, he was in no hurry to take charge during the present crisis. As long as Pike judged himself fit for command, Spock could afford to wait until circumstances warranted further action. He was only too aware, however, that the time was coming when the captain would be too ill to carry out his duties, at which point the responsibility would definitely fall upon Spock for as long as Number One remained occupied on Cypria III.

Would it perhaps be prudent to recall her from the planet?

An indicator light above the hangar entrance signaled that the deck had been repressurized following the arrival of *Climber One*. As the door slid open, Spock saw the Cyprian shuttlecraft unload its passengers.

"I have arranged accommodations for our new guests," he informed Pike, "as well as for the pilot. Their luggage will be delivered to their guest quarters shortly."

"Thank you, Mister Spock." Pike prepared himself to greet the visitors. He straightened his tunic; as the Murshes were not actually diplomats, neither he nor Spock was wearing full dress uniforms, nor was an honor guard in attendance. "And what is Merata's attitude toward this impending reunion?"

"That remains to be seen, Captain."

The newcomers crossed the deck to emerge from the landing bay. The party consisted of an older Cyprian woman and a younger male, whom Spock identified as the mother and brother of both Soleste and Merata. A family resemblance was evident in their sharp noses and chins.

"Welcome aboard the *Enterprise*," the captain said. "I'm Captain Pike and this is my science officer, Mister Spock. He's been personally looking after your family members while they've been staying with us."

That was a slight exaggeration since Soleste's care had largely been in the hands of Doctor Boyce and his staff, but Spock did not contradict the captain. Clarification was not required in this instance and, frankly, Spock was more interested in meeting the remainder of the Mursh family and observing their responses to the present situation. General Krunn and Soleste had both made their desires very clear concerning Merata's future. Spock was curious to see what the rest of her kinfolk made of the dilemma.

"Rosha Mursh," the woman introduced herself, although Spock had already briefed himself on the visitors' identities. She was a handsome woman who appeared to be roughly the same age as Spock's own mother. Short silver hair matched her silver eyes. She wore an embroidered vest over a dark green gown. "And this is my son, Junah."

"Pleased, I'm sure," the youth mumbled, although his bored, disaffected tone implied otherwise. Lank black hair fell past his shoulder and over his eyes. His lean, adolescent face bore a distinctly sullen expression. He avoided making eye contact with Pike or Spock as he glanced around the corridor. "So this is a Federation starship, huh? It's impressive, I guess." His hands were thrust into the pockets of his slacks. "So, is it true that you're all dying of fever?"

Rosha frowned, clearly embarrassed by her son's attitude. "Junah . . ."

"Nobody's dying on my watch," Pike said. "But you needn't concern yourself with that right now. I know you have to be anxious to see your family members."

"And we thank you for your hospitality, Captain, under these difficult circumstances." She spoke with an air of somber gravity. "I understand that we have you and your valiant crew to thank for both my daughters' lives."

"We just answered a distress call," Pike said, "as any ship would do."

"I fear you are not giving yourselves enough credit, Captain. Many would not be so brave or altruistic." A touch of bitterness infiltrated her voice. "The Klingons, for instance."

Spock recalled that, beyond stealing Elzura, the Klingons had also killed Rosha's husband and neighbors. A decade has passed since then, but Spock suspected the woman still felt the pain of that tragedy profoundly. Even Vulcans grieved for lives lost before their time, albeit in their own fashion.

"Well, the Federation is *not* the Klingon Empire," Pike conceded.

"Praise the changing seasons for that." She stepped forward and took Pike's arm. Her eyes implored him. "Captain, I don't want to impose on you so soon, but . . . surely it's not true what they're saying down on the planet, that you might actually give my baby back to those bloodthirsty savages?"

Pike placed his hand over hers. Spock did not envy the position the captain had been placed in.

"It's a complicated situation," Pike said honestly.

"Mer . . . Elzura is not exactly a baby anymore. And it's unclear where she truly belongs now."

Dismay spread across the woman's face; this was manifestly not what she wanted to hear. "But . . . but you don't understand. We're talking about an innocent child, carried off by heartless invaders. You must see what a miracle this is, that we've finally found her after all these years, after we'd practically given up hope. You aren't really going to let the Klingons take her from us *again*? That would be too cruel."

Spock took it upon himself to intervene on the captain's behalf.

"Excuse me, but Soleste is waiting for you in our sickbay. She has been looking forward impatiently to your arrival."

As Spock had hoped, the image of her older daughter in a hospital bed succeeded in distracting Rosha Mursh to some degree. "And Elzy?" she asked. "Doesn't she want to see us too?"

"It is a confusing situation for her," Spock stated, "but she has been informed that you were coming aboard."

In fact, Merata had been distinctively ambivalent about meeting the rest of her former family. Unlike Soleste, they had not abducted her, so she had no particular grudge against them, even as she continued to insist that her Cyprian roots no longer mattered, that she was thoroughly and irrevocably

Klingon now. It was possible, however, that, to use a human expression, she was protesting too much. He could not be sure but he thought he had detected in her some veiled curiosity regarding her Cyprian relatives, whom she possibly remembered to some degree. As she had not expressly ruled out meeting with their new visitors, Spock had reason to hope that curiosity—and perhaps old memories—would prevail in the end.

"If you are ready, I can escort you to sickbay now."

"Of course." Rosha let go of Pike's arm. "We mustn't keep Soleste waiting. Please lead the way." She looked at Pike. "Are you coming with us, Captain?"

"I'm afraid the captain is needed on the bridge," Spock said, to spare Pike from having to cope with both the family *and* his illness at the same time. "The demands of his position preclude a visit to sickbay at this time."

"Quite right," Pike agreed, giving Spock a grateful look. "As much as I would like to witness your reunion with Soleste, you hardly require a ship's captain for that. You're in good hands with Mister Spock, I assure you."

"If you say so, Captain," Rosha said, visibly disappointed. She lingered, reluctant to let the captain get away. "I trust we will have an opportunity to speak again, after I've met with my daughters?"

"In due time," he assured her. "Now if you'll excuse me . . ."

Spock was impressed by Pike's ability to carry on despite the fever steadily ravaging his body. He doubted that their visitors even realized the captain was sick, but Spock figured that the sooner he let the captain make his escape, the better.

"This way, please."

He led them away from the hangar deck to the nearest convenient turbolift. Gripping the rail, he instructed the mechanism to take them directly to the saucer's main deck, where sickbay was located. The lift ascended quickly from the lower levels of the ship, but perhaps not quickly enough for Junah, who paced restlessly around the compartment, not unlike his sister had done in the brig, while Rosha wrung her hands anxiously. An excess of nervous energy appeared to be a family trait.

"You said Elzura was . . . confused, Mister Spock?" she asked.

"Understandably." He attempted to prepare her for the reunion to come. "She was born a Cyprian, but has lived as a Klingon for many years now. It is only to be expected that she should be . . . conflicted about the possibility of returning to Cypria."

"My poor baby," Rosha said. "But it will be different once we're together again, Mister Spock. I know it will be. We just need to help her remember who she is, so we can be a family once more. Her *real* family."

"Such as it is," Junah muttered.

Rosha sighed and shook her head. "You must forgive my son, Mister Spock. He was only five years old when the raid occurred. He barely remembers Elzy."

"Not that I could ever forget about her," he grumbled, "since she's pretty much all I've ever heard about for my entire life, especially from my *other* sister, the homeless one." He chuckled mirthlessly. "The Klingons might as well have taken Soleste too, for all we ever see of her. Even when she comes back to Cypria, which is hardly ever, she's all about her endless, obsessive quest for little lost Elzy. It's been her whole life . . . if you can call that a life."

"Don't talk like that," his mother scolded. "It's been hard on all of us, since what happened, but it seems your sister was right all along when it came to not giving up on Elzy. She's sacrificed a lot, I know, and she hasn't always been there for us, but she succeeded in the end. She finally did what she set out to do."

"And nearly got herself killed."

"Nearly, but not actually," Spock stressed as the turbolift arrived at its destination. The door slid open to admit them to the corridor outside sickbay. "As you will soon see for yourself."

They entered sickbay, where he bypassed the quarantined fever ward to take them straight to the recovery room where Soleste was resting in a biobed, unattended by Doctor Boyce or any nurses, who were presumably busy with other patients. Her remaining eye lit up at the sight of her family.

"You're here!"

Rosha gasped and clutched her chest at the sight of her injured daughter. She hurried forward, arms outstretched, only to pause cautiously at Soleste's bedside. "Is it safe? Can I hug you?"

"Gently," Soleste advised.

Rosha embraced her daughter gingerly, then withdrew to take a closer look at Soleste. She wiped a tear from her eye. "My poor, brave darling! Look what those barbarians did to you."

Spock thought Soleste looked noticeably better than the last time he'd seen her, immediately after her surgery. Her burns were healing and her singed eyebrows were already growing back. A glance at the life-signs monitor revealed that her vitals were stable. No doubt she still needed time to recovery from surgery and blood loss, but she was in significantly less danger than the fever victims in the quarantine ward. He wondered if Merata would be pleased to know that her sister was doing better, or if Merata still wanted vengeance on her abductor.

"It's all right, Mom. The doctor and nurses here have been taking good care of me. I'll be back on my feet in no time." Soleste turned her attention to her brother, who was hanging back, away from the emotional scene. She held out her hand, beckoning him. "Junah. It's so good of you to come."

He shrugged. "Well, sure, what else was I going to do? Not like I had much of a choice, you know." He fidgeted and glanced around the ward, looking at everything except his sister's hand. He picked up a stray medical scanner and fiddled with it. "So, that broken-down old ship of yours finally blew itself to atoms, huh?"

Soleste's face hardened. She let her proffered hand drop limply back onto the sheets. Even Spock could tell that she was hurt by her brother's callous attitude, even if she was trying not to let it spoil the moment. For a moment, he was reminded of Captain Pike keeping up appearances despite the merciless effects of the fever. Whatever pain Soleste was experiencing, she would not let it show.

"It was a good ship," she said flatly. "It served its purpose."

"That's right." Rosha circled around to take the hand Junah had rejected. "You finally did it, just like you always said you would." Both joy and sorrow could be heard in her voice, along with what sounded to Spock like guilt. "I know we've quarreled in the past, that I didn't always support your quest the way I should have, even tried to talk you into getting on with your own life, but—"

"It's okay," Soleste assured her. "You meant well, I know. You didn't want to lose two daughters. I understand that. But that's all behind us now." She sat up straighter, seeming to grow stronger as she spoke of her triumph. "I found Elzura, Mom. I brought her home!"

"Well, not exactly," Junah pointed out. He glanced around the sterile sickbay. "This doesn't look much like Cypria to me."

Rosha turned to Spock. "What about Elzura? When can we see her?"

As a Vulcan, Spock found the intense family drama unfolding before him to be more uncomfortable than fascinating. And he feared that even more emotional turmoil was in store once mother and brother came face-to-face with Merata.

Still, there was little point in delaying the inevitable.

"Allow me to give you some privacy here, while I inform your other daughter of your arrival. When you are ready, we will see about visiting her in her quarters."

At least Merata was no longer confined to the brig, he reflected. That would have made for an even more potentially upsetting reunion.

If only slightly.

———

"My apologies for this unfortunate incident," Flescu communicated via holographic projection. "I can assure you it will not happen again."

Number One wanted more than apologies. Glass granules still littered the floor of the suite, while a team of Cyprian laborers were already hard at work replacing the shattered window. The interrupted luncheon, now spiced with broken glass, had been carted away, although Number One had taken the liberty of tucking a pair of knives under a seat cushion. The offending disk had been confiscated by the local security forces, who had confirmed that it was nothing more than a routine device ordinarily employed for advertising and entertainment purposes. There had been some talk of trying to trace the disk to its original owners, but the investigators had not sounded particularly optimistic—or motivated. Their manner had been notably brusque and unsympathetic, as though they'd figured the visiting aliens had had it coming. A few had even blamed Pike for the disturbances and expressed sympathy for the protestors.

"Thank you, Prime Minister," she replied, "but I remain concerned for the safety of my landing party. We were lucky this time, but this could have been much worse."

To her relief, the landing party had suffered only minor cuts and abrasions from the flying glass. Nurse Olson had treated the others with antiseptics and was presently applying a bandage to a nick on his forehead. Feeling an itch, Number One plucked a stray piece of window from her own dark locks.

She resisted a temptation to flick it directly at the hologram.

"*Let's not overreact,*" Flescu insisted. "*It was just a bit of political theater, that's all. Merely the people making their feelings known.*"

"At our expense," Number One said tartly.

"*I'm quite sure there was no serious intent to harm you and your party. My people assure me that the device posed no real threat.*"

"This time, perhaps," she said, "but you'll forgive me if I do not wish to take chances with my own people's safety. Perhaps we should relocate to our shuttlecraft for the time being, or, at the very least, you could return our weapons so that my security officers are properly equipped to carry out their duties."

She recalled how much she had yearned for a laser pistol before, so that she could have disintegrated the suspicious disk if necessary. A pair of purloined knives was a poor substitute for modern sidearms.

"*I hardly think that's necessary.*" The hologram's forced smile slipped a bit. "*I've ordered increased protection around Envoy House and launched a full investigation into this incident, but Cyprian forces must stay in charge of any security issues while you remain on Cyprian soil. That is non-negotiable, simply as a matter of planetary sovereignty.*"

"Then perhaps we should not remain on Cyprian

soil," she countered, "until you can fully guarantee our safety."

"*I thought I had just done so,*" he said curtly. "*But you are perfectly free to leave our beautiful planet if you so choose . . . although you will do so without the ryetalyn you came for.*"

And there was the rub. Despite the attack on the suite, Number One balked at returning empty-handed to the *Enterprise,* where the fever outbreak was, by all accounts, still burning through the crew unchecked. She had to weigh the safety of the landing party against the more than two hundred lives at risk aboard the ship, as Flescu damn well knew.

"I will have to consult with my colleagues," she said. "And my captain."

"*Of course,*" the hologram said, smirking. "*Let me know what you decide.*"

He vanished in a blink.

"Is it just me," Olson groused, "or is that guy not on our side?"

At this point, Number One doubted that any Cyprians were. Acutely conscious of the locals working to replace the window, she beckoned the team over to the other end of the living area so they could confer in relative privacy.

"You heard the prime minister," she said in a low voice. "Our options are limited. I would value your opinions."

"Don't worry about us, Commander," Giusio

said. The small cut on his cheek had stopped bleeding. "We're in this if you are."

Jones and Olson added their assent. "We came for the cure, right?" Olson said. "Not sure I want to face Doctor Boyce without it."

"Exactly," Jones said. "The captain is counting on us. If we give up now, we may never get that ryetalyn."

Number One agreed in theory, and yet the odds of them succeeding in their mission were looking slimmer by the minute, while the danger planetside appeared to be steadily increasing. The shouting of the protestors outside continued unabated. If anything, they seemed to have been emboldened by the "attack" on Envoy House. At what point did insurmountable odds dictate a prudent retreat? And what would become of the *Enterprise* if they called it quits? What posed the greater threat, the angry populace on Cypria III or the Rigelian fever waiting back on the ship?

"Very well," she said. "Thank you for speaking freely."

Good thing I stowed those knives away, she thought. *Here's hoping we don't need them.*

———

"Very well," Merata said. "Show them in."

Spock was relieved to find her willing to meet with her newly arrived family members, but could tell that she was uneasy about the impending visit. She fiddled with the pendant around her neck, while facing the sealed doorway with a tense, wary expression. He knew her well enough by now to sense her discomfort. Her shields were raised, so to speak.

"As you wish," he replied. Opening the door, he stepped out into the corridor, where Rosha and Junah were waiting. A security guarded remained posted in the hall as well. Spock blocked the open door with his body as he made a final attempt to prepare the visiting Cyprians for the encounter ahead. "Please keep in mind that Elzura is much changed, and that she prefers to be addressed as 'Merata' for the present."

"So you said," Rosha said, wincing somewhat, while Junah rolled his eyes in disgust. "I can't say I like that name, though. It's so . . . Klingon."

As is your daughter now, Spock thought, but refrained from belaboring the point.

Junah eyed the doorway apprehensively. He nodded at the looming security officer. "Is he coming in too?"

"He can, if that would make you more comfortable, but I do not believe it necessary."

Spock's own laser pistol rested discreetly on his hip. He did not anticipate violence, but felt it better to be prepared. Adding another armed Starfleet officer to this volatile mixture concerned him. He did not wish Merata to feel outnumbered.

"Don't be foolish, Junah," his mother said. "Your sister is waiting."

"That's what I'm afraid of," he groused. "But . . . fine. Let's get this over with."

Spock was inclined to agree. He stepped aside to let them enter the stateroom.

Unable to wait any longer, Rosha hurried inside, only to freeze at her first sight of Merata, who stood imposingly at the far end of the stateroom, still clad in full Klingon regalia, with her arms crossed atop her chest. She was uncharacteristically still and silent, her face betraying little emotion. Spock was uncertain if that was a good sign or not.

The door slid shut as he entered behind Rosha and Junah. Spock tried to see Merata through her mother's eyes. The intimidating Klingon teenager standing before them bore scant resemblance to the small Cyprian child lost so long ago. No matter how much Rosha had attempted to prepare herself for whatever changes had been wrought by the years, the reality of the transformation had to be shocking to her. She was looking at Merata, not little Elzura.

"Elzy?" she whispered.

"My name is Merata," the younger woman replied, but not as indignantly as Spock might have anticipated. If anything, she appeared unusually subdued, by Klingon standards. Her eyes widened as she gazed at Rosha and she swallowed hard, as though shaken by the sudden appearance of a ghost from her past. Rosha Mursh had also aged a decade since they had last laid eyes on each other, but Spock had no doubt that Merata recognized the woman before her. Her voice faltered under the weight of early memories. "You . . . you wished to see me?"

"Yes. Of course. I . . . I mean . . ."

An awkward silence ensued as Rosha found herself at a loss for words. No doubt she had been dreaming of a much more tender, heartfelt reunion, possibly involving tears and a loving embrace, as with her other daughter in sickbay. It was not logical that she should have expected such, but Spock could not find it in his own heart to condemn her for wishing for the improbable. He suspected that his own mother had sometimes nursed similarly unlikely fantasies—and been disappointed as well.

Truth to tell, he had never even told his mother he loved her.

He was about to say something, in an attempt to break the ice, when Merata took the initiative instead. "Was your journey uneventful?" she asked stiffly.

"Yes, thank you for asking." Rosha managed a weak smile. "I'm so glad you agreed to see us."

Merata shrugged, not unlike Junah had before. "You have come a long way. It would have been dishonorable not to greet you."

"Honor," Junah echoed sarcastically. He eyed

her with naked revulsion. "That's pretty, coming from a Klingon . . . of sorts."

Merata glared balefully at her brother. She dropped into a battle stance, her fists raised before her. A wolfish grin curled her lips; she appeared almost grateful for an enemy to oppose. "Klingons know nothing but honor, boy. Challenge me if you dare!"

Spock reached for his laser pistol, ready to intervene if necessary. Had he miscalculated by including Junah in this encounter? He should have anticipated that the surly youth might provoke Merata.

"Junah! Hush!" Rosha got between her squabbling children, perhaps not for the first time. "This is strange enough for all of us." She drew closer to Merata, who flinched at her mother's approach, but allowed the invasion of her personal space. Rosha peered at Merata's taut, suspicious face as though searching for some trace of her lost child. "Do you remember us at all?"

Merata lowered her shields slightly.

"Perhaps . . . I think." She spoke haltingly, sounding more vulnerable and unsure of herself than Spock was accustomed to. Her fists unclenched and her arms dropped to her sides. She shifted her weight restlessly. "I'm not certain. It was so long ago . . ."

"Ten years," Rosha confirmed, choking up. "I

can't get over how . . . grown-up . . . you are now. When I last saw, you were just a little girl . . ." Sobs shook her body as tears streamed down her cheeks. Trembling fingers fished a handkerchief from somewhere beneath her embroidered vest. "I'm so sorry. I promised myself I wouldn't do this, but . . ."

Merata raised her arms hesitantly, as though to comfort her mother, but they hung awkward in the air instead. She shot a desperate look at Spock, seeking direction—or perhaps simply blaming him for putting her in this position. It was said, he recalled, that Klingons had no tear ducts, although opinion was divided on whether that was literally the case or merely figurative. In any event, Merata clearly had no idea what to do with the weeping woman before her.

Spock sympathized. Vulcans were also not prone to tears.

"I regret causing you distress," Merata said.

"It's not just sadness," Rosha insisted. "It's joy, too." She gazed lovingly at Merata, somehow seeing past the scarred brow and pointed teeth. "You're back. You're finally back!"

"Yes," Junah said darkly. "Lucky us."

Spock pondered the youth's hostility. What did Junah see when he looked at Merata? The barely remembered sibling whose loss had haunted his upbringing, perhaps to an excessive degree, or simply one of the monsters who had killed his father and torn apart his family?

"Don't mind your brother," Rosha said. "He doesn't remember you like your sister and I do, but everything will be fine once we're back home on Cypria. You'll have a family again."

Merata's face hardened. She stepped back, putting more distance between herself and her mother. The uncertainly in her voice vanished.

"I have a family," she said firmly. "I do not wish to disappoint you, but we are not family anymore. Any prior blood ties were severed when I was adopted into the House of Krunn. You gave me birth and I honor that debt, but I am no longer your daughter. General Krunn is my father now."

Rosha stumbled backward, staggered by the crushing words.

"And what about our real father?" Junah erupted, unable to keep silent. "You know, the one your new father butchered?"

Merata opened her mouth, but no ready response came to her. She just scowled and clutched the pendant at her throat. Spock was grateful for her restraint.

"I . . . I would hope he died an honorable death," she offered finally. "For your family's sake."

"Stop it!" Rosha pleaded. "Both of you. We didn't come here to fight."

"I don't believe this!" Junah couldn't contain

himself. "Listen to her. She doesn't even care what her new Klingon friends did to us. She's a traitor to our people!"

"Junah, please." Rosha wrung her hands. "Whatever happened to your father, this is still your sister. Elzura."

"Are you joking?" Junah said. "For harvest's sake, look at her! She's one of them. A murderous Klingon savage, just like the ones who massacred your husband!"

The words were harsh, but not inaccurate. Spock considered interrupting the heated family dispute, but chose to stay out of it for the moment. In his experience, more emotional beings often needed to vent their feelings before a conflict could be resolved. It was not the Vulcan way, but he had observed aboard the *Enterprise* that humans did indeed sometimes benefit from "blowing off steam," as they termed it. Perhaps the same applied to Cyprians . . . and a Cyprian turned Klingon?

Watch and listen, Spock thought. *Provided there is no bloodshed.*

"You think I wish to claim you as a brother, you pitiful, ill-mannered pup!" Merata snarled at Junah, baring her teeth. "Your mother, although confused, has treated me with respect. But you . . . I show you hospitality and you rudely slander my people. Be thankful that I am not entirely the 'murderous savage' you think me!"

Caught up in the fury of the argument, Junah ignored the implied threat.

"You hear that? She called them *her* people." Contempt twisted his face. "This whole thing is a sick joke. I can't put up with this insanity any longer." Storming back to the exit, he pounded on the sturdy door. "Let me out! I'm done here!"

The door opened to reveal the security officer posted outside. Junah shoved past him in his haste to flee the stateroom.

Concern furrowed the guard's brow. "Is everything all right, Mister Spock? I heard shouting."

"Everything is under control," Spock stated, which was arguably stretching the truth. "Please keep an eye on young Mister Mursh, Lieutenant. He is in an agitated state."

"Yes, sir," the guard replied. "I'll do just that."

Rosha reeled about, torn between following her son and staying with her daughter. She started toward the door, then stopped to look back at Merata. "You have to forgive your brother. It's like I said before. He doesn't know you the way I do, the way Soleste does . . ."

"You *once* knew me," Merata corrected her. She nodded at the doorway through which Junah had departed. "He was rude and offensive, but he was not wrong. I am not the girl you remember. I am Merata, a Klingon, and the sooner you can accept that, the easier it will be for all of us."

"You can't mean that," Rosha said. "You're still Cyprian deep inside. You have to be."

"I am sorry," her daughter said. "But you are mistaken."

The pained look on Rosha's face was all too familiar to Spock. As before, a memory surfaced from his childhood:

"Part of you is human, Spock," Amanda had said. *"You will always be a child of two worlds."*

"You are mistaken," he had informed her, as gently as he could. *"I am and always will be Vulcan."*

The parallels with the scene before him were . . . unsettling.

Twelve

"Commander, you need to see this!"

Lieutenant Giusio called from the balcony, where he had been keeping a watchful eye on the demonstrations outside. Number One halted recording a new log entry into her tricorder to hurry out onto the balcony to see what was up, with Jones and Olson right behind her. Even though it was starting to get dark outside, stepping out into the muggy climate was like beaming directly from the *Enterprise* into a swamp, but the stifling heat and humidity were the least of her concerns right now.

"Yes?" she asked crisply. After the earlier attack on the suite, her nerves were slightly more on edge than she would have preferred. Her eyes searched the night sky for another flying metal disk. "What is it?"

"Something's got the crowd all riled up," Giusio reported. "Even more than usual, that is."

That was hard to imagine; the demonstrations and been going nonstop for days now. Number One had briefly hoped that the Cyprian authorities might dispel the crowd after the incident with the disk, but that had proved wishful thinking on her part. Politics appeared to have trumped security where the protests were concerned, or perhaps, to be more charitable, the Cyprians simply prized free speech over the safety of their guests.

Either way, Number One found the security measures lacking.

Accompanied by a chorus of angry shouts, a lone individual charged onto the dais and attempted to seize the attention of the crowd. The man's image supplanted the portrait of Elzy on the floating holographic display above him. Number One didn't recognize him, but the man's face was flushed with anger. Veins bulged at his temples and at his throat. His silver eyes were crazed and bloodshot. He shouted furiously, even though his voice was already being amplified.

"Listen to me, everyone! It's true. The *Enterprise* has struck a deal with the Klingons. They're going to give Elzy back to the savages!"

The crowd erupted thunderously. Fists, signs, and banners were shaken in the air.

Jones looked at Number One. "Is that true, Commander?"

"I doubt it," Number One replied. "Probably just a rumor. But rumors don't have to be true to be dangerous. They just need to be believed."

"Oh, it looks like they're believing it all right," Nurse Olson said sourly. "Tough luck for us."

His prediction, while pessimistic, proved all too accurate. Number One watched with alarm as the crowd turned into an angry mob, surging toward Envoy House like a sentient tidal wave. The Cyprian security guards posted in front of the building issued warnings and brandished their batons, but lacked the numbers to halt the mob even if they had been truly motivated to do so. The protestors smashed through the temporary barricades, trampling them underfoot, and shoved past the outnumbered guards, who offered only perfunctory resistance at best. As nearly as Number One could tell, the guards hadn't even tried to employ their disruptor pistols. She had to wonder if they had been specifically instructed not to fire on their own people or if they had simply chosen not to of their own volition.

Not that it truly mattered at the moment. She heard the front doors crash open downstairs. Irate voices and threats of violence penetrated the penthouse suite, even from five stories below. Footsteps pounded through the lower levels of the residence, accompanied by the sound of random vandalism. Glass shattered audibly. Furniture was overturned. Rumor or not, the spurious news had obviously incited the crowd, who were eager to take out their anger on the nearest targets available: Number One and her landing party.

Olson's face went pale. "What now, Commander?"

She swiftly assessed their situation. Without proper weapons or a ready avenue of escape, the best they could hope for was to buy time for help to arrive. Starfleet provided exemplary training in hand-to-hand combat, but that was not going to be sufficient to repel a bloodthirsty mob, even though Number One had excelled in her self-defense classes back at the Academy. At the moment, she would have gladly traded all her awards and citations for a single working laser pistol.

"Bar the door and secure it," she ordered. "Arm yourselves as best you can."

Guisio and Jones hopped to immediately. Grunting with effort, they shoved a sofa up against the door to the suite, then piled more furniture onto the makeshift barricade, while Number One retrieved the pair of knives she had hoarded before. Olson cracked open his medkit and took out a laser scalpel and hypospray. His hands shook as he loaded the hypo with what Number One assumed was a powerful tranquilizer or anesthetic.

Not a bad idea, she thought.

Footsteps stampeded up the stairs toward the fifth floor. Number One handed a knife to each of the two security officers. Jones accepted the crude weapon with obvious distaste.

"Maybe if we tell them that it's not true?" she suggested. "That it's just a dumb rumor?"

Her partner shook his head. "Doesn't sound like that crowd's in the mood to listen to anything, except maybe our skulls cracking."

Number One had to agree. While she admired Jones's faith in nonviolent conflict resolution, a crazed mob, inflamed by emotion and egged on by each other, could seldom be reasoned with. She and the others had to assume that they were in mortal jeopardy—and act accordingly. Spotting a fire extinguisher mounted on one wall, she claimed it as a possible means of crowd control. It was that or break off a chair leg to use as a club, and the former made her feel somewhat less like a Vetrian cave woman. She was still representing Starfleet after all.

"We don't want to hurt or kill anyone if we can avoid it, but I'm ordering you all to defend yourselves to the best of your abilities. Is that understood?"

"Yes, Commander," Olson said, swallowing hard. He gripped the scalpel in one hand and the hypospray in the other. He stared anxiously at the barricaded door. "I don't suppose we can make a run for the shuttlecraft?"

"Through a city of enraged Cyprians out for our blood?" Number One shook her head. "The spaceport is kilometers outside the city. I would not rate our chances of success very highly, even assuming we could somehow get past the mob outside."

As if to prove her point, the first wave of protestors reached the fifth floor and started hammering at the entrance to the suite. The sturdy wooden door shuddered from the impact of insistent bodies throwing themselves against it, the violence of which rattled the furniture propped up against the entrance. Number One found herself pining for the reinforced steel bulkheads and hatches aboard the *Enterprise*. The Cyprians' fondness for using wood wherever possible had its downside when it came to home invasions . . .

"Open up!" a hostile voice demanded, while others added further threats and curses to the hubbub. "We'll teach you Starfleet busybodies to help steal our children!"

Number One did not bother replying. The fact that the nameless speaker apparently expected the landing party to cooperate with the violent mob attacking them was a good indication that the rioters were not thinking rationally at this point. Instead of wasting her breath, she quickly surveyed her surroundings and concluded that the besieged suite offered little shelter once the mob inevitably made it through the door, which left only one option available to her.

"To the roof!" she ordered. "On the double!"

The roof was only slightly more defensible than the penthouse, but at least allowed for the possibility of being airlifted to safety, provided help arrived in time. She snatched her communicator from an end table as the landing party hustled for the roof, just as the door to the suite began to crack alarmingly. Clenched fists and groping fingers reached through the splintering door like the starving hordes on famine-racked Clephron V before the first Federation aid ships arrived. Cyprian faces, contorted with rage, could be glimpsed through the straining door as the weight of the rioters pushed against the barricade. Klingons in full battle mode could not have looked more ferocious.

"They're in here!" somebody shouted. "Don't let them get away!"

If only it were that easy, Number One thought.

A spiral staircase, carved from a single tree trunk, naturally, led to a rooftop garden, copiously bedecked with blooming flowers and greenery. The heady floral aroma seemed distinctly at odds with the dire circumstances. Sapprus was aglow with city lights and holographic advertising that all but drowned out the starry night sky. A crescent moon hung above a less occluded sibling. A monorail whooshed by on elevated tracks, so near and yet too far away to do the endangered landing party any good. The tumult below was practically loud enough to be picked up from space. The shouts of the rioters combined into a roar worthy of some gigantic predatory beast, like the semi-mythical dragons of the Kraken Nebula. Number One might have preferred a dragon.

"Secure the door," she ordered.

The verdant rooftop had less in the way of furnishings than the suite had, but Guisio and Jones hefted a solid wooden bench up against the door to the roof, then set to work sliding some heavy potted plants into place as well. It was a delaying tactic at best, but Number One took advantage of the time they'd bought to set her communicator to the prime minister's personal frequency. The holographic communications device in the suite was lost to them, but she'd had the foresight to make sure she had the means to contact Flescu's office directly if necessary.

In theory, at least.

"Envoy House to Prime Minister," she said sharply. "We are in immediate distress. Please respond."

To her dismay, her hail went unanswered.

"Envoy House to Prime Minister. Repeat: We are in immediate distress. Emergency assistance is required."

She moved to the edge of the roof, where only a carved rail stood between her and a five-story drop to the mobbed streets below. Working her way along the perimeter, she located a metal fire escape leading to an alley below, only to discover that another pack of rioters were already scaling the steel steps and ladders toward the roof, eliminating the fire escape as an avenue of retreat. Worse yet, it appeared as though they were only minutes away from having another pack of hostile Cyprians to contend with.

Unless she acted promptly.

Hefting the fire extinguisher she'd commandeered earlier, she twisted the nozzle and let loose a stream of fire-retardant foam against the rioters climbing the fire escape. The pressurized contents of the apparatus sent the belligerent climbers tumbling back down the metal structure while rendering the upper rungs and steps too slick and sudsy to safely navigate. She emptied the extinguisher of its contents, then hurled the empty tank down at the lower landings to further discourage any attempts to scale the side of the building. For a moment, she felt like Victor Hugo's famous hunchback defending Notre Dame, but, alas, there was no true "Sanctuary!" to be found here at Envoy House.

"No way down, sir?" Olson asked her.

"Not that I can determine."

Scanning the scene, she searched in vain for some indication that Cyprian security forces were responding to the attack on the building. No emergency vehicles appeared to be converging on the site by ground or air. She heard no sirens or alarms. Dead air greeted her desperate hails. Nobody was picking up.

"Commander?" Olson asked. "What are they saying? Is help on the way?"

"I doubt it." She lowered her communicator. "Looks like we're on our own."

Olson didn't want to hear it. "But what about the Cyprian authorities? They can't just abandon us to the mob, can they?"

Number One shrugged. Either the Cyprian police were in sympathy with the rioters or, more likely, nobody in authority, least of all the prime minister, wanted to be seen as siding with Starfleet against the righteous fury of the Cyprian people. Either way, the prospects for a timely rescue were not encouraging.

"I think they just did," she said.

———

"I wondered when you would visit me."

Soleste remained abed in the recovery ward, but appeared alert and well-rested as Merata entered the chamber, accompanied by Spock, who watched his charge's every movement carefully. Only days had passed after all since Merata had attacked her sister in the transporter room immediately upon their arrival aboard the *Enterprise*. Merata had since managed another family reunion without violence; nevertheless, Spock remained on guard, even as he'd agreed to facilitate this meeting at Merata's request.

As before, they had the recovery room to themselves. Rosha and Junah Mursh were presently recovering in their own guest quarters. After the near-altercation with Junah earlier, Spock had thought it best to limit this encounter to Soleste and Merata alone. Reuniting the two sisters was likely to be fraught enough without adding any additional variables.

"Does it surprise you that I delayed?" Merata replied icily. "When last we met, it ended badly for both of us."

Spock pondered Merata's motives. In truth, he was uncertain why the prisoner had finally consented to meet with Soleste. Perhaps her earlier encounter with her mother had somehow inspired this change of heart? He suspected that even Merata was not entirely clear on why had she had come to see Soleste or what she hoped to accomplish.

"Sorry about that," Soleste said. "The kidnapping and all, I mean. At the time, it seemed smarter to grab you when I could and explain later."

Merata's expression darkened in a way that worried Spock. He quietly took a step forward.

"A poor excuse for treachery," she snarled. "You betrayed my trust and stole my liberty."

Soleste didn't deny it. "But you understand now why I did it? Who I really am?"

Merata scrutinized the other woman from the foot of the bed. She frowned as she compared the injured tracker to whatever decade-old memories she retained of her elder sibling. "I recall a girl with *two* eyes."

"Yeah. I remember her too," Soleste said wryly. "Hang on. Let me show you something." She reached up and unscrewed her ocular implant from its socket. She turned the crystalline device around so that its inner lens was pointed away from her. "Ordinarily, this pricy souvenir projects images directly to my optic nerve, but it has other uses."

Merata tensed. "As a weapon?"

"More like a scrapbook," Soleste explained. "To remind me why I kept hunting for you."

She put the crystal eye in backward, then activated it by blinking her other eye rapidly. A lambent white glow lit up the implant as it projected a holographic recording into the empty air between the two women. Spock was impressed by the clarity of the three-dimensional image, which occupied a sphere approximately thirty-five centimeters in diameter. The Cyprians had clearly made great strides in holographic technology, putting many other civilizations to shame.

Inside the luminous sphere was what appeared to be a "home movie" of a sort. Images of a young girl, whom Spock assumed to be Elzura, playing happily with her family, including her mother, father, older sister, and baby brother, unfolded before his eyes. The girl, who bore scant resemblance to Merata, grinned and laughed and ran barefoot through a grassy field beneath a sunny sky while clutching a plush toy fashioned to resemble some manner of indigenous saurian. A split velvet tongue protruded from the toy's jaws.

"Forko," Merata whispered, visibly moved by the images. Unable to look away, she stood transfixed by the illuminated fragments of her lost childhood. Her fingers went involuntarily to her cropped left ear, as though comparing it to the scalloped lobes of the little girl in the hologram, while her other hand toyed once more with the Klingon pendant at her throat. Wide eyes misted noticeably.

"You loved that silly lizard," Soleste said, one eye aglow. "We found it in the ruins . . . afterward."

Her sister's words broke the spell cast by the flickering images. Eyes wet, Merata glared angrily at Soleste. She jerked her hand away from her ear. "Why would you show me this? Those days are long gone. That girl is no more!"

Soleste's face hardened. Spock could not help comparing the scarred, careworn Cyprian with the carefree older sister glimpsed in the recording. Soleste's transformation was arguably less dramatic than Elzura's, but it was striking in its own right. A decade tracking her lost sister across the quadrant had aged Soleste in ways beyond the merely chronological.

"You didn't like that?" she said acerbically. "All right. Let me show you something else."

She blinked and the idyllic family scene was replaced by a much more brutal glimpse into the past. Security camera footage captured the same little girl alone amidst a scene of fresh devastation. Soot and dust and tears streaked the face of the child, who was still recognizably Elzura. Surrounded by smoking rubble, she crouched warily behind a pile of charred debris. Smoke and flames flickered at the periphery of the image. A still and lifeless limb jutted out from beneath a collapsed wall or rooftop. More bodies could be glimpsed around the fringes of the scene. Small fingers clutched a jagged piece of torn metal as Elzy stared wide-eyed at an approaching menace. Her whole body shook with fear or anger or some combination thereof.

The attack on the mining complex, Spock realized. *Obviously.*

Long shadows preceded the arrival of a squadron of Klingon soldiers. The raiders sported no insignias and wore civilian garb rather than uniforms, but their military bearing and gleaming disruptor rifles betrayed their true affiliation. The soldiers advanced confidently through the ruins, no doubt conducting a cleanup operation, until they spotted the small survivor crouching in the wreckage. Elzura did not wait for the Klingons to threaten her before going on the offensive. Grabbing a fist-sized chunk of rubble with her free hand, she hurled it at the enemy.

The crude missile smacked against the chest of the lead Klingon, whom Spock now recognized as Krunn, albeit ten years younger than the grizzled commander of the *Fek'lhr*. The blow had little impact on Krunn, but provoked an angry snarl from another soldier who turned his rifle toward Elzy and took aim. Just as he fired, however, Krunn turned and knocked the barrel of the rifle aside so that the other Klingon's shot missed its target. An emerald pulse vaporized a piece of mangled equipment while leaving Elzy unharmed for the moment.

The foiled shooter protested angrily, but Krunn barked back at him. Brushing off the dust from the thrown fragment, Krunn thrust his own rifle into the arms of a subordinate and drew nearer to the cornered child. Grinning wolfishly, he held out his hand as though trying to entice a feral *sehlat* from hiding, while the other Klingons looked on with varying degrees of impatience and amusement. Backed up against a collapsed wall, Elzy had nowhere to run.

So she attacked instead. Knife in hand, she lunged at Krunn, going for his heart. It was a valiant effort, but, of course, she was no match for the full-grown Klingon warrior, who effortlessly grabbed her by the wrist and wrested the knife from her grip. Even still, Elzy refused to surrender. Fighting tooth and nail, she threw herself at the laughing Klingon, kicking and scratching and biting.

Appearing amused and/or impressed by the girl's spirit, Krunn tucked her under his arm and carried her off like a trophy of war. Elzura was still thrashing wildly, desperate to break free, as the Klingons continued on their way, taking the helpless child with them.

With a blink, Soleste froze the image, so that it hung motionlessly in the air between the sisters like an accusation. The frantic look on little Elzy's face was preserved for posterity.

"*That's* who your new family is," she said bitterly. "That's how they 'adopted' you . . . over the bodies of our dead."

Merata looked away from the projection, unable to face this jagged fragment of yesterday. The expression on her face defied easy interpretation. Spock could only wonder what turbulent thoughts and emotions were churning behind Merata's troubled eyes. He doubted that even a mind-meld would bring much clarity to this moment; delving into her psyche here and now would likely be akin to diving head-first into a seething matter/antimatter reaction—and just as dangerous.

"Shut it off," she said, half-pleading, half-demanding. "Shut it off now!"

Thirteen

"Captain!" Garrison called out. "There's trouble on the planet. I'm picking up reports of an attack on the Envoy House in Sapprus."

"What?" Pike asked. A jolt of adrenaline combatted the fatigue and fever wearing him down. He sat up in his chair and called out hoarsely, "Who is attacking? What's happening?"

Garrison adjusted his earpiece. "Details are sketchy, sir, but it's sounding like a crowd of angry demonstrators have invaded the residence. There are scattered reports of violence, vandalism." He looked up from his console. "It doesn't sound good, sir."

Damn, Pike thought. He'd been afraid of something like this, especially after the incident earlier. *I knew I should've have gotten them off that planet, despite Number One's stubborn insistence on completing her mission.*

Granted, that might have been easier said than done.

"What about the Cyprian authorities? Are they protecting our people?"

Garrison looked like he wanted to give the captain a different answer. "That's . . . unclear, sir."

"Understood," Pike replied. "Get me Number One, if you can."

"Aye, sir!"

Moments dragged on like eons, as though time itself was warping, as Pike waited tensely for Garrison to get in touch with the landing party. For all Pike knew, Number One and the others had already been taken hostage, injured, or worse. His head throbbed with each interminable tick of the chronometer. His chest ached.

"I'm running into some interference, sir." Garrison cupped a hand over his ear to filter out the ambient noise on the bridge. "It appears somebody is attempting to jam communications from Envoy House."

Pike clenched his fists. "The authorities or the protestors?"

"Impossible to tell, sir. It appears to be a localized effect."

To keep the landing party from calling for help, Pike wondered, or to give the Cyprian authorities an excuse not to respond promptly to the threat? Pike couldn't be sure, but this reeked of plausible deniability to him. But who was behind this and why didn't matter at the moment, only finding a way around the obstacle in time to reach Number One and the others.

"Can you get past the interference?" he asked.

"I think so," Garrison said, "if I can boost the signal by narrowing the frequency." His arm stretched across his console to reach the external communications panel. "Just give me a few seconds."

"A lot can happen in a second, Mister Garrison. Make every one count."

"Yes, Captain! Boosting the signal now."

Pike crossed his fingers.

"Got her, sir!" Garrison announced with visible relief. "Putting her through."

There was no visual, but Number One's voice echoed across the bridge. *"Captain? I was just about to contact you."* She sounded admirably cool and collected under the circumstances. *"I'm afraid things have taken a turn for the worse, sir."*

She quickly briefed him on the landing party's perilous situation. Pike was relieved to hear that she and the other crew members had not been harmed yet, but "yet" appeared to be the operative word. Straining his ears, he thought he could hear lots of noise and commotion in the background. Number One had to raise her voice to be heard above the din.

"We could use a lift, sir," she concluded. *"Sooner rather than later."*

"Copy that, Number One." Pike made the decision without a moment's hesitation. "We're on our way. Hold on as long as you can."

"*We're not going anywhere, sir. At least not willingly.*"

"I'm going to hold you to that. Expect us soon. *Enterprise* out." Pike coughed and cleared his swollen throat. It hurt just to breathe, let alone issue commands. "Helmsman, take us into a lower orbit . . . within transporter range."

"Aye, sir," Mohindas replied, sounding healthy enough for now.

Pike trusted Mohindas to do her job. He hit the intercom button on his armrest. "Transporter room, prepare for an emergency beam-out. We're going after our landing party and time is of the essence."

Sam Yamata responded at once. "*Message received, sir. We'll be ready.*"

Pike had expected to hear Pitcairn's voice instead. "Is Chief Pitcairn on hand?"

"*The chief has taken ill,*" Yamata explained. "*But we can handle this, sir. Don't worry about it.*"

"No worries, Mister Yamata," Pike said, even as he regretted hearing that one of his senior officers had been taken out of commission by the implacable fever. "Stand by."

Pike kept the line open to the transporter room. He sat back in his chair and watched Cypria III draw nearer upon the viewscreen. Ryetalyn or not, he was developing a serious dislike for the planet. Painful breaths tortured his breathing. His eyes felt like they were being speared by lasers.

Colt approached his chair. "The Cyprians aren't going to like this," she said quietly, not as a criticism but merely as an observation. "They wanted us to keep our distance."

Tell me about it, Pike thought. "Then they should've taken better care of our people."

"That's telling them, Captain," Tyler said. "We can't just—"

The rest of his remark was lost to a vicious coughing jag that sounded as though he was trapped on a Class-L planet without a respirator. His face was pale and sweaty and looked like death warmed over. He gripped the edge of his console with shaking hands.

"You all right, Joe?" Pike asked.

"I've felt better, Captain." Tyler managed to bring his coughing fit under control, mostly. He clipped his words, obviously short of breath. "But I can manage."

Pike hoped that was the case. He probably should have had Tyler relieved earlier, but at this point there were few crew members well enough to take the navigator's place. The *Enterprise* was already close to running on a skeleton crew. *If I dismiss every crew member who's looking under the weather,* Pike thought, *we'll be down to bare bones.*

"Yeoman," he addressed Colt. "I think Mister Tyler could use a cup of that restorative tea of yours."

She jumped to it, albeit not without a worried backward glance at Pike.

"I'll be right back," she promised, starting toward the turbolift.

"Captain," Garrison interrupted. "We're being hailed by the planet. They're ordering us to return to our previous orbit."

That was fast, Pike thought, impressed by the Cyprian's orbital defense monitoring. *Too bad they couldn't respond to the attack on Envoy House so promptly.*

"Tell them this is a rescue mission. Remind them our landing party is in danger."

"Yes, sir." Garrison spoke in a low voice to whoever was at the other end of the transmission. "They're not buying it, Captain. They insist that they can deal with any unrest on the planet."

"Like they have so far?" Pike shook his head, which just made it throb all the worse. He felt like he was on the receiving end of a Klingon agonizer. "That's not good enough. Tell them we're coming in . . . with or without their permission."

Garrison gulped. "Yes, sir."

This may vaporize our chances of ever getting our hands on that ryetalyn, Pike realized, but what else was he supposed to do? He wasn't about to let the landing party face death in the performance of their duty. *Not after what happened on Rigel VII . . .*

"Incoming, Captain!" Tyler blurted. "They're targeting us with their laser satellites!"

"Shields at maximum!" Pike ordered. "Red alert!"

A klaxon sounded and annunciator lights flashed crimson all around the bridge as the *Enterprise* came under fire from Cypria III's orbital laser cannons. White-hot beams lit up the void, narrowly missing the ship. Pike blinked, surprised that they hadn't taken a hit from the lasers.

"Are those satellites near-sighted?" he asked aloud. "Not that I'm complaining, mind you."

An explanation was not long in coming.

"Those were warning shots," Garrison reported. "They're saying that the next blasts won't be."

Colt returned to the command circle, calling off her tea run in light of the red alert. She clearly had her priorities straight. "Guess they don't like people getting too close."

"Can't say I blame them," Pike said, "considering their history with the Klingons, but they're not giving us any choice." He turned toward Garrison. "Remind them that Elzura is aboard, along with the entire Mursh family."

"Right on it, sir!" Garrison said.

"Should I stay on course, Captain?" Mohindas asked. "Despite the Cyprians making a fuss?"

"Absolutely," Pike replied. "Don't even think about slowing down."

"Figured you'd say that, sir," Mohindas said as the *Enterprise* continued her descent into a lower orbit. "Just checking."

Pike knew that disregarding the Cyprians' warnings would have consequences. They weren't long in coming.

"Brace yourself!" Tyler croaked. "We're under fire!"

A blinding white flash lit up the viewscreen, momentarily overwhelming the brightness filters, as a powerful laser blast slammed into the *Enterprise*'s shields, rocking the bridge. Comparable in punch to the Klingons' disruptors, the white-hot energy beams ricocheted off the spaceship's deflectors, but the impact was still felt inside the ship. Colt staggered and grabbed on to the safety rail to keep from falling. Pike gripped his armrests and gritted his teeth. The massive jolt hadn't done his aching head any good. A thunderous din hurt his ears.

"Status," he demanded.

"Shields holding," Tyler said weakly, swaying slightly in his seat. He hugged himself as though chilled. "But down to seventy-nine percent."

"Receiving damage reports," Garrison added. "Nothing major yet. Mostly burned-out control circuits and transfer coils, coolant leaks, and a few small fires, all being brought under control." He paused to absorb more data from the comm board. "Sickbay is objecting to the disturbances."

I'll bet, Pike thought. He took comfort in knowing that sickbay was one of the most heavily protected areas on the ship. At least Boyce and his patients weren't taking the brunt of the attack, such as it was. The captain guessed that the Cyprians hadn't unleashed their full firepower yet, due to the presence of Elzura and the others aboard, but things had obviously progressed beyond warning shots. The Cyprians were serious about defending their orbital borders.

Too bad he was just as serious about rescuing his people.

"Should we retaliate, sir?" Tyler asked. "I could try to target their defensive satellites."

"Belay that," Pike said. As tempting as it was to strike back, that was a line he wasn't going to cross. Encroaching on the planet's airspace without their permission for the sake of the endangered landing party was one thing; opening fire on Cypria's defense forces was something else altogether. "We're Starfleet, not the Klingon Empire."

"Yes, sir," Tyler said between coughs. "Understood, sir."

A second blast shook the *Enterprise*, testing Pike's resolve not to fire back. The bridge shuddered and sparks erupted from an overloaded sensor station, forcing an ensign to jump backward to avoid being shocked. Pike was impressed by the woman's reflexes, as well as the way she quickly diverted power to a secondary relay. Loud booms, echoing across the bridge, made it sound like the *Enterprise* was flying through a minefield. Pike suddenly understood why the Klingons hadn't raided Cypria in years.

"Shields at seventy percent, sir!"

Pike turned toward Garrison. "The Cyprians aren't backing down, I take it."

"Not yet, Captain."

"Talk faster." Pike looked to the helm. "Time to transporter range?"

"Two minutes," Mohindas reported. "Almost there."

Pike nodded. *Hold fast, Number One. Here comes the cavalry . . . assuming the Cyprians don't blow us out of the sky first.*

"Captain!" Tyler blurted. "The Klingons . . . they're closing in on us!"

Blast it, Krunn! Pike thought. *Not now!*

A red alert disturbed sickbay, interrupting the highly emotional confrontation between Merata and Soleste. Spock was almost grateful for the distraction.

"What is it?" Soleste exclaimed. The hologram

emanating from her ocular implant blinked out. "What's happening?"

Merata instinctively looked for a martial explanation. "Is that a call to arms? Is the ship going into battle?"

Excellent questions, Spock thought. Before he could attempt to ascertain answers, the ship was jolted by an unknown force. The deck listed beneath Spock, and he braced himself against the nearest bulkhead to keep his balance, while Merata gripped the foot of her sister's bed. The diagnostic monitor above the bed shorted out briefly before rebooting itself. A forgotten data slate slid off a counter to crash onto the floor. A rolling chair toppled over. Confusion and commotion sounded in the adjacent wards. Spock's keen ears heard Boyce and his staff scrambling to cope with the aftermath of the tremor. Keeping a close eye on Merata, lest she take advantage of the chaos to flee or fight, he hurried over to a wall-mounted intercom unit.

"Spock to bridge," he said. "What is the nature of the emergency?"

The most probable explanation was that the ship was under attack, but from whom? The Klingons? The Cyprians? Both? Too many equally plausible scenarios flashed through his brain as he waited for additional information to dispel any uncertainty. As a scientist, he was reluctant to jump to conclusions without sufficient data. As a Starfleet officer, he needed to know how much danger the *Enterprise* was in and what he could do to defend both ship and crew.

"Repeat: Spock to bridge. Please advise."

To his frustration, which required some effort to suppress, the bridge did not respond immediately to his query. He suspected that the comm station was preoccupied with whatever crisis was at hand; under ordinary circumstances, auxiliary personnel would have been available to handle the overflow, but the Rigelian fever outbreak had apparently taxed the ship's resources. Backup personnel were few and far between.

Accepting reality, he used the comm unit to summon assistance instead. Doctor Boyce responded with commendable alacrity. "Yes, Spock?" he asked brusquely, looking and sounding like a man with rather too much on his hands. A filter mask covered his nose and mouth; Boyce lowered the mask and peeled off a pair of protective gloves. "What is it?"

"I am needed on the bridge. Please look after our guests." He handed his laser pistol to the startled doctor, who accepted it without thinking. "I recommend that you summon a security officer to escort Merata back to her quarters."

"Hold on there, Spock," Boyce protested. "Do I look like a prison guard to you?"

"I do not have time to debate the matter, Doctor.

Feel free to delegate the task to a nurse if you prefer, but I cannot remain here while the ship is in jeopardy and the captain may require my services." He turned to Merata. "Can I trust you not to give the doctor cause for concern?"

"I make no promises, Vulcan."

Spock found her response worrisome, if not unexpected. Boyce retreated a few steps and raised the pistol. Normally unflappable, he looked as though he would've rather been performing dental surgery on an Uttrian razor sloth. "Retirement is sounding better and better," he muttered.

"Go, Spock," Soleste said from her bed. She unscrewed her ocular implant and returned it to its original orientation. "I can keep an eye on my sister."

"We'll see about that," Merata said ominously. Her gaze followed Spock as he headed out of sickbay. "Is it my father, Vulcan? Has he come for me at last?"

Spock wished he knew.

———

"The Klingons are hailing us!"

"Of course they are," Pike said irritably. As if the Cyprians weren't posing enough of a threat at the moment, both to the *Enterprise* and to the landing party, the Klingons had to raise a ruckus too. "Onscreen."

Krunn's glowering countenance took over the viewscreen. *"What are you up to, Pike? I warned you not to deliver Merata to the Cyprians!"*

"That's not what this is about," Pike insisted, all the while suspecting that he was wasting his time trying to allay the general's suspicions. He straightened his posture and put plenty of iron into his voice, the better to conceal his debilitated state. With any luck, Krunn would mistake his raspy delivery for a guttural growl. "We're just going to pick up some of our own people."

"And I'm supposed to believe you? What's to stop you from beaming my daughter down to those weaklings?"

"Captain!" Tyler interrupted. "The *Fek'lhr* is still following us down toward the planet. The Cyprians are opening fire on the Klingons!"

Sure enough, the image on the viewscreen shook violently as the battle cruiser apparently came under attack from the Cyprians' orbital defenses. Tossed about in his seat, Krunn barked commands to his subordinates. Smoke and dust added to the already murky atmosphere of the cruiser's bridge before the image blinked out completely. Cypria III, looking closer than ever, returned to the screen.

"Status of the *Fek'lhr*?" Pike demanded.

"Still in one piece," Tyler reported, "but they're taking a walloping. The Cyprians aren't holding back, sir."

Silver linings, Pike thought. If nothing else, the *Fek'lhr* was probably drawing plenty of fire away from the *Enterprise.* Certainly the colonists had better reason to fear the Klingon ship than the Starfleet vessel and considerably less incentive to moderate their fire. Whether he intended to or not, Krunn was possibly doing Pike a favor by providing the Cyprians with a much more tempting target.

A Cyprian defense satellite came into view directly ahead. The unmanned orbital weapon resembled a cactus, with remote-controlled laser cannons bristling like spikes from an armored core that was approximately ten meters in diameter. Coruscating white energy crackled within the barrels of the satellite's annons as it rotated toward the *Enterprise*, preparing to unleash another salvo at the trespassing space ship while firing at the *Fek'lhr* with its other weapons.

"Evasive act—" Pike began, but before he could finish the command, twin disruptor beams bombarded the satellite, sending it spinning wildly out of orbit and control. Moments later, a photon torpedo delivered the *coup de grâce*, blowing the vulnerable satellite to kingdom come, or whatever the Cyprian equivalent was. It exploded into a fireball of blazing plasma and debris that spread out harmlessly in all directions before flying out of view.

"Let me guess," he said. "The Klingons firing back at the Cyprian defenses?"

"Affirmative," Tyler said. "They're shooting at each other now."

Figures, Pike thought. *Unlike us, Krunn has no reason not to retaliate when fired up by the laser satellites. Naturally, he's going to respond in kind.*

"Works for me," he said. "As long as it keeps both of them busy while we're doing our job." He turned toward the helm. "Mohindas?"

"Coming within transporter range," she reported. "Four thousand kilometers and counting."

"And none too soon." Pike took a deep breath, or tried to at least. He was getting shorter and shorter of breath. "Here comes the tricky part."

Lowering the ship's shields while caught between the Klingons and Cyprians was a calculated risk, to say the least, but there was no way around it if they were going to beam the landing party to safety. They just needed to be quick about it and not keep the shields down any longer than absolutely necessary. Split-second timing was the order of the day.

"Transporter room, get ready to lock onto the landing party. Mister Tyler, prepare to lower shields at my command."

"Aye, sir." Tyler's hoarse voice was barely a whisper. He wiped his brow with the sleeve of his tunic while wheezing loudly. "Wait . . . incoming!"

A third blast proved that the Cyprians hadn't forgotten the *Enterprise* entirely, which made lowering the shields still a dicey proposition, particularly with the *Fek'lhr* closing in on the *Enterprise* as well. His head throbbing, Pike racked his brain for a way to discourage any further attacks for just a few precious moments.

"Garrison!" he said sharply. "Open channels to the Klingons *and* Cyprians. Let me talk to both of them."

"Aye, Captain." Garrison flipped a switch on his console. "You're on, sir."

"Attention all parties. This is *Enterprise*. Hold your fire! Our primary warp manifold has fractured. One more blast and we'll go up like an exploding star!"

That was stretching things a bit, but what was a little exaggeration between armed combatants? With any luck, the deception would make both sides think twice before taking another shot at the *Enterprise*—at least for a few minutes.

"Are we within transporter range?" Pike asked urgently.

"Aye, sir!" Mohindas said. "In synchronous orbit above Sapprus."

Here goes nothing, Pike thought. "Lower shields."

"Uh-huh . . ." Tyler reached groggily for the controls, only to collapse at his post. He tumbled from his seat onto the deck, moaning in distress. He writhed upon the floor, clutching his stomach as though gripped by severe pains. His face was gray and clammy except for the discolored yellow veins bulging across his face and neck. Straining lungs labored audibly. He was sweating profusely.

"Transporter room to bridge," Yamata piped in via the intercom. *"Standing by."*

Pike lurched from his chair, desperate to get to the shield controls, but Colt beat him to it.

"I'm on it, sir!" she declared as she dived into Tyler's seat and took over the console. "Shields down, Captain!"

Grateful for her quick thinking and initiative, Pike sagged back into his chair and leaned into the intercom receiver. "Transporter room . . . now!"

He prayed they weren't already too late.

Fourteen

Their second barricade lasted no longer than their first. With a resounding crash, the door to the roof broke apart and the Cyprian rioters shoved their way past the heaped obstacles meant to delay them. The furious mob stormed onto the rooftop, undaunted by the sweltering heat and humidity. Their wild eyes and murderous expressions reminded Number One of the barbaric Kaylar warriors who had massacred three of her fellow crew members not too long ago. These assailants brandished broken bottles, bricks, and chains instead of swords and spears, but the intent was the same.

This was Rigel VII all over again . . .

"There they are!" one of the ringleaders shouted, pointing at the outnumbered Starfleet personnel. "We've got them now!"

Number One and the rest of her team were backed up against a rail at the far side of the rooftop garden. Behind them was nothing but a five-story drop to the pavement below. Number One silently cursed the planet's Class-M gravity. What she wouldn't give for a few pairs of jet boots right now.

"Keep back!" she warned. Her hands gripped the shaft of a shovel she had liberated from a nearby tool shed. It was no *lirpa* or *bat'leth,* both of which she was fully trained in the use of, but it would have to do. "You don't want to do anything rash. We're here as guests of your government!"

"Never mind the politicians!" the ringleader said. He had shoulder-length blond hair, a ruddy complexion, bad skin, a potbelly, mean little eyes, and a construction hammer gripped in one hand. A patch bearing the iconic portrait of Little Elzy was affixed to his vest. Saliva sprayed from his lips. "You'll answer to the people now, for holding a Cyprian child hostage!"

A chorus of hostile voices echoed the sentiment, accompanied by a disturbing variety of suggestions as to what was to be done with the trapped landing party. "Throw one of them off the roof," a red-faced woman called out. "Show that human captain we mean business!"

"You do that," Number One said sternly, "and you'll likely never see your precious Elzura again. I don't know what you've heard, but—"

"Shut your lying mouth, human!" the ringleader snarled. "We've had enough of your stalling and excuses. Your captain will give us Elzy back all right . . . or he'll get you and your friends back in pieces!"

"Actually, I'm Illyrian," she corrected him. "So you should know better than to think you can frighten me."

Her bravado was at least partially an act, of course. Despite her composure, she was genuinely concerned for the safety of her team. Unless the *Enterprise* extracted them from this situation momentarily, bloodshed—or worse—was all but inevitable.

"Human, Illyrian . . . it makes no difference!" the ringleader shot back. "You have no right to keep a Cyprian child from her family!"

"You tell her, Tofrum!" a woman's voice called out. "We know how to deal with Klingons and anybody who sides with them!"

A rock came hurtling out of the crowd like a speeding meteoroid. Number One's superior reflexes came to her rescue as she deflected the missile with the blade of her shovel, sending it back the way it came. Tofrum grunted as the stone hit him in the gut, knocking him back onto his rear. That the rock had conveniently struck the mob's leader was no coincidence; Number One silently thanked all the hours she'd spent playing null-G lacrosse and racquetball in the *Enterprise*'s gymnasium. Calculating angles came easily to her.

"Witch! Child-snatcher!" Tofrum clutched his stomach as his cohorts helped him to his feet. His face flushed with anger. "You aliens don't care who you hurt, do you?"

The sheer hypocrisy of his accusation was rather breathtaking. Number One had dared to hope that a vigorous show of self-defense might give the mob pause when it came to attacking a team of highly trained Starfleet personnel, but it seemed she'd sadly underestimated the crowd's desire to lash out at the landing party. They were not to be deterred.

"Get them!" Tofrum bellowed. "For Elzy!"

The mob charged at them, surging forward like an avalanche. Number One counted a couple dozen hostiles, with more pouring through the breached door onto the roof, and still there was no sign that Cyprian security forces had any intention to intervene. The landing party was going to have to rely on one another and no one else.

"Close ranks!" she ordered. "Stick together!"

They contracted into a tight circle, back to back to back to back. Giusio and Jones staked out positions flanking Number One and Olson. The paired security officers wielded their knives defensively, keeping the crowd at bay with skillful combos of feints, thrusts, and slashes. Jones lobbed her knife back and forth between her hands, just to keep her attackers guessing, while Giusio used his intimidating height and build to full effect. They drew blood, but took pains to avoid killing or maiming; they sliced rather than stabbed, inflicting only shallow cuts on arms and chests and scalloped ears. Bleeding orange, a few chastened rioters fell back, but for every Cyprian who retreated, two more seemed to shove forward to take their place, while the minor injuries only seemed to madden some of the protestors more. It was like a feeding frenzy—and the landing party was the chum.

"Back off!" Jones flaunted her dazzling knifework. "This is all a misunderstanding! We can work this out!"

"Save your breath," Giusio said gruffly. He absorbed a punch with his knife arm, then delivered a crushing uppercut with his left. "We're past talking now."

And then some, Number One thought. *So much for this garden of tranquility.*

She spun the shovel before her like a battle staff, striking with both ends of the tool. The metal blade blocked a broken bottle thrust at her face, shattering it to splinters; a heartbeat later, she jabbed the handle at the opposite end into the shin of a charging Cyprian bruiser, who dropped to the rooftop whimpering and clutching his leg. Number One kicked him away from her before he got the bright idea to grab her leg instead, and the next wave of rioters tripped and stumbled over the fallen man, nearly trampling him. Broken glass crunched beneath their feet.

Remind me not to fall, she thought.

She took a second to firm up her grip on the shovel. Between the tropical climate and the ongoing melee, she was working up a sweat. Her palms were damp and slippery. Perspiration gleamed upon her face and dripped down her back, gluing her tunic to her skin. Her stamina was in the ninety-ninth percentile, but even she was wearing down. Her human comrades had to be tiring too.

"They just keep on coming!" Olson said, panting. "There's no end to them!"

She glanced briefly at him over her shoulder. Sweat drenched his face and hair. Bulging eyes were wide with fear. He waved the surgical laser before him like a talisman, trying to ward off the crazed Cyprians and succeeding to a degree. The red-hot tip of the laser could not fire a beam like a pistol, but it traced blazing patterns in the space between Olson and his foes, who looked inclined to give the scalpel a wide berth. Apparently, surgical instruments scared people more than knives or shovels.

Probably old news to Doctor Boyce, Number One thought. "Keep it together, Olson. The captain is on his way."

"But what if . . . ?"

"Speculation does not help us," she said bluntly. "Stay sharp."

"Yes, Number One. It's just that—"

A determined Cyprian, gripping a crooked wooden cane with both hands, swung the cane at Olson's legs, but Olson swiped the scalpel down in time to counter the attack. The laser sizzled through the cane at an angle, cleanly slicing it in two. The curved top half of the cane flew over the edge of the roof, where the clatter of its landing was drowned out by the tumult of battle and the shouting of the crowds remaining below. Left holding only a fraction of cane, the rioter stared aghast at her bisected weapon. She froze, uncertain if she still had enough of a club to fight with.

"Not so fast!" Olson said, savoring his narrow escape. He drove his would-be assailant back with the business end of his scalpel. "I know how to use this and—"

A chain whipped out of nowhere, wrapping tightly around his wrist. He cried out in pain, and the laser slipped from his fingers. The chain yanked him forward, away from Number One and others.

"Olson!"

Engaged with too many opponents of her own, she could not immediately rush to his aid. She could only watch out of the corner of her eye as a large, muscular Cyprian grabbed Olson and hurled him to the floor. Snatching up a heavy potted plant from the garden, the man raised it high above his head, clearly intending to crush the nurse's head with it. Olson threw up an arm to shield himself, but gravity was not on his side. Number One saw at once that Olson had only seconds to live.

Calculating quickly, she took the only action available to her. Flipping the shovel in her hand, she threw it like a javelin with the blunt end of the handle leading. The shovel struck the big Cyprian in the chest, knocking him backward into the garden. The raised pot tumbled away from Olson to crash into a flowering bush instead. Nearby rioters jumped out of the way to avoid being hit by an explosion of flying soil and jagged ceramic shards.

Good news, Number One thought. *Olson is still alive.*

Bad news, I just tossed away my only weapon.

"Guisio! Jones! Cover me!"

She moved to get behind the security team, but not quickly enough. A rock hit her forehead, barely missing her right eye, and she staggered to one side, momentarily dazed. A wooden board, swung by an anonymous rioter, struck her in the side and sent her reeling away from Jones and Guisio. She slipped on a loose clod of damp soil and tumbled to the floor, the jarring impact leaving her stunned and vulnerable. Someone grabbed her ankle and dragged her across the roof. Her aching head banged against the floor.

"Over the edge for you," a harsh voice gloated. "Let's see if Earthers can fly!"

Not Earth, Illyria, she thought irritably. *How many times do I have to explain that?*

Her back scraped against the floor of the garden as she was dragged toward the edge, unable to shake her leg free of her captor's grip. Her fingers groped for something to grab on to. Her head was still ringing from being hit by the rock, not to mention being bounced around; it would be a minor miracle if she didn't have a concussion, but that inconvenience paled in comparison to being thrown off the roof. Her bruised cranium wouldn't matter once it was shattered all over the sidewalk. If she could just get back on her feet . . . !

"Lieutenant! Catch!"

Olson's voice penetrated the fog around her brain. Turning her head toward him, she saw a small silver object arcing through the air toward her. It took her a second to place it.

The hypospray!

Her brain swiftly calculated its trajectory. She reached out and plucked it from the air even as her captor reached the low guardrail at the edge of the roof. He looked around for assistance. "Somebody help me toss out the trash!"

I beg to differ, she thought. Muscles honed to perfection by rigorous exercise, including daily situps, allowed her to sit up far enough to apply the hypospray to the Cyprian's thigh. A pneumatic hiss accompanied the act, which proved just as effective as a Vulcan nerve pinch. Whatever sedative Olson had loaded in the hypo knocked out the Cyprian in the space of a heartbeat. His fingers lost their grip on her ankle, and she rolled out of the way just in time to avoid having his limp body land on top of her. Another Cyprian, who had been rushing to help throw her off the building, froze briefly in his tracks. Number One rocked backward, slamming her heels into his lower body, before somersaulting back onto her feet. A third Cyprian, a woman this time, ran toward her, holding a sharp metal trowel like a dagger.

"No more!" the woman yelled as fiercely as any Klingon. "You're not going to get away with—"

Number One threw the empty hypo, nailing the trowel-wielder in the face and halting her charge. Joining up with Olson, she darted back to Jones and Giusio, who formed a defensive line between her and the crowd. Both security officers had taken some hits themselves. Their uniforms were torn and their faces roughed up. Jones had a split lip and a gash across her shoulder. Giusio spit out a broken tooth. Number One probed her own forehead with her fingers. There was no blood where the rock had hit her, but she could feel a nasty bump beneath the skin. It smarted unpleasantly.

"Thanks for the hypo," she told Olson. "Hope that didn't violate your Hippocratic oath."

"I'm a nurse, not a doctor," he reminded her, sweating and breathing hard. "And I like to think I saved a life."

"That you did, Nurse."

They were all running on adrenaline now, but the crowd had righteous fury on its side. Despite the security team's flashing blades, the landing party was forced to give ground as the roof filled up with crazed Cyprians out for their blood. The sheer weight of their numbers drove the Starfleet personnel back toward the brink. If the crowd didn't kill them, Number One realized, a five-story plunge soon would.

"Keep it up!" Tofrum cheered the mob on. He shouted and shook his fist in the air. "For Elzy . . . and Cypria!"

Jones slashed her knife back and forth, carving out a narrow space between the landing party and the crowd hemming them in. "I'm not sure they're getting the message, Number One," she stated. "Any suggestions?"

I wish, Number One thought. "Hope for the best . . ."

But expect the worst.

She suddenly flashed back to that moment on Talos IV when she had set her laser pistol for a forced chamber overload, choosing self-destruction over allowing the Talosians the opportunity to breed a colony of human slaves. *That,* she reflected, *would have been a rather more exemplary way to depart this mortal coil.* Falling victim to a misguided mob, worked up over a false rumor, was just embarrassing

"Let me through!" Tofrum pushed his way through the crowd. The ruby radiance of a laser burned at the tip of a weapon he brandished above his head. "I've got a score to settle with that dark-haired demon!"

Number One's heart sank as she recognized the device.

"Oh, hell," Olson moaned. "He's got my scalpel."

Tofrum grinned sadistically. "Let's give the Earthers a taste of their own medicine."

Number One kept her eye on the scalpel as Tofrum crept toward them, backed up by more berserk Cyprians than even she could count. Outside of jumping to their deaths, she really couldn't see any way the landing party could get away from the mob on their own. The *Enterprise* was the only hope left to them.

Any time now, Christopher . . .

The familiar tingle of the transporter effect filled her with relief. The beam locked her into place as the overcrowded rooftop seemed to blur into a crackling, golden haze. She wasn't sure she'd ever been quite so relieved to be taken apart on an atomic level. The process took just long enough for her to hear, over the energetic whine of the transporter, Tofrum howling in frustration.

"No! We had them!"

She could not find it in her heart to sympathize with him.

But we still haven't got that ryetalyn.

———

Yamata's excitement sounded over the intercom. "We've got them, Captain!"

Music to my ears, Pike thought. "Shields up, Yeoman!"

"Way ahead of you, sir!" Colt worked the controls at the nav station like a natural. "Shields up . . . at sixty percent, that is."

Not as much as Pike would have liked with a hostile battle cruiser bearing down on them, but beggars couldn't be choosers. "Helmsman, get us out of here!"

"Absolutely, sir!" Mohindas replied. "This neighborhood is rather too noisy for my tastes."

That's one way to put it, Pike thought. "Somebody see to Tyler."

The stricken navigator was still sprawled on the deck of the command circle, looking far from his usual chipper self. The Rigelian bug had him down for the count; he moaned and twitched spasmodically. If he wasn't in stage three of the fever, he was knocking on its door. Lieutenant Burstein, who had been manning the environmental systems station, scurried over to check on Tyler. He placed his hand against Tyler's brow.

"He's burning up, Captain."

"Get him to sickbay," Pike ordered. He could scarcely afford to sacrifice any more warm bodies on the bridge, but the environmental monitors would just have to go unattended for the moment. "Call security for assistance."

The turbolift door whooshed open, and Spock

hurried onto the bridge. Pike was glad to see him. Babysitting Merata had to take a back seat to defending the *Enterprise* at the moment. Spock's keen eyes instantly took in the unconscious navigator and the slagged consoles around the bridge, but betrayed neither shock nor alarm. Pike could always count on Spock to keep a cool head in a crisis. He was like Number One that way.

"Situation, Captain?" the Vulcan asked.

"Heading away from Cypria, Mister Spock, and straight toward the Klingons."

"I see." Spock arched an eyebrow. "A curious strategy, Captain."

"Not my first choice," Pike said. "Believe me."

The *Fek'lhr* could be seen on the viewscreen now, approaching the *Enterprise* head-on. Its bulbous prow seemed to increase in size as the distance between the two vessels shrank. Scorch marks on the battle cruiser's hull and a breached cargo hatch revealed that it had not come through the Cyprians' laser barrage unscathed. Pike had to wonder how much of the Klingons' shields were left.

"Hail Krunn!" he ordered. "Tell him we're coming through!"

Pike felt like he was playing a high-stakes game of chicken with the suspicious Klingon commander, who seemed to be in no hurry to let the *Enterprise* pass.

"Evasive action," Pike said. "Hard to port!"

"Aye, sir," Mohindas responded. A sharp turn pushed the limits of the ship's inertial compensators as the entire bridge seemed to tilt sharply before the artificial gravity adjusted itself. Pike's ribs smacked into the side of his chair while the rest of the crew fought to keep their balance. Spock stumbled across the deck, making his way to the science station, where he relieved Weisz. On-screen, the *Fek'lhr* seemed far too close for comfort as the *Enterprise* zoomed past it, barely escaping a collision. Pike held what was left of his breath, waiting to see if Krunn would take a shot at them.

Shields at sixty percent, he thought. *Barely a passing grade.*

Tense seconds passed as the *Enterprise* left both Cypria and the Klingons behind. To Pike's slight surprise, no Klingon disruptor beams assailed his ship. The bridge remained steady.

"Shall I return to our previous orbit, sir?" Mohindas asked.

"And then some," Pike answered. "Let's put a little more distance between ourselves and those lasers." He glanced at Spock. "What are the Klingons doing?"

"Coming about, Captain," he reported, "and veering away from the planet as well."

Pike hoped that Krunn was simply taking his own ship out of range of the Cyprian defenses and not preparing to attack the *Enterprise* at last. By now, he guessed, the Klingons were already scanning the *Enterprise* in hopes of finding out whether that fractured warp manifold was real or not.

Let them, he thought. The ruse had served its purpose. Number One and the landing party were safely back aboard and the *Enterprise* was still intact, despite lowering her shields for a crucial instant. *That was victory enough for the time being.*

A ragged cough tore at his lungs, shaking him like a leaf. He squeezed his eyes shut for moment, to shut out the sharp pains stabbing his eyes. He just needed the universe to go away for a few seconds.

"Captain!" Spock shouted, yanking him back into the crisis. "A hasty review of the sensor logs indicates that the Klingons also lowered their shields at the same time we did . . . and took advantage of the opportunity to beam a boarding party onto the *Enterprise!*"

Fifteen

Seven Klingon soldiers, in full environmental suits, beamed onto the *Enterprise*'s spacious hangar deck. One of them did not survive the experience.

An anguished howl escaped Mokag as he materialized midway into the port nacelle of a parked Cyprian shuttlecraft. His flesh and bone fused with the unyielding metal on a molecular level as two objects sought in vain to occupy the same space at the same time. Death was inevitable, but a brilliant green disruptor blast from his commanding officer spared him needless suffering. The top half of Mokag's body disintegrated into a blazing shower of atoms.

Lieutenant Guras scowled as he lowered his pistol.

"An ugly death, but a brave one," he pronounced to his surviving men. "Mokag knew the risks."

The assault team had deliberately beamed into the shuttle hangar, which was believed to hold the largest open space aboard the *Enterprise*, in hopes of avoiding just such an accident, but fate had not been kind to Mokag. Still, Guras was grateful to have only lost one soldier in the risky operation. Beaming blind into an enemy vessel was always fraught with peril. Guras could only fight to ensure that Mokag's sacrifice would not be wasted.

"Move out!" he barked to his troops. There would be time enough to toast Mokag's memory after they had achieved their objectives. Guras's deep voice reverberated inside his sealed helmet, which he'd worn just in case the hangar had been depressurized. Heavy magnetic boots stomped across the deck. "Move, you lazy *targs!*"

A pair of marksmen, armed with long-range disruptor rifles, opened fire on the control booth overlooking the hangar deck in order to keep any startled Starfleet operators from responding too quickly to the incursion. And if a few humans were killed in the process . . . well, such were the fortunes of war.

They should have thought twice, Guras thought, *before holding the general's daughter hostage.*

Twin blasts from the rifles shattered the control booth's transparent observation window. Seared fragments rained down on the deck and empty shuttlecraft. Had he more time, Guras would have paused to sabotage the Cyprian shuttle, but the large clamshell doors at the end of the hangar were already beginning to open, exposing the hangar to the deadly vacuum outside. Some clever human had finally roused himself to action, apparently, and was attempting to flush the intruders out of the hangar. Emergency alarms began blaring as well.

So much for the element of surprise, Guras thought, not overly concerned. He had never expected the humans to overlook their arrival for long. *Let them try to halt us!*

Opening the space doors was a good idea, but the humans had not reacted fast enough. The rest of Guras's team, minus the unlucky Mokag, had already reached the nearest exit from the hangar. Guras rushed to join them, his heavy boots weighing him down only slightly. A mighty wind blew against him as the voracious vacuum outside the ship swiftly sucked the air from the hangar, but the Klingons had come prepared for that tactic. Guras was grateful for his helmet and magnetic boots as he arrived at the hatchway, which had automatically sealed itself when the space doors started to open.

"Stand aside!" Guras ordered. "Must I do everything myself?"

A well-aimed blast from his disruptor pistol destroyed the locking mechanism, so that his men were able to pry the door open with their gloved hands. They scrambled through the doorway just as an emergency force field activated to seal off the hangar. Intended to merely keep the rest of the ship's atmosphere from escaping into the void, it was a feeble field that Guras pushed through with

little difficulty to reach the pressurized corridor beyond. At worst, he felt a mild static shock through
his spacesuit.

"Stay sharp!" Guras said. "Fire at anything that
moves!"

A gauge on his wrist confirmed that the corridor held sufficient air to breathe. Guras tugged off
his bulky helmet to reveal a ridged brow and stern
features, along with a neatly trimmed mustache and
goatee. He took a deep breath and quickly surveyed
his surroundings, which struck him as surpris-
ingly deserted. According to Klingon Intelligence, a
Starship-class vessel like the *Enterprise* housed more
than two hundred crew members; Guras would
have expected the halls to be bustling with activity
instead of empty of targets. Was the entire ship taking a nap?

His lip curled in disdain. Such idleness would
never be tolerated on a Klingon warship.

But now was no time to mock the enemy, not
when there was still a mission to carry out. Guras
consulted a handheld scanner that verified the presence of the ship's warp core only a few decks above
them. Shunning the turbolifts, he quickly located
an emergency access ladder leading upward. He
called to his men, who were busy removing their
own helmets.

"Over here! Climb!" he growled. "Or would you
prefer to wait for the humans to come looking for us?"

"Pity the human who does!" said a young soldier, grinning in anticipation. His dark face was agleam with the joy of battle. "It will not end well for them!"

"Save your breath for battle!" Guras snarled impatiently. "Climb!"

Getting the message, the other warriors clambered up the ladder, one after another, save for a single sergeant, who broke off from the rest of the team as planned. Wragh was a brash young soldier, replete with the cockiness of youth and handsome despite his regrettably smooth brow. Slick black hair tapered to a widow's peak above his eager eyes. A thick mustache bristled above his upper lip, but his chin was clean-shaven, the better to show off its strong lines. Like Guras, he too carried a handheld scanner, albeit calibrated to detect a different kind of signal. He squinted at the readout.

"Is it working?" Guras demanded. "Do you have her?"

Wragh nodded. "The transceiver is functioning perfectly."

"Then make haste . . . and do not return without our prize."

Wragh grinned confidently. "I will recover her or die trying!"

Preferably the former, Guras thought as he watched the sergeant dash off in another direction. This was supposed to be a rescue, not a suicide mission, and they had already lost one man. Guras did not fear death, but he loathed the idea of failure. *May fortune be with us.*

Turning his back on Wragh, he hurried up the ladder after his men. Speed and stealth remained paramount if they hoped to succeed in their mission. They had encountered little resistance so far, but Guras knew that was bound to change any moment now. The blaring alarms proclaimed that the human captain and crew were awake to the danger and were surely mobilizing in response. Guras had never invaded a Federation starship before, but humans, to their credit, were known to fight back when challenged.

They were almost Klingon that way.

———

"Intruder alert!" Pike announced shipwide. "The *Enterprise* has been boarded by an unknown number of Klingons. All security forces on high alert. All other personnel, clear the corridors and secure your posts."

The turbolift opened and all eyes turned warily to the entrance, as though half-expecting a horde of Klingon berserkers to storm the bridge. A few able-bodied security officers drew their weapons, only to lower them as Number One strode briskly onto the bridge. Pike heard more than a few audible sighs of relief.

"Reporting for duty, Captain," she said dryly. "Is this a bad time?"

Pike noticed that she was not her usual immaculate self. Her uniform was ripped in places, not to mention sweaty and dirty. An ugly purple bruise marred her smooth white brow. Nicks and scratches on her face and hands hinted at the hardships she'd endured down on the planet. She had obviously been through the wars and come straight from the transporter room, but Pike still found her a sight for sore eyes. Given that the ship was at red alert, he could see why she wouldn't waste time freshening up first. He would have done the same.

"To the contrary, your timing is impeccable, Number One," he greeted her. "Although you may wish you had stayed on Cypria."

"Unlikely, sir." She took her usual place at the helm, relieving Mohindas. "I believe I am exactly where I need to be."

Pike had to agree, especially with his own health deteriorating. He wasn't sure how much longer he could keep fighting the fever, which didn't seem inclined to take a time-out while he dealt with an equally relentless adversary. His chest felt like it was being squeezed by shrinking duranium bands. His brain threatened to burst out of his skull. If he didn't know better, he'd swear he was taking a spacewalk without a pressure suit.

Of all times, he thought, *for the ship to be*

boarded by hostiles, when half the crew is down with fever and I'm not exactly at full strength myself. The Klingons have caught us at a bad moment.

"Shut down the turbolifts," he ordered, hoping to contain the invasion, and looked urgently at the science station, where Spock was peering intently into a gooseneck monitor. "What about it, Mister Spock? Have you pinpointed our gate-crashers yet?"

"Negative, Captain," Spock replied. The glow from his monitor highlighted the angles of his face, making him look older than his years. "I am attempting to employ the ship's internal sensors to detect specifically Klingon life-forms, but they are, for better or for worse, not easily distinguishable from humans . . . or Vulcans."

"Don't let the Klingons hear you say that," Colt remarked from the nav station. "They would probably consider those fighting words."

"In my experience, Yeoman," Number One commented, "Klingons consider all words 'fighting words.'" If she was surprised to find Colt serving as a navigator, she gave no indication of it. "That's what makes them so distinctly . . . Klingon."

Pike lacked the strength or inclination to take part in the banter. He briefly flirted with turning command over to Number One, now that she was back aboard, but, no, he wasn't about to step down while his ship was being overrun by Klingons. If the intruders wanted the *Enterprise*, they'd have to drag him off the bridge.

"Captain!" Garrison said. "I'm getting reports of weapons fire in the hangar deck."

"Of course." Spock looked up from his monitor. "That would be the most advisable location to beam an uninvited boarding party." He frowned ruefully. "I apologize for not thinking of that immediately."

"Never mind that, Mister Spock." Pike needed answers, not apologies. "Where do you predict that the Klingons will strike *next*?"

Spock and Number One came to the same conclusion almost simultaneously.

"Engineering."

Sixteen

Chief Engineer Caitlin Barry was already having a rough day.

It was bad enough that most of her crew was out sick, and she felt like maybe she was coming down with something herself, but the Cyprians' laser cannons had really done a number on the deflector grids. Holding down the fort in main engineering with just a single green technician to assist her, she ran a hand through her disheveled auburn hair as she studied the damage reports and tried to prioritize the repairs, given the ever-shrinking manpower at her disposal. Exasperation and fatigue were written all over her freckled face.

And then the intruder alarms went off. Captain Pike's voice rang out over the shipwide address channel, warning that a Klingon boarding party had invaded the *Enterprise*.

"Seriously?" Barry asked. "On top of everything else?"

Main engineering consisted of a large chamber accessible by a single entrance. A long bank of control panels lined one side of the room, across from a row of glowing blue standby power units. A wall-sized metal grille occupied the rear of the chamber, shielding it from the thrumming warp manifold assembly beyond. As the ship was currently cruising on impulse power, the warp engines were merely idling, but could be fired up on a moment's notice. Barry looked up abruptly from the damage reports, which were displayed on a monitor at her desk by the front entrance. Unlike the captain, she had little use for hard copies, which struck her as messy and inefficient.

"Chief Barry?" the young technician blurted over by the power relay station he had been working on. Anxiety tweaked his pronounced British accent. An antigrav lifter, loaded with fresh stem bolts and transfer coils, floated beside him. "Are we under attack again?"

It took her a moment to recall his name. *Collier, that was it.*

"Just a minute." The alarm had startled her too, but she knew what to do. The door to the corridor swished into place as she locked it shut. Repairs to the deflector grid would have to wait. Protecting the engineering room from intruders had just hit the top of her to-do list. "There we are. Locked up tight, like the crown jewels on Sadmi Prime."

Her breezy assurance masked some serious worry. Locks or no locks, she couldn't defend engineering indefinitely, especially if the worst occurred and the captain lost control of the ship. Just off the top of her head, she could think of far too many ways to break into the sealed-off chamber, like lasering through a bulkhead to get at the wall circuits. Granted, that would take some time to do safely, but she doubted that the Klingons worried much about safety factors when they pillaged an alien ship.

Collier hefted a wrench defensively. A scrawny blond Englishman with a baby face and no chin to speak of, he looked vaguely ridiculous holding the tool like a weapon. He was a tinkerer, not a fighter. "What do you think is happening out there, Chief? With the Klingons?"

"Let me find out."

But before she could hit the intercom to hail the bridge, a bosun's whistle sounded, alerting her to an incoming transmission. She leaned over the comm unit. "Engineering here. Talk to me."

"Heads up," Pike warned. *"We have reason to believe the Klingons are heading your way. Needless to say, we don't want them gaining access to the main engineering controls."*

Even over the intercom, the captain's voice sounded hoarse and strained. Barry guessed that the captain was under the weather like so many others, but refrained from commenting on that. "You can say that again, Captain. Don't worry. I'm not about to let any Klingon vandals get their grubby hands on my engine room."

"*Security teams are en route to you,*" Pike promised. "*Hold tight.*"

He signed off abruptly, without any wasted words, but Barry didn't begrudge him the curtness of the communication. They both had better things to do than chit-chat. She sprang from her desk and darted over to the primary control banks. Skilled fingers expertly manipulated the dials and toggles as she called out to Collier.

"Quick!" she said. "Help me transfer control of the main systems to the bridge."

Collier responded promptly, hustling over to one of the auxiliary stations to her right. His fair complexion looked even paler than usual. His Adam's apple bobbed up and down as though trapped beneath alternating magnetic poles. "But couldn't the Klingons override the bridge from here?" he asked. "If they capture engineering, that is?"

Barry rolled up her sleeves.

"Not if I can help it."

———

Kutth was the first Klingon to reach the engineering deck. Taking point, he stepped off the maintenance ladder and poked his head around an alcove wall to scope out the curving corridor beyond. To his surprise, and disappointment, no Starfleet targets immediately presented themselves; aside from the blaring alarms and flashing alert lights, it was starting to feel as though they had boarded a ghost ship.

"All clear," he grunted, signaling the rest of the squad, who quickly climbed up the ladder and onto the deck. Kutth hefted his disruptor rifle. "I don't like this. Where are this ship's defenders?"

"Patience," Guras said. "They'll be here soon enough." He consulted his tracking device before gesturing to the right. "Engineering is this way. Kutth, secure the corridor. All others, with me."

"Yes, Lieutenant." Kutth gripped his rifle. "None will pass except over my dead body!"

"I should hope not," said Guras, whose tongue was known to be as sharp as his blades. He marched the rest of the troops away at a brisk pace, leaving Kutth behind to guard their backs, while the other rifleman, Tras, hurried ahead to secure the other end of the corridor. Kutth heard his comrades' heavy boot steps recede behind him as he assumed a defensive post within the alcove, which served as excellent cover. He kept his rifle raised and his vigilant gaze fixed on the empty corridor, like a hunter hidden behind a blind, awaiting his prey.

New footsteps and grating human voices heading toward him alerted him to the arrival of three *Enterprise* crew members in gold and blue uniforms, rushing down the hall on errands both unknown and irrelevant. As they were unarmed, and therefore not worthy of his marksmanship, he fired above them at the overhead lights, which exploded in a shower of sparks and jagged transparent shards, eliciting startled gasps and exclamations from the humans, who turned and fled around the curve of the corridor. Rather than chase after them, he held to his post.

Excellent, he thought. *That should bring some real foes my way.*

His finger, poised expectantly on the trigger of his rifle, was not idle long. Peering around the corner of the alcove, Kutth spotted a team of Starfleet security officers rushing toward him down the now dimly lit corridor. He opened fire immediately, blasting the few first humans before they spotted him. Ducking back into the alcove, he grinned as blood-red laser beams shot harmlessly past him. No one, least of all Starfleet, had yet to invent an energy weapon that could shoot around corners, not without literally bending the laws of physics.

Go ahead, he thought. *Waste your fire.*

He could not rest easy, however. Before the enemy could regroup, he plucked a concussion grenade from his belt and hurled it around the corner into the hallway. He ducked for cover, shielding his ears as the bomb exploded gloriously. The deafening echoes of the explosion accompanied the shrieks of battered metal and humanity. Risking a peek around the corner, Kutth saw that the grenade had achieved the desired effect. Smoke and debris and groaning bodies filled the murky corridor, obstructing the path of any reinforcements. Kutth looked forward to picking off the next wave of human soldiers as they tried to get through the rubble-strewn corridor. He smiled coldly as he patted the remaining grenades on his belt. He still had several more bombs—and a fully charged disruptor rifle.

What more did any Klingon need?

Aside, that was, from worthy foes and the sweet promise of victory?

Come, Starfleet. Try to get past me. I dare you!

He heard a second explosion go off at the other end of the corridor, beyond engineering. Clearly, Tras was doing his part to secure the deck as well, taking advantage of the fact that, unlike their opponents, Klingons would not hesitate to wreak havoc on a Starfleet vessel.

He readied another grenade.

———————

"Captain! The Klingons have seized control of deck nineteen," Garrison reported. "Our people have engaged the enemy, but the intruders are dug in outside engineering and are firing back at our security officers."

Pike could readily imagine the stand-off. A couple of good snipers, positioned correctly, could probably secure a single corridor for a time. He remembered holding off a whole tribe of cannibalistic mutants from a narrow gorge in the Sepeth

Mountains year ago, during a rather eventful visit to Yortob IV. It was all about sight-lines, positioning, and narrow passages.

"A logical strategy," Spock observed. "Capturing the engineering room would allow them to shut down power to the ship's shields, leaving the *Enterprise* defenseless."

"And Krunn free to reclaim his daughter." Number One looked apologetically at Pike. "And all because you lowered the shields long enough to beam me and the landing party back to the ship."

"Don't blame yourself, Number One," Pike said. "That was my call, and I'd make same one in an instant." A thought occurred to him and he turned toward Spock. "But speaking of Krunn's daughter, where is Merata during all this?"

"In good hands," Spock said, "I believe."

———

"Where the devil is that security guard?" the doctor grumbled.

Merata could not blame Boyce for his impatience. Some time had passed since Spock had left her in the doctor's keeping, yet no guard had arrived to escort her from sickbay to her quarters. No doubt the *Enterprise*'s soldiers were otherwise occupied.

"Stay where you are and don't try anything," Boyce cautioned her as he made his way to the wall intercom unit while gripping Spock's laser pistol uncomfortably. As a physician, he no doubt preferred a scalpel or hypo to a firearm. "Sickbay to security. I need an armed escort here. Stat."

"I'm sorry, Doctor," a voice replied. *"We're shorthanded as is, and all forces are needed to deal with the intruders. I'm afraid you'll have to wait for that escort."*

"For how long?" Boyce asked. "I've got patients to attend to."

"Sorry, Doctor," the voice repeated. *"In any event, the captain has ordered the corridors kept clear. Just sit tight until we have things under control. Security out."*

"Blast it." Boyce stepped away from the comm, visibly displeased. "I've got better things to do than babysit a teenage Klingon." He shrugged apologetically at Merata. "No offense."

She paid little heed to the old man's grousing, having far more urgent matters on her mind. Her fingers toyed with the pendant at her neck as she silently rejoiced at the news of the ongoing intruder alert. At last the liberation she had been waiting for had arrived.

I knew my father would come for me, she thought. *He would not leave me in the hands of an enemy.*

"Looks like we're stuck together for the time being," Soleste observed from her sickbed. "Might as well take advantage of it."

Perhaps for not much longer, Merata thought. To her surprise, she felt a slight pang at the prospect of abandoning her one-time family. Misguided and maddening as they were, they wanted only their lost Elzura back. She regretted that their foolish dreams would be crushed once more, and hoped, for their sakes, that her imminent departure would not wound them too deeply.

"Why didn't you stop looking for me?" she asked. "Why not just mourn and move on with your life?"

"Because you're my sister," Soleste said bluntly. "Wouldn't a Klingon do the same?"

Once again, Merata found herself with no ready answer. *My father has not abandoned me.*

"That would . . . depend on the circumstances," she hedged. "As a rule, Klingons fall in battle. They do not go missing or permit themselves to be taken captive. We honor our dead, but believe life is for the living."

"On Cypria, we don't give up on family," Soleste said, "and we look out for each other, no matter what." She gestured toward a cardboard box resting on a nearby counter. "Do me a favor and fetch me that box if you don't mind."

Merata saw no harm in the request. "Doctor?"

"Go ahead," he said, "but keep your hands where I can see them."

Merata was amused by the doctor's wariness. "You are not a trusting soul, old man."

"How do you think I got to be so old," Boyce replied. "Clean living?"

A canny response, she decided, and one she could respect. Gray hairs, like scars, were the emblems of a survivor. Crossing the ward, she retrieved the box and handed it to Soleste. The paper container struck Merata as notably flimsy, but she recalled that the Cyprians were overly attached to nature and vegetation. Organic materials appealed to them.

Soleste opened the box to reveal an assortment of small frosted cakes, each the size of a biscuit. Icing of various colors hinted at a variety of flavors. A pleated paper cup kept each cake separate from the rest, which Merata thought was unnecessarily extravagant. Klingons did not require such frills.

"Homemade nutberry cakes," Soleste explained. "Mother brought them up from the planet as a taste of Cypria." She bit into a cake, which clearly met with her approval. A satisfied sigh spoke highly of the treat. Selecting another cake, she offered it to Merata. "Care for one?"

Merata regarded the sugary-smelling pastry with disdain. "Klingons do not eat . . . cakes. And I have had enough unappetizing fare these last few days to last a lifetime."

That was an understatement. As she had discovered since being brought aboard the *Enterprise,* Starfleet cuisine was quite literally lifeless; she hadn't eaten anything squirming for days. And despite what Spock had claimed was an extensive menu, the ship's galley had been unable to provide her with bloodwine, *gagh*, skull stew, or anything else remotely palatable. She'd been forced to consume burned meat, cooked not nearly rare enough to her taste, merely to keep her strength up.

"You sure?" Soleste held out the cake. "You couldn't get enough of these as a child. We used to fight over who got the last one."

"I told you before. I am not that girl anymore."

And yet . . . the aroma coming off the cakes was oddly tantalizing, awakening memories long dormant: *A toasty kitchen with golden sunlight pouring in through the windows. Freshly baked cakes hot from the oven. Sitting at the kitchen table with her mother, who smiled warmly at her. Licking the extra frosting from a bowl while waiting for the cakes to cool. The smell of the treats filling her senses . . .*

Merata's mouth watered. She licked her lips.

"Go ahead," Soleste tempted her. A knowing smirk indicated that she felt confident that she was succeeding. "Just a bite. Try it."

"Fine," Merata snarled. She snatched the sticky pastry from the other woman's hand. "If you insist."

She bit into the cake—and was taken aback at how delicious it was.

It was much sweeter than proper Klingon fare, true, leavened by both a fruity tartness and a nutty undercurrent that complemented each other more effectively than one might expect, but the taste, both strange and hauntingly familiar, landed pleasantly on her tongue, even as it triggered yet more memories and feelings from her vanished childhood.

A picnic in a park, beneath the shade of a leafy canopy tree. Sunlight reflecting off the shimmering azure waters of a nearby swimming hole. The intoxicating fragrance of freshly bloomed spring flowers perfuming the air. Song lizards chirp in the branches overhead. A cool breeze brings added relief from the heat. A band is playing music somewhere in the distance.

A man is there, with long brown hair, a warm smile, and kind silver eyes. It's Father—her dead, Cyprian father—then very much alive. He sits peacefully, resting his back against the trunk of the tree, while he shares the lovely afternoon with her and Mother and Soleste and even bratty little Junah, who keeps trying to grab up handfuls of grass and dirt and throw them at people. Mother gently swats his hand and tells him to behave. He sulks and pouts, as usual.

Mother unrolls a wicker mat atop the lawn. Opening a cooler, she lays out an enticing feast: merry plum cider, ivy butter sandwiches, and, best of all, her favorite dessert . . .

Soleste watched her expectantly. "Well?"

"It is . . . not disagreeable," she conceded, before taking another bite.

"I knew it!" Soleste grinned triumphantly. "You may call yourself a Klingon now, but your taste buds are still Cyprian at least." She offered Merata a second cake. "Here. Have another."

Merata cursed her treacherous sweet tooth. The tale of Kulara, who was trapped on the Barge of the Dead forever after she was tricked into feasting on shadows, suddenly made sense to her. Disgusted with herself, she spit a mouthful of half-eaten mush onto the floor.

"I think I've had enough."

"Hey!" Boyce protested. "That's my sickbay you're—"

A sudden uproar in the adjacent ward cut off the doctor's objections. Shouts and screams could be heard, along with the unmistakable sizzle of a Klingon disruptor pistol firing. Merata's hand went back to her pendant, all thoughts of enticing Cyprian pastries driven from her mind. Her heart thrilled at the sound of the blasts.

This is it, she realized. *Freedom has found me at last.*

"What in blazes?" Boyce blurted. Startled and alarmed, he spun toward the commotion in the next room, turning his back on Merata, who knew that she would never have a better chance to seize control of her destiny once more.

My apologies, Doctor, she thought. *But my path is clear.*

She struck swiftly and without hesitation.

Seventeen

"Permission to lead additional forces to deck nineteen," Spock requested. "A counterassault of sufficient force may succeed in dislodging the Klingons from their current position outside engineering."

Pike weighed Spock's offer. "It may come to that, but I'm uneasy about escalating a firefight that close to the warp core." He searched for a better solution. "We need a less incendiary way to neutralize the invaders. One that, preferably, doesn't involve a heavy-duty exchange of laser beams and disruptor blasts."

He paused to catch his breath. When did the simple act of inhaling become so hard?

"Hang on," he said as his respiratory difficulties gave him an idea. "What about the environmental controls? Klingons need to breathe as much any other humanoid. Suppose we cut off the flow of oxygen to the deck until they black out? Granted, this would temporarily incapacitate our own people as well, but that might be safer for them in the long run than being menaced by Klingons."

"Perhaps," Spock said, sounding unconvinced, "but there is a significant flaw to that strategy. No offense intended, but Klingons are in many ways physically stronger than humans and, on an average, possess a greater degree of stamina. In particular, Klingons possess three lungs, giving them approximately thirty percent more lung capacity. By the time the Klingons finally succumbed to lack of oxygen, any humans on deck nineteen, including those trapped in engineering, would be at serious risk of permanent brain damage or death."

"Three lungs, you say." Pike remembered hearing something about that at a Starfleet briefing once, but he was not quite ready to give up on his idea just yet. "Is there any way to use that against them?"

Number One spoke up. "Down on the planet, Nurse Olson thought to employ a powerful sedative as a weapon. Perhaps we can attempt the same on a more ambitious scale?" Her voice took on confidence as she warmed to the idea. "Three lungs means the Klingons would absorb a knock-out gas thirty percent faster than our own crew."

"Yes!" Spock said with unreserved enthusiasm. His agile mind quickly tackled the technical challenges. "If one could introduce a quantity of aerosolized anesthezine into the air conduits feeding into deck nineteen, the Klingons could conceivably be subdued without undue violence."

"That's the best idea I've heard all day," Pike said, despite feeling like hell. "Get on it, but quickly! The Klingons aren't wasting any time, so neither can we. Every second counts."

"I quite agree, Captain." Spock sprang from his seat and made good time toward the turbolift. "If you can release the lift, sir."

Pike overrode the command shutting the turbolift down. The action took far more effort than it should have. He needed a moment to recuperate.

"Sir?" Colt asked. She and Number One both gave him worried looks, which he did his best to ignore. Colt tried to do double duty, as a navigator *and* yeoman. "Anything I can do for you, Captain?

Pike wasn't about to treated like an invalid on his own bridge.

"Cross your fingers, Yeoman, that Mister Spock can work as fast as he thinks."

———

A sharp blow to his neck rendered the doctor unconscious. He crumpled to the floor of sickbay, and the laser pistol slipped from his fingers. Merata bent quickly to claim it.

"Elzura . . . no!" Soleste gasped. "What have you done?"

Merata did not bother correcting the name. "He will recover. The injury is not a permanent one."

She spoke the truth. In order to compensate for

her relative weakness compared to other Klingons, she had trained extensively to become proficient in advanced hand-to-hand combat techniques. A swift but effective chop to a certain nerve cluster had allowed her to disable the doctor with a minimum of fuss. The old man had earned his years. He deserved better than to end up in one of his own sickbeds.

"But why, Elzura? Why are you doing this?"

"Isn't it obvious? I'm leaving."

The horrified look on Soleste's face jabbed Merata in the heart. "No! I won't let you!"

"You cannot stop me." The taste of cake lingered upon Merata's tongue like a bittersweet memory. She paused long enough to offer a few last words of parting. "Bid good-bye to our—*your*—mother for me. Tell her . . . I am sorry I cannot be the daughter she lost."

"Like hell I will!"

Despite her injuries, Soleste hastily climbed out of bed and limped toward Merata. She winced with every step, but the pain did not slow her. Anguish showed in her single good eye.

"It took me years to find you! I'm not going to lose you again!"

"Silence!" Merata shouted, alarmed and angry. "Get back in bed!"

"Or what? You'll try to kill me again?"

A single Klingon soldier burst into the recov-

ery ward, sparing Merata from having to face that
question. She recognized him as Wragh, a sergeant
under her father's command. He clutched a tracking device in one hand and a disruptor pistol in the
other. A whiff of ionization in the air confirmed
that the weapon had been fired very recently. She
found herself hoping that any inconvenient sickbay
workers had merely been stunned and not killed
or disintegrated. Soleste might require their care
before this was over.

"Success!" Wragh grinned triumphantly at
Merata. "I knew I could find you!"

He thrust the tracker back into his belt now that
it was no longer needed. Like the transceiver hidden in her pendant, it had served its purpose, leading him straight to Merata. His eyes registered the
unconscious doctor sprawled upon the floor and
his wolfish grin grew even wider.

"I see you were expecting me." He beckoned to
her. "Come. Lieutenant Guras and an entire squad
of warriors are seizing control of the engine room
even as we speak. We need only fight our way to a
transporter room to be beamed back to the *Fek'lhr*
as soon as the *Enterprise*'s shields are down."

A fine plan, Merata thought. Indeed, the *Enterprise*'s main transporter room was not far away, on
the same deck as sickbay; she recalled passing it on
the way here. "Excellent. Follow me."

"No!" Soleste grabbed Merata's arm with surprising strength. She glared at the intruder. "You Klingon bastards can't take her, not again! I won't let you!"

Comprehension dawned on Wragh's face. "This is her, isn't it? The vile jade who kidnapped you?" He looked as though he could not believe his good fortune. "How convenient to find her here as well. Shall I kill her for you, or would you rather take your own revenge upon her?"

"Forget about her." Merata yanked her arm free and stepped between Wragh and Soleste. "My father awaits."

Wragh's smooth brow furrowed in confusion. "I don't understand. She abducted you. Honor demands that she pay for her crime with her life."

He stepped to one side, attempting to get a clear shot at Soleste.

"I said, forget about her!" Merata sneered at her sister—for everyone's sake. She moved to obstruct Wragh's aim once more. "She's not worth it."

Wragh stared at her in shock, as though she had suddenly sprouted antennae or pointed ears. "Have you taken leave of your senses?"

While they quarreled, Soleste staggered to the exit and blocked it with her body. She winced with every movement, which surely aggravated whatever pains remained from her recent surgery. Her face was ashen beneath its sun-baked tan. Her features were drawn and taut, betraying her discomfort. Her crystal eye glowed from within while a tear leaked from the flesh one.

"Listen to me, Elzura! You don't want to do this. We can still go home to Cypria!"

"My name is Merata!" she roared, only partly for Wragh's benefit. Perhaps she could ease this final parting for Soleste as well, by making it as rancorous as possible. "A daughter of the Empire—and I care nothing for your pitiful world." She growled and bared her teeth. "Stand aside, Cyprian!"

"Never!" Soleste refused to budge. "You're my little sister, Elzy, and you always will be!"

"Enough of this lunacy!" Wragh's scant patience reached its limit. Charging forward, he seized Soleste by the shoulders and hurled her aside. She went flying across the ward to crash loudly against a steel bulkhead. Crying out in pain, she bounced off the wall onto the floor. She hit the deck face-first, hard enough to rattle a tray of instruments nearby. A vial of pills spilled over a counter.

The awful sound of the impact made Merata cry out as well.

"That was not necessary!" she yelled at Wragh. "Can you not see she is badly injured?"

Wragh shrugged. "Then let us put her out of her misery."

"Better killers than you have tried, Klingon," Soleste said from the floor. Battered by her brutal collision with the wall, she nonetheless climbed

to her feet and came at them again. She teetered
unsteadily, clutching her abdomen and gasping in
pain. She wiped her lips with one hand, which came
away bloody. "I gave an eye for my sister. You think
I won't risk the rest of me to stop you from taking
her again?"

No! Merata thought. *Stay down!*

Wragh took aim with his pistol. "Go to *Gre'thor*,
you maddened sow."

"Don't!"

Merata reacted without thinking. A crimson
beam shot from her stolen laser pistol, blasting
Wragh before he could fire on Soleste. Jolted by the
beam, he stayed on his feet long enough to turn
startled eyes toward her before crashing to the floor
like a toppled statue. Disbelief had flared briefly
upon his face like the final rage of a collapsing star.

She was no less stunned by what she'd just done.
She stared numbly at the weapon in her grasp.

"I knew it," Soleste said weakly, only a few paces
away. "I knew you were still my sister . . ."

She barely got the words out before collapsing
onto the floor, joining the fallen figures of Boyce
and Wragh, so that the recovery ward resembled
a battlefield more than a place of healing. Merata
found herself the last person standing, still gripping the pistol she had used against a loyal soldier
who had come to rescue her. Guilt and confusion
tangled themselves in her mind and soul.

I can still get away, she thought. *I just need to make it to the transporter room on my own.*

She could say that Wragh sacrificed his own freedom to save her, that she had been forced to leave him behind. She could still escape the *Enterprise* and return to her father. She could live as a Klingon should.

But what of Soleste?

The conflict with Wragh, on top of her previous injuries, had left the other woman in a dire state. She lay sprawled upon the floor, senseless and deathly pale. Blood trickled from the corner of her mouth. Her single eye rolled in its socket so that only the silver could be seen. Merata feared that Wragh's rough handling had reopened Soleste's wounds. She was likely bleeding internally.

She could die, Merata realized.

A doctor also occupied the floor, none too far away, but Boyce showed no sign of regaining consciousness soon. By the time he recovered, it might be too late.

Indecision paralyzed Merata. Her desperate gaze swung back and forth between the open exit and the bleeding woman before her. She knew she had to choose between them, but what was more valuable: her freedom or Soleste's life?

She bit down on her lip. Her mouth still tasted of cake.

Merata hurled the pistol away.

"Help me!" she shouted, dropping to Soleste's side. She prayed to whatever deities looked after Cyprians that there was still a doctor or nurse within earshot. Scooting across the floor, she took Boyce by the shoulders and shook him violently in a desperate attempt to rouse him. "Wake, Doctor! Rise, curse you! My sister is hurt!"

Eighteen

"Guras to Wragh! Respond!"

Only a worrisome silence greeted Guras's snarled command. Scowling, he lowered his communicator. His inability to contract Wragh was troubling; Guras feared the young sergeant had been foiled in his attempt to rescue Merata. Why else would he not respond?

General Krunn will not be happy if we fail to recover his daughter.

The stirring sound of weapons fire, coming from both ends of the curved hallway, did little to ease his mind. His marksmen were doing a commendable job of holding off the human soldiers out to reclaim this section of the *Enterprise*, but they were only two men after all. Granted, two Klingons were worth a dozen humans in a fight, but Guras was not so myopic as to deny reality. They needed to take possession of the engineering room if they were ever to escape the *Enterprise*. Time was not their ally in this conflict.

"Faster!" he growled at a pair of demolitions

experts who were rigging explosive charges to the sealed doorway standing between him and the engineering room. The men were not working quickly enough for his satisfaction, so he employed two of his most effective weapons: scorn and sarcasm. "Are you planting bombs or baking a blood pie?"

"Just a few more moments, Lieutenant," a sapper named Kaln insisted. He adjusted the settings on a photon grenade, recalibrating its charge and orientation. "This is delicate work."

"Klingons do not do 'delicate.'" Guras sneered at the man's excess caution. "Blow that accursed door down before we die of old age!"

"Yes, Lieutenant!" Spurred to movement, Kaln affixed the photon grenade to the door, only to be hurled backward by a powerful electric shock. A bright blue spark flared and crackled. Kaln's dark hair stood up like the quills of an angered Z'Rojjian spike ape. Smoke rose from his fingertips as he bellowed obscenities at the top of his lungs. He hastily deactivated the grenade before glaring murderously at the booby-trapped entrance. "Human slime! They electrified the door. I'm lucky the grenade didn't go off in my hands!"

An engineer's trick, Guras thought, with grudging respect, *but a good one.*

"Can you counter it?" he demanded.

"Yes. I should be able to rig up an electrostatic field that will cancel the opposing charge, or I might be able to ground the current to a neutral bulkhead."

"Then why are you not doing so?" Guras didn't care how it was done, just that it was. He stifled an urge to kick Kaln into action. "Did the shock fry your brain cells?"

"No, sir! The door will fall, sir!" He turned to his partner, Dograk. "Get me an EM field inducer."

The men ran an insulated cable from the door to a compact, boxlike mechanism that emitted an irksome high-pitched hum. Kaln flipped a switch and electricity crackled across the surface of the door before dissipating. The technician scanned carefully before pronouncing it safe.

"Electrostatic countermeasure deployed. The door has been de-charged."

"Then get back to blowing it open!" Guras snapped.

He tapped his foot impatiently against the deck of the corridor. This entire operation was taking far too long. It was often said that four thousand throats could be cut in one night by a running man, but nobody ever talked about how many locked doors the runner might have to break through first. Guras could hear weapons fire being exchanged at opposite ends of the corridor. Was it just his imagination, or were the Starfleet forces drawing nearer?

"All this," Kaln muttered under his breath, "for a female who isn't even a true Klingon."

"Look who is talking, smooth-brow," Dograk jeered. Unlike Kaln, the other sapper had proper

Klingon ridges. "I know Merata. Her heart is as Klingon as any."

"More than Mokag's? Was his life worth hers?"

In truth, that thought had crossed Guras's mind as well, but now was no time for petty arguments.

"We have our orders," he said in a tone that brooked no dissent. "What Klingon questions any opportunity to wage war against the enemies of the Empire?" He glowered at the bickering soldiers. "Are the charges set?"

"Yes, Lieutenant!" The men backed away from the door. "All is in readiness."

Guras also put a safe distance between himself and the rigged entrance. In theory, the directed charges would expend their explosive wrath against the door, but a wise Klingon did not fall victim to his own weapon. Not even for a general's daughter.

"What are you waiting for?" he snarled. "Do your duty!"

The grenades went off with an impressive roar. A scorching white flash stung his eyes even as the stubborn door crashed inward, reduced to a mangled sheet of charred and smoking metal. The barrier had been breached. The *Enterprise*'s main engineering room was theirs for the taking.

That's more like it, Guras thought.

Now if only Wragh would check in with good news!

Nineteen

It was evident at once that much had transpired in sickbay since Spock had left Merata there at the onset of the red alert. Confusion and commotion reigned in what appeared to be the aftermath of a violent incident. Scorch marks could be seen on the walls, along with shattered glass shelves, spilled medicines and instruments, overturned chairs, and other evidence of a physical conflict. Frantic nurses and orderlies were in the process of restoring order, tending to anxious patients as well as to their own injuries. Observing the tumult, Spock could only hope that the ship's stores of anesthizine had not been compromised; if so, his vital mission would be over before it could begin.

What if the sedative was among the casualties of the attack?

An angry voice, employing notably offensive profanities, called Spock's attention to a lone Klingon soldier under heavy restraint in a biobed. His vital signs, as displayed on the overhead monitor, indicated an excessive degree of agitation, even for a Klingon. He strained vigorously at his bonds.

"Let me loose, cowards! I must avenge myself on the traitor!"

Traitor?

A nerve pinch silenced the Klingon's disruptive shouting, restoring at least a measure of calm to the unruly environment. An orderly, bearing a supply of medical dressings and dermal applicators, crossed Spock's path. Spock stepped forward to detain him.

"Mister Howell," he said. "What has happened here?"

Overwrought and emotional, Howell was only too eager to tell him.

"You wouldn't believe it, Mister Spock. A Klingon invaded sickbay, shooting up the place, sending everybody scrambling for safety, but that Klingon-looking girl stopped him. She stunned him with a laser before anybody got killed!"

Spock's inner eyelids blinked in surprise. He did not often doubt his own senses, but the sheer improbability of the orderly's statement made him wonder if he had indeed heard correctly.

"Merata? Merata foiled the incursion?"

"So they say," the man said. "Go figure."

Spock recalled leaving Merata in Doctor Boyce's care. He glanced around, but did not immediately see either individual. "The doctor? Where is he?"

Howell gestured toward the surgical ward. "He's performing an operation right now."

"On whom?"

"The Cyprian woman. The one with the crystal eye. She's supposed to be pretty messed up."

Soleste, Spock thought. *In surgery once more?*

Despite the urgency of his mission to obtain the sedative, concern drove Spock to investigate. Proceeding swiftly to the surgical ward, he was confronted by an ominous and rather unlikely tableau. As reported, an unconscious Soleste was being operated on by Doctor Boyce, with the assistance of Nurse Carlotti. A surgical support frame fitted over Soleste concealed her torso while generating a sterile field in which the doctor could work. Insulated sheets protected the patient's lower limbs. A steady blue glow from the interior of the frame lit up Boyce's haggard face as the nurse handed him a calibrated autosuture. Focused on his labors, Boyce did not immediately acknowledge Spock's arrival.

"All right," he said to Carlotti. "I think we've staunched the bleeding from her lower abdominal organs, but I want to run a complete circulatory scan just to make sure."

"Yes, Doctor." She handed him a specialized scanner before consulting a diagnostic monitor. "Blood pressure low, but within acceptable safety margins, at least according to the recorded baselines for her species."

"If we can trust those," Boyce muttered. "It's not like I've operated on a whole lot of Cyprians before, although I'm getting much more familiar than I'd like with the insides of this particular specimen."

All of this was to be expected, Spock noted, given the data provided by the orderly. What surprised him was the sight of Merata lying in the adjacent bed, obviously donating blood to her sister. Orange plasma flowed through clear tubing from a micro-stent in Merata's bare arm to an intake in the solid-steel exterior of the surgical frame. After serving alongside red-blooded humans, Spock paid little heed to the peculiar orange hue of Cyprian blood, but it was certainly striking, and strangely moving, to see the sisters' blood connection reestablished so literally.

Merata, who had been watching the doctor intently, took note of Spock's entrance. She turned her weary gaze toward him. "Vulcan."

He noted, upon closer inspection, that she too was under restraint. In addition, a grim-faced security officer stood watch nearby, keeping a close eye on the proceedings. It seemed her apparent cooperation with the medical procedure had not dispelled a reasonable degree of distrust on the part of Boyce and the others.

"You are not in your quarters," Spock observed. "As I instructed earlier."

She shrugged, resting her head on a silver cushion. "Fate deemed otherwise."

Boyce snorted. "That's one way to put it." He looked up from the operation. "Can I help you, Mister Spock?"

The needs of the ship outweighed his personal curiosity regarding the drama in sickbay.

"I am in need of a sizable quantity of concentrated anesthizine," he informed the doctor, "as well as the facilities required to produce an aerosolized form of the same."

"Anesthizine?" Boyce gave him a puzzled look. "For medical purposes?"

"Tactical," Spock replied. "I would explain further, but time is short and my mission imperative."

To his credit, the doctor took Spock at his word and did not waste precious minutes interrogating him.

"Fair enough. I'm going to guess you know what you're doing." Boyce nodded at the nurse. "I can close up here, Gabrielle. Show Spock to our inventory and help him use my lab." He turned his attention back to his comatose patient. "But I'm going to want a full explanation somewhere down the road."

Spock contemplated the fraught scene in sickbay. He was still not entirely certain how matters here had come to such a pass in the short time since he had left for the bridge.

"As will I, Doctor."

He followed the nurse out of the ward.

———

Disruptor pistol in hand, Kaln was the first through the breached entrance into the engineering room. Whether he was trying to make up for his earlier lapses or simply intent on revenge against whoever had electrified the door, Guras neither knew nor cared. All that mattered was that victory was at hand, provided they encountered no further delays.

"Eyes open!" Guras ordered as he and Dograk charged in after Kaln, leaving the two riflemen in place in the corridor to guard their backs. Their boots clanged atop the twisted remains of the fallen door. Swirling fumes from the explosion fogged their vision even as Guras searched for the cornered Starfleet engineers, who were bound to attempt to defend their domain. He sniffed the air, but smelled only the ionized residue of the photon grenades. "Arms at the ready!"

He knew they could not be alone, but, to his frustration, he could not immediately detect any lurking foes. He turned about slowly, sweeping the barrel of his disruptor pistol through the smoky air before him. The layout of the chamber bore a certain similarity to the *Fek'lhr*'s own engine room, although the bland, tasteless air lacked the pungency of that found on a proper Klingon vessel. The lights were irritatingly bright and colorless. No weapons or trophies adorned the walls.

Fine, he thought impatiently. Let the human technicians hide, as long as they stayed out of his way. He had better things to do than track down cowards who chose their own safety over defending their post. He was starting to wonder if Starfleet's reputation as a force to be reckoned with had been woefully exaggerated. So far he was not impressed.

"Shut down power to the shields!" he ordered. "I'll stand watch!"

Disabling the *Enterprise*'s shields took priority above all else. Even if Wragh had failed to rescue Merata, a defenseless *Enterprise* would be in no position to refuse General Krunn's demands. Nor would the humans be able to stop the boarding party from beaming back to the *Fek'lhr* once Pike finally surrendered Merata. Success was still within Guras's grasp.

Reluctantly lowering his weapon, Kaln commandeered a control panel. Guras waited impatiently to hear that the shields were indeed down. He wondered what was taking so long.

"Well?" he growled.

"I'm trying, Lieutenant!" Kaln fought the machinery as though it were an enemy, trying to pound it into submission. "I'm locked out of the controls!"

Guras felt like shooting the man. "Then unlock it!"

"I'm doing my best, Lieutenant! It's resisting me!"

Guras saw the cunning hand of a Starfleet engineer at work. It seemed the chamber's defenders were not completely worthless. He was tempted to shove Kaln aside and try the controls himself, but suspected that would be an exercise in futility. Mastering technology was not his strength; he left that to lesser warriors like Kaln, whose technical prowess was sharper than their blades. If Kaln could not overcome the humans' computer trickery, it was doubtful that Guras could.

"Show me how strong your brain is," he challenged Kaln, "unless you want to spend the rest of your days in a Starfleet holding cell!"

"I can do it!" Kaln vowed. "Just give me time!"

"Request denied! Time is the one thing we cannot spare!"

The smoke began to clear, offering a better view of the engine room. Guras noted an odd rectangular shadow moving across the floor before him. Tilting his head back, he peered up at the ceiling . . .

"Hah!" Kaln laughed triumphantly. "I see it now! The trick is to—"

A wrench flew like a missile from above, smashing into the man's skull. Knocked unconscious, he collapsed over the control panel even as Guras spotted the underside of an antigrav lifter cruising just below the engine room's high ceiling. The lifter banked to one side, and he glimpsed a flame-haired human female stretched out atop the device, riding it like a sled. She brandished a gleaming metal cylinder like a club. It took Guras a moment to identify the weapon as an EPS control rod.

"Keep your hands off my controls!" she threatened. "And you owe me for that busted door. Like I didn't have enough repair jobs on my plate!"

"Insolent she-devil!" Dograk raised his disruptor and fired at the flying sled. A blazing green blast barely missed its target, scorching the ceiling instead. He spun about, trying to catch the lifter in his sights, but Guras angrily knocked his arm aside.

"Fool!" Guras cursed him. "Firing a disruptor next to the warp core? Do you want to kill us all?" Holstering his own disruptor, he drew a dagger from his belt. The razor-sharp *d'k tahg* had tasted the blood of many a foe, both Klingon and otherwise. "I'll deal with the human. See to the shields!"

"Yes, Lieutenant!"

Dograk hurried to take Kaln's place at the controls, roughly shoving the unconscious soldier aside. Kaln's limp form landed in a heap upon the deck.

"Oh, no you don't!" the human engineer protested. She swooped down toward Dograk, swinging the metal rod with clear intent to brain Dograk before he could finish what Kaln had started. "Keep away from those controls!"

Guras saw his chance. Placing his knife between his teeth, he sprang onto one of the standby power batteries and from there launched himself at the diving sled. If he missed, he was in for a hard tumble.

But he did not miss.

Tackling the human in midair, he landed atop the lifter, which went into a spin. Biting down hard on his knife, he grappled with the woman as the out-of-control sled crashed to the deck and went skidding toward the EM shield grating at the far end of the engine room. Sparks flew as the lifter scraped against the metal deck. For a heartbeat, Guras feared that the sled would crash straight thought the grille into the warp core, but the grating proved to be more solidly constructed than that. The skidding lift slammed to a stop against the grille, spilling its jarred passengers onto the deck, where neither human nor Klingon could take a moment to recover.

"Ouch," the female said. "I'm going to feel that later."

Her club had hit the deck a few meters away. Shaking off the jolting crash with admirable speed, she scrambled to her feet and dived for the lost weapon, but Guras was on her even more quickly. Knife in hand, he lunged for the fleeing engineer, only to be tackled from behind by another human, who burst out of a cramped storage compartment beneath one of the secondary control stations. Puny arms attempted to restrain Guras.

"Leave the chief alone!" demanded a boyish voice. "You have some nerve, barging in—"

Guras rammed the back of his skull into the human's face. The impact loosened the male's already meager grip and sent him tumbling backward, clutching a bleeding nose. Annoyed by the interruption, Guras spared a moment to spin about and deliver a backhanded blow with his fist that dropped the youth to the floor, where he lay dazed and moaning. Guras debated whether he was worth finishing off.

"Forget him!" the female shouted. "It's me you need to worry about."

She gripped the metal rod with both hands as she faced off against him while keeping one eye on Dograk as well. Despite the breached doorway behind her, she made no effort to flee but stood her ground instead. Her face was bruised and sooty. She spit a mouthful of crimson onto the deck. Guras wondered if she had any Klingon in her blood.

"And you are?" he asked.

"Caitlin Berry, chief engineer of the *Space Ship Enterprise*, and you're trespassing on my turf, mister."

Under other circumstances, Guras might have enjoyed engaging her in combat, but duty and expedience prevailed. He placed his boot over the throat of her downed male subordinate. "Drop your weapon, or I'll crush his windpipe."

A trace of fear appeared in her eyes. "You wouldn't!"

"I am Klingon," he reminded her. "Why would I not?"

She glanced briefly back over her shoulder, as though hoping that reinforcements were on the way. The furious exchange of energy weapons could be heard out in the corridor. Clearly, the battle for control of the deck waged on and would for at least some time more.

"Help will not arrive to save him." He ground his heel into the boy's throat, just enough to make the human gasp for breath. "Drop the weapon. I will not ask again."

"Hellfire," she swore. The rod fell from her fingers onto the floor. "Guess you think you have the upper hand now, don't you."

"I know I do."

As she had fought bravely, he honored his offer of mercy. He lifted his boot from the boy's neck.

"Sorry, Chief," the youth squeaked. A broken nose distorted his speech, making it even more grating to Guras's ears. "I thought I had him . . ."

"It's okay, Collier," she said. "You did good."

"Enough!" Guras strode across the chamber to place his dagger at Barry's throat. He snarled at her, his fierce countenance barely a hand's width from hers. "Unlock the control panel at once."

Barry met his gaze boldly, as though death was not only a short length of steel away. A smirk lifted her lips. "Sure you want to get so close? I'm contagious, you know."

He blinked in confusion. "Contagious?"

"Oh, haven't you heard? There's a nasty bout of Rigelian fever going around." She coughed in his face. "Nasty way to go, they say."

A shudder ran through him. Like all Klingons, he dreaded disease. To die in battle was a glorious end, but to die in bed, sickly and weak, was every warrior's worst nightmare. He had to fight a sudden urge to retreat from the woman and flee her presence at once.

"You're lying," he insisted, as much to himself as to her. "You think to distract me."

"Take my temperature if you don't believe me. Trust me, I'm running hotter than my engines . . . and not in a good way."

Was she trying to taunt him into killing her before she could betray her captain? Or was she simply stalling for time? Either way, he refused to be baited any longer.

"Curb your tongue!" He dragged her over to the control panel, dislodging Dograk, and spun her around so that she faced the frozen mechanism. Trying his best not to think of germs or sickness, he came up behind her and placed the edge of the blade against her neck. "Release the controls to us, or you won't have to worry about your fever any longer!"

Twenty

"Excuse me, sir," Garrison said. "It's the Cyprians. They're still upset about us defying their orders and coming within transporter range of the planet."

"I'm sure they are," Pike said irritably, "but I've got a Klingon boarding party running amok on my ship at the moment." As far he was concerned, smoothing the Cyprians' ruffled feathers could wait. "Tell them to file a formal protest—in writing—but clear that board, mister!"

"Message received, Captain." Garrison kept any Cyprian signals confined to his own station. "Loud and clear."

Number One sighed ruefully. "I'm sorry, Captain. Rescuing me and the others is not going to endear you with Prime Minister Flescu."

"Belay that, Number One," he replied. "Don't even think of apologizing. The way I see it, Flescu owes me a favor. Thanks to our unauthorized detour, he doesn't have four dead Federation citizens on his hands. Now *that* would be a diplomatic incident."

Any trace of guilt vanished from Number One's features as she considered the captain's reasoning. "That's certainly one way to look at it, I suppose, but I wouldn't expect any thank-you notes from the prime minister in the immediate future."

I can live with that, Pike thought. He activated the intercom via his chair. "Pike to engineering. How are you holding out?"

Worryingly, no one responded.

"Repeat: Pike to engineering. Barry, are you there?"

The engineer's failure to reply suggested various possibilities, none of them good. His heart pounded inside his aching chest. "Garrison?"

He shook his head dourly. "I'm trying to reach engineering, sir. No luck."

Pike would have hit something in frustration if he had the strength. Had the Klingons already seized control of the engine room? If so, then the *Enterprise* could be losing power to her shields and engines at any moment, which would leave the ship a sitting duck. Krunn wouldn't even need to wait for his reinforcements to take the ship.

Spock's plan had better work, he thought, *and soon.*

———

Spock wriggled through the Jefferies tube to reach the central air conduit servicing deck nineteen.

Navigating the cramped access tunnel while transporting a pressurized tank of concentrated anesthizine gas posed a challenge; Spock was grateful that he was still relatively young and limber and that his half-human genetics had not significantly impaired his upper body strength. He had every reason to believe that he possessed the strength of a full Vulcan, which made it easier to carry the heavy tank under one arm while pulling himself along with the other. Given that the tank weighed 10.4 kilograms and was approximately 46.8 centimeters in length, he doubted that anyone else aboard could have made better time through the tube.

Nonetheless, he remained all too conscious that time was elapsing at an unsettling rate. Despite his haste, procuring and preparing a sufficient quantity of the gas had taken longer than anticipated. It was a pity, he reflected, that the *Enterprise* did not already have a gas-based security system in place to deal with such eventualities. Something to consider, perhaps, the next time the ship was due for refit, some years hence. He resolved to recommend consideration of such an innovation in his log entry on this incident, assuming that he survived to compose one. The ability to painlessly subdue intruders by pumping a tranquilizing gas into selected areas of the ship might well prove a boon to future starship captains and crews in years to come.

But more pressing issues demanded his attention now. Arriving at the proper junction, he was confronted with what might have been a bewildering array of pipes, joints, and cables to anyone less versed in the intricacies of starship design or less capable of absorbing and processing complicated diagrams at a glance. He took only a moment to verify that he had the correct outlet pipe before wrestling the tank into position and commencing to hook the tank into the system. This required care, lest he accidentally gas himself in the process or contaminate the air on other decks of the ship. He held his breath as he opened the valve on the tank. A faint hiss lasted only long enough for him to tighten the seal. He let go of the tank after making sure it was secure and lifted a communicator to his lips.

"Spock to bridge. The procedure is under way. Stand by to respond accordingly."

"Copy that," Pike responded. *"Our people have acquired respirator masks and are ready to move in."*

"The gas should take effect in approximately two point four minutes," Spock stated, "allowing for a reasonable margin of error."

Calculating the correct dosage of gas, in parts per milliliter, had involved factoring in a number of variables, including the comparative metabolisms of humans and Klingons, the atmospheric pressure and air volume on deck nineteen, and the estimated rate of dispersion of the aerosolized sedative, but

Spock was reasonably confident in his result. Just for a moment, he wondered if perhaps he should have double-checked his figures one last time before releasing the gas, but he quickly dismissed such doubts as illogical and unworthy of him.

He *was* Vulcan.

Twenty-one

"You heard me!" Guras tickled the human's throat with the edge of his dagger. "Unlock the control panel!"

He watched her hands carefully and wished he was better acquainted with the workings of Starfleet engine rooms. Would he even spot any sleight of hand if she attempted it?

"No tricks," he warned. "Or both you and your underling will pay the price."

"Yeah, yeah, I get it," she shot back. "It's just a little hard to concentrate with a knife to my throat, you know?"

Guras doubted that. From what he'd seen so far, she coped well under pressure.

"Try harder."

Dograk coughed hoarsely nearby. "My apologies, Lieutenant. The smoke, I think . . ."

What smoke? Guras thought. The fumes from the explosion had long since dissipated, yet he too felt something irritating his throat and lungs. For a moment, his blood went cold as he feared that he had indeed contracted some debilitating sickness from the humans, then his eyes spied the swirling white fumes entering the chamber through the air vents. The fumes spread quickly, contaminating the atmosphere and filling up the engine room and corridor outside.

"Gas!" he realized. "They're trying to gas us!"

"Sneaky," Barry said. "Wonder who thought of that."

"Tell them to cut it off!" he snarled. "Or I'll slash your throat!" He turned to shout at Dograk, who was already reeling from the fumes. Guras felt his own wits dulling. His tongue felt thick and cumbersome in his mouth. "Kill the boy . . . to show them that Klingons do not . . . make empty threats!"

"With . . . pleasure . . ." the soldier said, slurring his words. He staggered unsteadily through the thickening vapors, which resembled a heavy fog on Argelius II. He gripped the haft of his own dagger. "Been . . . wanting . . . to kill . . ."

He got only a few steps before stumbling sideways into one of the standby power units. He threw out an arm to steady himself. He gasped for breath, sucking in even more of the insidious gas, while getting no closer to the downed male human. Guras saw his mission falling apart.

"Finish it!" Guras ordered, gasping as well. "You are Klingon. Act like it . . ."

His head swam and the deck seemed to tilt beneath him as though rocked by an ion storm. His knife felt heavy in his hand, weighing down his arm so that it drooped beneath Barry's throat. Ordinarily, he would not have been so sloppy, but the gases dulled his reflexes, giving her time to grab his knife arm with both hands, yanking it farther away from her neck while simultaneously bending forward and flipping him over her shoulder onto the control panel. Losing contact with the deck, his heels collided with the displays above the controls as Barry ducked out from beneath him and sprang away, out of reach. Guras slid headfirst off the console onto the deck, but kept hold of his dagger. He clambered haltingly to his feet, all too aware that the gas was his true enemy now.

But he would settle for the human engineer.

"No more games," he said, coughing. "Only vengeance!"

"Uh-uh," Barry said. "I'm going to take a rain check on that one."

She sought out her rod, which still rested where she'd dropped it before. Cupping a hand over her nose and mouth, she kicked the rod so that it rolled directly into the path of Dograk, who tripped over it and crashed to the floor, not far from the insensate form of Kaln. Labored breaths suggested that he too was out cold. Barry half-ran, half-stumbled to Dograk's side and snatched the fallen soldier's disruptor from his holster. Crouching beside the man's prone body, unable to stand, she took aim at Guras as he lurched toward her clumsily. His neatly trimmed black hair was mussed, his ridged brow scratched and scraped from the tussle. His head lolled atop his neck, even as he forced himself to stay on his feet through sheer force of will. He was Klingon; he would not be brought down by an insubstantial mist!

Just a few more steps, he thought. *Keep marching. Do your duty.*

"That's far enough," she warned him. She swayed back and forth upon her knees, visibly succumbing to the gas. She needed both arms to hold the disruptor steady, more or less. "I *think* I've got this blaster set on stun, but I wouldn't swear to it . . ."

Guras refused to let victory slip from his grasp. He stomped through the swirling fog toward the infuriating engineer. All he needed was one valuable hostage to trade for the general's daughter. There was still a chance to avoid the sour taste of defeat.

"You wouldn't dare," he challenged her. "Not here . . . not by the warp core . . ."

She managed a defiant smirk.

"This is my engine room, remember? I know just where to shoot."

The blast knocked him out before the gas did.

———

"We have your soldiers, Krunn. I assume you want them back?"

Pike addressed the general via the viewscreen on

the bridge. Less than an hour had passed since their improvised gas tactic had incapacitated the Klingon invaders with no loss of life to the *Enterprise* and its crew. The recovering Klingons were now confined to the brig, minus the soldier whose remains were currently being cleaned out of one of *Climber One*'s nacelles by technicians with—hopefully—strong stomachs. Pike didn't envy them that task, which he thought it best not to dwell on, and wanted the surviving Klingons off his ship as soon as possible. He needed to resolve this crisis, not escalate it by taking on a load of prisoners-of-war.

"*And my daughter?*" Krunn grumbled. Unsurprisingly, the failure of his boarding party had not improved the general's mood any. An angry vein throbbed along his hairless pate. He absently rubbed the ancient bite mark on his hand. "*What of Merata?*"

"That's another matter," Pike stated, "but I strongly advise you not to attempt to take her by force again." He chose his words carefully, trying to walk the fine line between taking a firm stand and provoking Krunn into launching another assault. Said diplomacy was not made any easier by the fact that he felt like a shuttle had landed on his chest. Speaking was almost as exhausting as breathing. "Next time we may be less inclined to . . . overlook . . . such incidents in the interest of peace."

His thoughts turned to the unexpected drama

in sickbay during the invasion. According to Spock, Merata had passed up an opportunity to escape and join forces with the other Klingons in order to stay by her injured sister, who was now in critical condition. Pike debated mentioning this to Krunn, but decided against it; who knew how Krunn would react to the news that Merata had chosen Soleste over a chance to return to her father?

Better not to take that chance, Pike thought. *Krunn looks unhappy enough.*

But from where Pike was sitting, Merata's unexpected actions only complicated the already murky question of where she truly belonged. Was it possible that Merata was no longer quite so adamant about being a Klingon, now that she had been reunited with her Cyprian family? Was she confused or changing her mind about where she wanted to be? If anything, the dilemma posed by the twice-stolen young woman seemed even less cut-and-dried than before.

Pike decided he needed to get Spock's latest thoughts on the subject, if and when the opportunity arose. In theory, Spock was attending to the Mursh family at present, while Pike dealt with Merata's more belligerent "family." Pike suspected that he had drawn the short straw here. At least the Murshes were not equipped with disruptor cannons and photo torpedoes.

"Make no mistake, Pike," the general said. *"We*

will *reclaim Merata, one way or another. It is a certainty.*"

Pike took that as a barely subtle reminder that Klingon reinforcements were converging on the system and were now only hours away. He wondered briefly why Krunn had not simply waited for the other battle cruisers to arrive instead of attempting to liberate Merata on his own by means of the boarding party. Probably a matter of Klingon pride, Pike guessed. No doubt Krunn would have preferred to reclaim his daughter without any other Klingon's help.

Tough, Pike thought. "About your men . . . ?"

Krunn grudgingly got back to the topic at hand, with all the enthusiasm of a junior lieutenant assigned to a graveyard shift in the ship's bowels. *"What do you propose, human?"*

"I am prepared to beam the soldiers back to your ship on the condition that you give me your word of honor that you will not launch another attack on the *Enterprise* the minute we lower our shields."

He did his best impression of a marble statue, solid all the way through. He breathed shallowly through his teeth to keep from coughing or wheezing.

"Are you well, Pike?" Krunn leaned forward, as though sensing advantage. *"We have been monitoring the news transmissions on Cypria III. It is said*

that there is sickness aboard your ship, human. That you are all dying of fever."

Pike silently cursed the Cyprians' loose tongues.

"Reports of our imminent demise have been greatly exaggerated," Pike lied. "Cyprian media coverage is highly sensationalized. Don't tell me you've fallen for such shameless yellow journalism?"

A cough clawed at the back of his throat, demanding release. Pike struggled to talk past it.

"The only exaggerated claims I know of were yours, concerning that fractured warp core," Krunn said, calling Pike on his earlier deception. *"So you expect me to believe that you are* not *gravely ill?"* Skeptical eyes regarded Pike across the void. *"You look worse than I remember."*

"I'm getting pretty tired of your looks too," Pike shot back. "And I'm choking only on your stubbornness. Do you want your men back or not?"

Krunn leaned back in his seat, considering.

"Very well," he agreed finally. *"My soldiers deserve better than to be confined to a stinking plague ship. You have my word as a Klingon that I will not open fire as you beam the rescue party back to the* Fek'lhr. *Is that good enough for you?"*

"Works for me," Pike said. "I have no reason to doubt your word . . . or your honor."

Not that he planned on trusting Krunn too far. The battle cruiser would have to lower its own shields to receive the prisoners and Pike intended the *Enterprise* to be fully armed and ready to retaliate if the Klingons tried to pull a fast one.

"Consider this a gesture of good faith," he said.

"*Fah.*" Krunn dismissed the overture with an impatient wave of his hand. "*Do not think to buy any goodwill here, Pike. You still have my daughter and, on my honor, there will be a reckoning.*"

That cough was getting most insistent with every breath. Pike was practically choking on it.

I need to wrap this up, he thought, *before Krunn sees just how sick I really am.*

"Let's hope for a resolution rather than a reckoning. For now, however, I'll have my crew arrange to get your rescue party off my ship. *Enterprise* out."

Krunn's visage had barely vanished from the screen before Pike started coughing violently, causing him to double over in his chair, hacking and gasping as though he was trying to cough up an organ or two. Pike envied the Klingons; he could use an extra lung right about now.

Number One looked back at him from the helm. "With all due respect, Captain, you belong in sickbay. I can manage the bridge."

"And prove to Krunn that I'm unfit for battle?" Pike shook his head while trying to bring his coughing under control. "Not a chance. We might as well roll over and present our belly to that battle cruiser."

Colt made a face. "There's a picture I didn't want in my head."

"But, sir," Number One protested, "I am quite capable of—"

"I know you are, Number One, but that's not the point." He sat up straighter as the coughing fit mercifully subsided. "Do me a favor, though, and work out the details of returning those Klingons to the *Fek'lhr*. Let's make this happen sooner rather than later."

"Aye, Captain," she replied. "I'll see to it at once."

He could tell from her tone that she thought he was making a mistake, but he appreciated her not making an issue of it. He imagined that she and Doctor Boyce would gang up on him at some point, when the fever truly had him on the ropes, but right now the prospect of lying sick in bed while his ship was in danger was worse than any physical distress he could conceive of. He'd sooner face another dose of illusionary hellfire and brimstone back on Talos IV.

"Thank you, Number One. I've had all the Klingon bluster I can take for now"

At least until those extra battle cruisers arrive, he thought. *Somehow I doubt that they're going to be as "easy" to repel as Krunn's boarding party.*

If the fever didn't beat him first.

Twenty-two

"Be reasonable, Chris. You belong in sickbay."

Boyce had come straight to the bridge from sickbay, after performing emergency surgery on Soleste Mursh. Minute traces of Cyprian blood still speckled the doctor's rumpled blue jumpsuit. Pike regretted calling Boyce away from his numerous other patients, but he needed the doctor's expert assistance if he was going to be able to stay in command of the bridge.

"Not now, Doctor," Pike said as firmly as he could in his present condition. Between his killer headache, increasing shortness of breath, and sinking strength, he felt like he was practically ready for a burial in space. "Our Klingon friends are expecting their friends any time now. I need you to keep me going for as long as you can."

"I'm no miracle worker." Boyce stood beside the captain's chair. "Without that ryetalyn, I can only treat your symptoms, not the fever, and I can't even promise you much in the way of relief there, certainly not in the long term. You're approaching stage three. There's only so much I can do for you."

Boyce spoke quietly, for the captain's ears only, but Pike was all too aware of the remaining bridge crew as they did their best to pretend that they weren't listening. He hated showing weakness before his crew, but that cat was out of the bag at this point. Better that the crew knew he was sick than that the Klingons did, especially with two more battle cruisers bearing down on them.

"Do what you can, Doctor. That's all I ask."

Boyce produced a hypospray from his portable medkit. "This is a combined stimulant and anti-inflammatory. It may help . . . a little."

He pressed the hypo against Pike's neck. A brief hiss accompanied the introduction of the medicine into Pike's bloodstream. He felt a slight stinging sensation.

"Thank you, Doctor." Pike waited impatiently for the drug to kick in. So far he wasn't feeling much of an effect, although *maybe* the tightness in his chest was loosening—barely. "You can report back to sickbay. I'm sure you have other patients to attend to."

"Does Wrigley's Pleasure Planet have beaches?" Boyce lingered in the command circle, eyeing Pike with concern. "But if you need me here . . ."

"Get going, Doctor. Unless you've got a working vaccine against Klingon disruptors."

"Still working on that one, I'm afraid." Boyce

made his way to the turbolift, only to pause at its entrance. He called out to the helm. "Keep an eye on him, Number One. Doctor's orders."

"You are preaching to the converted, Doctor," she replied. "But I'll do my best."

Boyce stepped into the turbolift, vanishing from view. Pike rubbed his neck where the hypospray had been applied, as though he could massage the medicine deeper into his system. He inhaled experimentally, testing his lungs. Maybe it was just a placebo effect, but it seemed he was wheezing less. And at least he hadn't coughed for a moment or two. His head still hurt, though, and it was hard to keep his head and eyelids from drooping. He wanted to lie down, but was afraid he'd never be able to get back up again. He found himself envying the crews of those old-time sleeper ships. He could use a two-hundred-year-long nap.

"Captain!" Weisz said at the science station, his eyes fixed on the gooseneck monitor. "Two additional battle cruisers have entered the system. They're closing in on us, sir."

"The *Ch'Tang* and the *BortaS,* I presume." Number One had already familiarized herself with the names of the addition Klingon warships. She glanced down at the ship's chronometer. "Arriving somewhat ahead of schedule."

"And the party just got more crowded," Colt said. "Oh boy."

Pike was getting used to having Colt at the nav station. "Tactical analysis. On-screen."

"Aye, sir," she replied. "Coming up."

A computer-generated graphic appeared on the viewer, charting the relative positions of the various ships in three-dimensional space. Blinking red triangles indicated the Klingon vessels while a glowing blue delta represented the *Enterprise*.

Pike studied the graphic as the crimson triangles converged on his ship. One of the realities of space combat was that it was all but impossible to completely surround a ship unless you had a full armada. On the downside, there were always a multitude of angles and orientations from which the enemy—or enemies—could come at you. Within minutes, the battle cruisers were facing off against the *Enterprise* from above, below, and, in the case of the *Fek'lhr*, head on. Pike noted that Krunn had shrewdly positioned his forces so that Cypria III and its laser defenses blocked at least one avenue of retreat.

Just what I would have done, Pike thought, *if I had a fleet at my disposal.*

"The *Fek'lhr* is hailing us," Garrison said.

"Of course it is." Pike coughed to clear his throat and lungs. He still whistled when he breathed, but not quite as badly as earlier; it seemed the doctor's remedy had helped some after all, even if his voice still sounded raspier than he liked. His throat felt like it had been dragged over rocks. "Let's hear from the good general again."

Krunn reappeared on the screen, like a recurring bad dream Pike just couldn't shake. It occurred to Pike that he and his Klingon counterpart had never actually met in the flesh, not that that would have likely made any difference. Krunn was more about making threats than shaking hands.

"Captain Pike," Krunn addressed him smugly, looking in far better spirits now that he had numbers on his side. He cracked his knuckles loudly. *"I assume you are aware that my reinforcements have arrived."*

"That did not escape my notice," Pike said. "Your friends made good time."

"Never underestimate the speed and strength of the Klingon military," Krunn gloated. *"Remember that, should you live to see another day."* He fixed his gaze on Pike. *"This is your last chance, human. Return my daughter, and I may let you and your pitiful ship go limping back to the Federation."*

Pike doubted he could talk his way out of this fix, but felt obliged to try.

"Have you spoken to your boarding party yet?" The Klingon prisoners had been beamed to the *Fek'lhr* some time ago. Pike assumed that they had been debriefed by Krunn by now. "Did they tell you that Merata *chose* to stay behind? Perhaps matters are not as simple as you make them out to be."

Krunn's temper flared, burning away his earlier smugness.

"Merata chose nothing of the sort! You have con-fused my daughter's mind, making her forget where her true allegiances lie." He peered suspiciously across space. *"I am informed that you have a Vulcan science officer, Pike. If he has employed some foul Vulcan mind trick on Merata, I swear by the honor of my house that—"*

"There have been no tricks," Pike interrupted, "Vulcan or otherwise. It's just what I've been telling you all along, that this situation is complicated and confusing by its very nature, and for Merata most of all."

He was tempted to summon Merata to the bridge, have her speak to her father directly, but there was no way to guarantee what she might say or to predict whether she would even want to try to mollify Krunn. An old-fashioned lawyer Pike knew on Starbase 11 always said that a smart attorney never asked a question he didn't already know the answer to, or called a witness to the stand whose tes-timony had not been carefully rehearsed. Merata had already proven herself highly unpredictable, trying to kill Soleste one day and saving her another. Letting her talk to Krunn *might* calm matters—or it could just as easily inflame an already incendiary situation.

Was it worth the risk?

"Let me clarify matters for you, Pike," Krunn

growled. *"You are outnumbered, three to one. Give us back Merata or we will take her by force . . . and your ship as well!"*

He could do it too, Pike realized. The battle cruisers didn't even need to risk destroying the *Enterprise* with Merata aboard. All they needed to do was bombard the ship with disruptor blasts until her shields collapsed. They could then easily take out the *Enterprise*'s weapons and propulsion units, leaving her unable to defend herself or repel any more boarders. Krunn could beam aboard as many soldiers as he needed to capture the ship, and the fact that a hefty percentage of the crew were down with fever would just make that all the easier for the Klingons.

"Then let me make one thing clear to you, Krunn. We don't want this fight, but we will defend ourselves if necessary."

"Good!" Krunn said. *"That will make your surrender all the more satisfying!"*

The transmission ceased abruptly, replaced by the ominous sight of the *Fek'lhr* cruising toward them. Bursts of emerald energy flared from the ship's twin disruptor cannons.

"They're opening fire!" Pike shouted. "Brace for impact!"

———

"Your family is here to see you," Spock said.

Merata remained confined to her quarters.

There had been talk of returning her to the brig following her attack on Doctor Boyce, but mixing her with the other Klingon prisoners had seemed inadvisable at the time. The fact that she had ultimately aborted her escape attempt in order to attend to her injured sister had also mitigated in her favor.

"Send them in," she said quietly, sounding unusually subdued. She rose from the bed to greet her visitors. No pendant adorned her throat; the hidden transceiver had been discovered in the wake of the Klingon incursion, after the sergeant's tracking device was identified as such. "You need not stay if you are needed elsewhere, Vulcan. They are in no danger from me."

Spock was tempted to return to the bridge. Even though Number One was now on hand to assist the captain during the present crisis, he was uneasy being away from his post while the *Enterprise* was anticipating the arrival of two more Klingon battle cruisers. Yet Pike had urged Spock to keep close to Merata in hopes of winning her trust and cooperation. Perhaps Merata could convince her father to call off the assault for the sake of her newfound Cyprian family?

Moreover, the last time I left her alone, the consequences were dire.

He admitted Rosha and Junah Mursh to the chambers. The older woman brought with her the same stuffed lizard Spock had glimpsed in Soleste's holographic "home movies." Junah brought only his usual surly attitude and expression. Spock had been reluctant to include Junah in this visit, but his mother had insisted. Spock resolved to keep a close eye on the discontented Cyprian youth lest his presence prove disruptive or unnecessarily provocative.

"We just came from sickbay," Rosha said wanly, obviously under stress. "From your sister . . ."

Merata nodded. "How does she fare?"

Spock considered what he had learned of Soleste's condition, as well as the circumstances surrounding it. As Doctor Boyce had put it, matters had been "touch and go" with the injured sister after the disturbance in sickbay. The injuries sustained during the Klingon raid had reopened old wounds and traumatized an already weakened system. There was some concern as to whether she was strong enough to survive this latest surgery or any resulting complications.

"She hasn't woken from the surgery yet." Rosha wiped a tear from her eye with her free hand. "The doctor says she should recover, but that there are no guarantees, after everything she's been through already. He says she's fighting for her life."

"She is not one to surrender readily," Merata observed. "That much I have learned these past few days."

Rosha accepted Merata's words in the spirit in

which they were clearly intended. "Yes, that is very true." She gazed warmly at her Klingon daughter. "The doctor says we have you to thank for saving your sister's life. If you hadn't found him in time, and then volunteered your own blood for the operation . . ."

Merata shifted uncomfortably, avoiding eye contact. "The doctor is too generous in his praise."

Spock thought that a fair assessment. Apparently, Boyce had omitted the part where Merata herself had rendered the doctor unconscious before rousing him in time to treat Soleste. Nevertheless, Merata *had* redeemed herself to some degree by choosing her sister's life over the prospect of escape.

"I don't think so," Rosha insisted. "If not for you—"

"If not for her, none of this would be happening," Junah said, interrupting her. "Soleste wouldn't be dying, we wouldn't be stuck on an alien starship menaced by Klingons, and you wouldn't be making a fool of yourself by pretending that this bloodthirsty savage is family." He regarded Merata with undisguised loathing. "We'd all be better off if Soleste had never found you!"

Spock tensed, expecting Merata to react ferociously to her brother's harsh words, but, to his surprise, she merely looked back at Junah from across the room. When she spoke, her tone was more somber than irate.

"You may be right," she said.

"Don't say that, either of you." Rosha frowned at her offspring. "We need to be here for each other, now more than ever."

"Too late for that," Junah said. "Her Klingon friends blasted that possibility to bits a decade ago, along with Father."

"Please, Junah," his mother pleaded. "This isn't helping."

Merata nodded at the plush lizard Rosha had with her, perhaps in an effort to defuse the situation. "Is that for me?"

"Why, yes, of course." Rosha looked painfully grateful to be asked. "I've held on to Forko all these years, ever since . . ." Unable to finish the sentence, she started over. "I would have brought him before, but I wasn't quite sure what to expect that first time, or if you would even remember . . . ."

"I remember." Merata accepted the gift from her mother. "Thank you."

Spock noted that the stuffed lizard had been seared in places and stitched back together in others, having somehow survived the Klingon raid on the mining complex so many years ago. He wondered momentarily what Klingon children played with. Toy weapons, he imagined, or miniature soldiers. Nothing cute or soft or comforting.

Or was he guilty of stereotyping Klingons too broadly? Despite their well-deserved reputation for ruthlessness and aggression, surely they were not entirely about war and conquest, just as Vulcans were not entirely without emotion or sentiment, save for those rare few who had attained the ultimate ideal of *Kolinahr*. Spock thought of his own childhood pet, lost to him so many years ago. I-Chaya had been a true companion to him as a boy. Spock missed him still.

"Red alert! Battle stations!"

The announcement resounded throughout the ship. Spock knew that he could not delay any longer. If ever there was a time to test his tentative bond with Merata, this was it. They needed her help to talk Krunn down from the brink of war.

"Merata," he began. "I fear matters have come to a head. Only you may be able to—"

A sudden tremor jolted the room as the *Enterprise* came under attack, even sooner than Spock had anticipated. The shock sent everyone stumbling across the floor. Books and manuals tumbled from shelves. The overhead lights flickered ominously, creating a strobe-like effect. Gasping, Rosha lost her balance and fell against the large triangular viewer console facing the bed. Her head struck the edge of the unit, and she dropped to the floor.

"Mother!" Merata called out.

Spock rushed to check on the fallen woman, who moaned and stirred fitfully upon the floor. At first glance, she appeared only dazed by the blow and there was no evidence of blood, but he was anxious to verify that she had not suffered any serious injuries.

"Madam Mursh!" he asked urgently. "Are you able to respond?"

Distracted, he noticed too late that Junah had come up behind him. Greedy fingers plucked Spock's laser pistol from his hip. He spun around in alarm.

"Sorry, Vulcan," Junah said. "I need your weapon . . . and you out of the way."

A crimson beam struck Spock at the speed of light.

Twenty-three

Disruptor beams assailed the *Enterprise* from three directions, causing the bridge to pitch back and forth like a raft on stormy seas. A blast from above hammered the ship, causing Pike to glance up anxiously at the transparent aluminum dome overhead; the bulb had been designed to withstand everything from a rogue comet to an ion storm, but even Starfleet engineering had its limits. Dust, ash, and minute particles of ceramic and plastiform fell like an unexpected snow flurry, aggravating Pike's already raw throat and lungs. Deafening booms accompanied the pounding in his skull.

"More power to the forward deflectors," he croaked. "And return fire!"

Colt somehow managed to keep from being thrown from her seat. "At which ship, sir?"

"All of them, any of them," Pike answered. "Whoever you can lock onto, Yeoman!"

"Understood, Captain." She unleashed a laser blast, which bounced off the *Fek'lhr*'s shields. "I always liked shooting galleries."

The lead battle cruiser banked away from the
Enterprise's lasers, then came around for another
strafing run. At the same time, a blast from the
BortaS hit the *Enterprise* from below, causing the
entire ship to tilt upward at a nearly ninety-degree
angle. Pike was thrown against the back of his chair,
so that he seemed to be staring straight "up" at the
main viewer, while loose papers, microtapes, data
slates, digital styluses, coffee mugs, and other para-
phernalia tumbled past him to collide with the rear
of the bridge. A flying slate cracked a display panel
above Garrison's head, causing the enlisted man
to yelp out loud, and a standing crew member fell
backward over a safety rail, landing hard in front of
the helm and navigation stations, before the ship's
gravity corrected itself and the bridge tilted back
into its usual orientation. Up and down went back
where they belonged.

"Shields at fifty-eight percent!" Colt shouted
above the chaos. "And falling!"

And the worst part was, Pike realized, that the
Klingons were actually holding back. They were
fighting—and winning—a war of attrition here.
These were controlled blasts, calibrated to chip
away at the *Enterprise*'s shields, not destroy the
ship. The Klingons weren't even using their photon
torpedoes.

Perhaps he could convince them that they were
doing more damage than they were?

"Hail the Klingons," Pike ordered. "Ship to ship!"

"Yes, sir!" Garrison swept shattered bits of display screen off his console. "Opening a channel!"

"*Enterprise* to Klingon vessels," Pike said. "This is Captain Pike speaking. Hold your fire if you don't want to destroy this ship and everyone on it!"

Krunn's voice replied over the bridge's loudspeakers. "*Do you think me a fool, Pike? I shall not fall for this pathetic trick again!*"

"What about Merata?" Pike challenged him. "Are you willing to bet your daughter's life on that, after all you've done to rescue her?"

"*At least she would die a Klingon. I would sooner see her lost in battle than let you turn her against my house . . . and back into a worthless Cyprian tree worshipper!*"

"I think he means it, Captain," Number One said. "I fear Merata's conduct during the Klingon raid may have realigned the general's priorities somewhat." Another blast jostled her in her seat. "He wants her back, or he wants her dead. No other outcomes will satisfy him."

That sounds about right, Pike thought.

Colt managed to hit the *Ch'Tang*'s starboard wing with a well-aimed laser beam, but that wasn't going to be enough to turn the tide of the battle. Swirling smoke and ash began to fog the atmosphere aboard the bridge. The fallen crew member limped back to his post, clutching his ribs. A blast from the *BortaS* nearly sent the *Enterprise* into a spin. Emergency klaxons and malfunction alerts sounded from nearly every console. Warning lights flashed all over the bridge, like the stardust festival on Ivar VI but without all the gaiety. Pike's ears rang. He felt foggy and lightheaded, as though whatever Boyce had injected him with was already wearing off. For a moment, as his anguished body reeled before the sensory onslaught, and the chaotic scene took on the surreal quality of a nightmare or fever dream, Pike had to wonder if he wasn't still on Talos IV after all, and everything that had happened since was just another disturbingly lifelike illusion . . .

"Vina . . . ?" he whispered.

Colt and Number One both cast him sideways looks.

"Damage reports flooding in," Garrison reported, snapping him back to reality. "We've lost gravity on decks ten through twelve. Life-support on minimal in the cargo bay and maintenance. Injuries reported in main engineering and elsewhere"

"Institute damage control procedures on all decks," Pike ordered. "Instruct sickbay to prepare for additional casualties. Standard triage protocols in effect."

"Shields down to fifty-two percent," Colt added. "Sorry, sir."

This is all about Merata, Pike realized. Maybe only she could end this.

He hated putting the future of his ship and crew in the hands of a short-tempered Klingon teenager, but he had run out of options. It was time to roll the dice and hope for the best. His finger stabbed the intercom button.

"Pike to Spock. Get Merata up here now."

To his surprise, his second officer failed to respond with his usual promptness. Pike checked quickly to see the intercom was still working, but it appeared in order. He pressed down on the speaker button.

"Pike to Spock, respond immediately. Repeat: respond at once."

The Vulcan did not answer.

"Spock!" Pike said, growing alarmed. "Answer me, Spock!"

———

"This is all your fault!" Junah snarled, swinging Spock's laser pistol toward Merata, who found herself hard-pressed to keep up with the rapid cascade of events in her borrowed quarters. His lean face, contorted with rage, bore an uncomfortable resemblance to her own. He braced himself against a curved wall as disruptor blasts continued to pummel the *Enterprise* and Pike's voice called for Spock somewhere in the background. The deck rocked beneath them. "You're a disgrace to our father's memory. You should have died years ago!"

Unarmed save for the stuffed toy lizard, she faced her treacherous brother across the sprawled forms of both Spock and their mother. A fury equal to his set her blood aflame. Alone among her Cyprian kin, Junah had never sought to find common ground with her. His hatred of all things Klingon, and blatant disgust at her upbringing, had made them enemies from the start.

She should have known it would come to this.

"You'd best set that laser on kill, then," she taunted him, "if you mean what you say."

He glanced down at the unfamiliar weapon. His fingers fumbled with the settings on the barrel.

"Catch!" She hurled Forko at him with all her strength. The toy smacked him in the face, throwing off his aim. He fired wildly and a red-hot beam sizzled past Merata to burn a hole in the empty bed while she sprang at him like an unleashed grint hound, knocking him onto his back. He fought back furiously, striking her face with the pistol so hard that she tasted blood, but she grabbed his arm and bit down on his wrist until he released the weapon, which went clattering across the floor. Pinning him to the floor, she bloodied his face with her bare fists, exulting in her wrath. After days of bitter frustration and confusion, it felt glorious to finally do battle against a deserving foe. The thunder of the space battle waging outside was like war drums, spurring her on to victory. To his credit, Junah refused to surrender, demonstrating that they had at least one trait in common, but the outcome of the contest was never in doubt. No Cyprian youth was a match for a true Klingon warrior.

"Barbarian!" He spit at her through broken teeth. "Filthy animal!"

"Hold your ignorant tongue!" she shouted back. "You have no idea who I truly am or what it means to be Klingon!"

Groping for something to shut him up, her fingers latched on to Forko, which had landed barely within arm's reach. She snatched up the stuffed toy and pressed it down on his face so that he couldn't breathe. He thrashed wildly and tugged at it, trying to yank it away from his mouth and nose before he suffocated, but she just pressed down harder, holding it in place.

"Choke on this, 'little brother' . . ."

"Elzy! Stop!" Rosha stumbled toward them, clutching her head. "You're killing him!"

That's the idea, Merata thought, relishing her victory. It was past time she reminded all concerned that they crossed a Klingon at their own peril. Junah's frantic efforts faded as his flailing limbs lost their strength. Bloodshot silver eyes bulged in panic. *Only a few moments more and his slanderous tongue will be still forever.*

"Stop it, please!" Rosha took hold of Merata's shoulders and tried unsuccessfully to pull her away from Junah. "You can't do this. He's your brother!"

"Not much longer!" Merata fought an impulse to knock the older woman away. "He chose this fight. This is his doing, not mine!"

"Please, Elz—Merata! I'm begging you! I can't lose another child!"

The naked pain and desperation in her mother's voice tugged on Merata like a tractor beam, staying her hand. Letting out a howl of frustration, she flung the toy across the room. Junah gasped for breath, sucking in air as though he had never tasted it before. Merata wondered if he appreciated her act of mercy or how much it had cost her.

Most likely not.

"Thank your mother for your worthless life," she said, before knocking him unconscious, much as she had the doctor before. "I'm not sparing you. I'm sparing *her*."

She rose to her feet and stepped away from her defeated foe. Rosha rushed to embrace her.

"Bless you," Rosha said tearfully. "I knew he was wrong about you!"

Merata gently pushed her away.

"No. He wasn't."

Twenty-four

"Wake up, Vulcan! I need you!"

Something slapped Spock hard across the face as an urgent voice shouted at him. Blinking, he struggled to orient himself, even as full consciousness eluded him. Merata's blurry face leaned over his. She slapped him again, harder this time, and a primordial anger flared within him, slipping the reins of culture and discipline. He reached up and grabbed her wrist before she could strike him again, squeezing it until she winced in pain. Bones ground against each other.

"Let go!" she exclaimed. "Release me!"

The violence of his action shocked him back to himself. Regaining his self-control, he let go of her wrist and looked around. His vision came into focus as he quickly took in the sight of a bloodied Junah lying unconscious on the floor of Merata's temporary quarters. His muscles stung from what he recognized as the lingering effects of a laser set on stun. The memory of Junah helping himself to the pistol came back quickly to the recovering

Vulcan, who climbed hurriedly to his feet. Violent jolts shook the guest quarters, forcibly reminding him that the *Enterprise* was under attack. The floor seesawed beneath his feet. Random articles were strewn about the room. Red alert sirens sounded outside.

"What has happened here?" he asked. "Quickly, please."

Merata did not waste words. "My brother made to kill me. I stopped him."

Spock saw with relief that Junah's chest was still rising and falling, although he had clearly taken a beating at his sister's hands. He observed Merata closely, noting her blood-stained knuckles, an ugly bruise upon her cheek, and the pistol in her grip.

"You did not kill him?"

Merata shrugged. "His mother persuaded me otherwise."

"That's true," Rosha confirmed. She knelt by her injured son, wiping the blood from his face with a cloth from the lavatory. "She could have killed him, but she chose not to."

Fascinating, Spock thought, although more pressing matters asserted themselves. "You said you needed me. How?"

She held the pistol at her side, not threatening him with it. She shook the circulation back into her bruised wrist, where he had gripped it before. Spock regretted his momentary lapse. He would have to work harder at keeping control of his emotions, even under the most arduous circumstances.

"I don't belong here, Vulcan. Isn't that obvious now?" She indicated the battered form of Junah. "There is no place for me on Cypria III. Even my own brother could not accept me as I am, and I nearly killed him for it. I *wanted* to kill him. I still do."

Spock believed her. That was the Klingon way, after all.

"But that was in self-defense," Rosha argued. "You can't blame yourself for retaliating like you did, considering . . . what you've been taught."

"I regret nothing . . . and everything." Anguish rang out in Merata's voice. "I've tried to kill my brother, fought and saved my sister, and betrayed my Klingon father, firing on a soldier under his command, acting on his orders. I cannot live like this, Vulcan, torn between two peoples, two families." Desperate eyes implored him. "Tell me you don't understand that, Spock of Vulcan."

That was the first time, Spock noted, that she had ever addressed him by name. And, yes, he knew exactly what she meant.

"You are a child of two worlds," he agreed, "but only you can choose your own path."

"I have chosen. I am Klingon, and I must live as a Klingon. There is no other way." She offered him the stolen pistol. "Can you help me return to my people, Spock, before more blood is spilt?"

She made a convincing argument, but Spock had to consider the larger picture. The *Enterprise* still needed ryetalyn to stem the fever rampaging through the ship, and letting Merata go back to the Klingons would almost certainly eliminate any chance of securing the Cyprians' cooperation. On the other hand, the hostile battle cruisers were arguably the more immediate threat at the moment. Logic dictated that a cure to the fever would do the crew little good if they were killed or captured by the Klingons first, especially if the Klingons succeeded in reclaiming Merata anyway. At this point, he calculated, the odds of ever trading "Elzura" for the ryetalyn were becoming too minimal to factor significantly into the equation.

"I believe I have determined the proper course of action." He accepted the laser pistol from her. "But we will have to work together and with all deliberate speed."

"Wait!" Rosha protested. She stared anxiously at Merata. "Are you truly going to do this? Leave us again, after all these years?"

Merata spared a moment to address the grieving woman. "You know I have to," she said, with more gentleness than Spock would have previously guessed a Klingon capable of. "You saw with your own eyes what just happened, what's been happening ever since Soleste found me and tried to bring me back to Cypria." She shook her head. "That homecoming was never meant to be. It's better this way. You *have* to see that now."

Rosha's moist eyes looked back and forth between her children. A look of pained resignation came over her face. She nodded sadly.

"You won't forget us, will you?"

"Never," Merata promised. "I will honor the memory of the family we once were and keep you in my heart all the way to *Sto-Vo-Kor.* And, please, take comfort in the knowledge that I am where I choose to be. You need not worry about what has become of me anymore." Her voice caught in her throat. "Tell my sister to stop looking for me, for her sake as well as mine. Tell her . . . that Elzy is safe and well. That little girl does not need to be rescued."

Rosha nodded again. "I will."

Rapid-fire blasts from the Klingon warships shook the *Enterprise* like an animal caught between the jaws of a predatory *sehlat.* Along with the two women, Spock lurched clumsily across the wildly pitching floor of the chamber. He braced himself against the central viewer unit while readily imagining the crisis on the bridge. Spock did not need access to his science station to know that the *Enterprise*'s shields could not long withstand this relentless barrage.

General Krunn has all the advantages, Spock thought. *We are fighting a losing battle.*

He cleared his throat. Although reluctant to rush the emotional parting between the two women, time did not allow for long good-byes. "My apologies for interrupting, but we must make haste if we hope to avert further hostilities."

"You are quite right, Vulcan." Merata turned away from her mother without protest; Spock suspected that she had no desire to prolong the difficult farewell. "Let us proceed, by all means. What is our strategy?"

But Rosha was not quite ready to see her daughter depart. "Wait, before you go—" She retrieved the stuffed lizard from the floor and held it out to Merata. "You can't forget Forko."

Orange smears stained the toy's scaly hide. Spock arched an eyebrow, but Merata accepted the sentimental offering as though it was unblemished by her brother's blood. She tucked it under her arm.

"I'll keep him safe," she promised. "You may rely on that."

Spock couldn't tell if she was only humoring her mother or not.

———

"Mister Spock? Do you require assistance?"

The security officer, going about his business, was obviously startled to find Spock escorting Merata at gunpoint down the shaking corridor. He regarded the Klingon warily while eyeing the stuffed lizard under her arm with understandable confusion.

"Negative, Ensign," Spock replied with his usual

measured calm. "I am transferring the prisoner to the brig. You may continue with your duties."

Ensign Williams accepted Spock's explanation. "Yes, sir. If you think you can manage the Klingon on your own."

Spock found himself grateful for the widespread myth that Vulcans could not lie. In fact, while his people certainly placed great value on the truth, they were also fully capable of subterfuge when logic dictated its use. The needs of the many often outweighed a strict adherence to veracity.

"I have the situation fully under control, Ensign." Spock's laser pistol remained aimed at Merata's back. "On your way, mister."

Another salvo from the enemy punctuated Spock's command. Williams missed a step as the deck reeled beneath them. The lights dimmed for a moment, so that only the flashing red annunciators lit up the quaking hallway. The blast served to remind the ensign that he had other places to be.

"Aye, aye, Mister Spock!"

Spock repressed a sigh of relief as Williams hastened to carry out whatever vital task required his attention. If nothing else, the rapacious fever had significantly cut down on the number of personnel roaming the halls, which worked in Spock's favor at this moment. He hoped to avoid too many inconvenient encounters of the sort that had just transpired; the fewer people who were aware of his present activities, the better. It was just as well that the guard posted outside Merata's quarters had been called away to help defend the ship against the battle cruisers. That had eliminated one variable from what was already a risky endeavor.

"You lie well for a Vulcan," Merata observed in a low voice. "Your human half showing through?"

He saw no need to tarnish his homeworld's reputation. "Let us say so."

Fortuitously, they made it to the turbolift with no further complications. The door slid shut, hiding them from scrutiny. Spock gripped the control handle, which activated at his touch. He lowered the pistol in his other hand.

"Hangar deck."

The lift descended rapidly, bypassing the brig while moving down and across the ship toward the entrance to the hangar deck. Spock passed the pistol over to Merata, exploiting the fact that there were no security sensors in the turbolifts. He spoke freely while he could.

"From this point on, our story must be that you somehow overpowered me."

"A Klingon overpowering a Vulcan?" Merata chuckled. "Who could doubt it?"

He hoped the captain and Starfleet would feel likewise. Never before had he deliberately violated the chain of command in this fashion. He resolved not to make a habit of it.

Unless absolutely necessary.

The lift dropped them off outside the hangar deck, which still bore a few scars from the Klingons' sneak attack hours ago. Merata shoved him roughly through the doorway onto the deck ahead of her. Brandishing the laser pistol, she marched him across the hangar toward the waiting Cyprian shuttlecraft, *Climber One*. Spock held his hands above his head, so that he would clearly resemble a hostage to any onlookers in the control booth above them. He feared this would not reflect well on his record.

"Move, Vulcan!" She prodded him forward. "I won't ask again!"

An anxious voice sounded over the public-address system: *"Halt where you are! Lower your weapon, and keep away from the spacecraft!"*

Merata fired a warning shot into the air. "Do not hinder me . . . or the Vulcan dies!"

In fact, the laser was set on stun, or had been when Spock had turned it over to her. He trusted Merata not to take this performance too far.

"Do as she says!" He kept his hands in the air as he raised his voice to be heard by all present. "Clear the deck! That's an order!"

A handful of overworked technicians scurried to safety, leaving him and Merata alone on the deck. Spock noted that much of the damage done to the site by the Klingon boarding party had already been repaired. A replacement observation window shielded the flight controllers, while the outer space doors appeared in working order. No debris or Klingon remains littered the floor of the hangar. He trusted that the shuttle was operative as well.

Commendable, he thought, *as well as convenient.*

Acting as though he was under duress, he opened the hatch to the shuttle's cockpit and climbed inside.

"Are you certain you can pilot this craft?" he asked sotto voce.

"Watch me." She confidently took her place at the helm and closed the hatchway before activating the control panel and engines. As they surged to life, she turned to look at Spock. Their eyes met in communion. "Many thanks, Spock of Vulcan, for your hospitality . . . and understanding."

He refrained from offering a traditional Vulcan salute, lest the gesture be observed and cast doubt on the scenario they had labored to create. Only the slightest tip of his head acknowledged her words. "Live long and prosper, Merata, daughter of the Empire."

She snorted at the salutation, which was doubtless too pacifistic for her tastes. "And may you die honorably in battle, but preferably not today."

He appreciated the sentiment, to a degree.

"I have done what I can," he told her. "The rest is up to you . . . and Captain Pike."

She nodded grimly. "And my father."

Twenty-five

"Captain!" Garrison sounded startled. "I'm receiving a transmission from *Climber One*." A nonplussed expression conveyed his bewilderment. "It's . . . from Merata, sir."

Merata?

Pike recalled that the Cyprian shuttlecraft was still stowed in the *Enterprise*'s hangar bay, and so apparently did Number One.

"What's she doing on the hangar deck?" Number One asked aloud. "Last I heard, she was confined to quarters."

Pike could think of only one possible explanation.

Spock.

The Vulcan had never responded to Pike's urgent requests to bring Merata to the bridge, and Pike had been too busy and too short-handed to send anyone in search of him. That might have been a mistake . . .

"Let's hear her," he said tersely. Short of breath, barely able to stay upright, he hoarded his words as though he was running out of them, which he probably was. "Tie her in."

"Aye, sir."

Merata's face appeared on the viewscreen. There was a nasty ocher bruise on the left side of her face, but she still looked better than Pike felt. Her sardonic voice burst from the speakers

"I have taken your pet Vulcan hostage, Pike, and commandeered this shuttle. Know that I will shortly attempt to exit your ship at top speed. I suggest you open the space doors and lower your aft shields or the consequences will be most uncomfortable for all concerned, including Mister Spock."

Despite his fever, Pike knew what she meant. A shuttle slamming into the space doors and shields at impulse speed would inflict severe damage to both vessels and almost certainly pulp anyone inside *Climber One.*

"That's suicide," he rasped. "You'd never survive the collision. You'll be crushed."

"I'm not bluffing, Pike. As my people say, today is a good day to die."

"Captain," Garrison interrupted. "This is going out on all frequencies. The Klingons are hearing this, too."

Pike assumed that was intentional. Merata wanted her father to know what was happening.

"Sensors detect engine activity in the hangar

deck," Weisz confirmed from the science station. "*Climber One* is ready to launch."

Pike remembered what he'd told Spock earlier about playing the hand you're dealt. It seemed to him that the time had come to lay down his cards and hope for the best.

"Open space doors," he ordered. "Number One, get our backside away from those battle cruisers for as long as you can."

"A challenging task in three dimensions," she observed, "but I'll do my best. Hold tight, everyone."

The inertial dampers were tested once more, this time on purpose, as Number One threw the *Enterprise* sharply into reverse, so that she shot backward away from the Klingons at full impulse. White knuckles gripped armrests and consoles as the sudden shift in momentum tugged hard on Pike and his crew. Pike could practically hear Caitlin Barry swearing profanely at the abuse her engines were taking, but at least the stern of the ship was leading the flight away from the Klingons, taking the hangar deck out of the line of the fire for a few crucial moments. Pike's stomach twisted painfully.

"Colt!" he grunted. "Lower shields at my command."

She looked back at him from the nav station. "But the Klingons—"

Number One called out to him. "Our stern is clear, Captain, for now."

Pike noted that the Klingon barrage seemed to have paused for the moment. He suspected that Krunn was holding his breath while monitoring the situation closely.

"Do it, Yeoman!"

"Yes, Captain. Lowering aft shields."

Pike hailed Merata. "Pike to *Climber One*. You are cleared for takeoff."

"A wise decision, Captain," she said from the viewer. *"You'll forgive me if I take my leave now."*

Her face vanished from the screen.

"Get that shuttle on-screen," Pike ordered. "Now!"

"Aye, sir," Weisz responded. "Switching to aft view."

The image changed in time for Pike to see *Climber One* rocket away from the *Enterprise*. Merata's voice was picked up by the ship's communications array.

"Hailing Klingon forces. This is Merata, daughter of Krunn. Hold your fire!"

"Is the shuttle shielded?" Pike demanded.

Colt consulted her tactical sensors. "Negative, sir."

He keyed the intercom. "Pike to transporter room. Mister Spock is on the fleeing Cyprian shuttle. Lock onto him immediately—and get him out of there."

"Yes, Captain," Yamata responded. *"What about the pilot?"*

Pike thought about Merata, and the Klingon battle cruisers poised to resume their attack on the *Enterprise* at the slightest provocation.

"Let her go."

So much for the ryetalyn. He hoped he had made the right call. *The Cyprians will just have to live with this, even if we don't.*

"Transporter room. Do you have Spock?"

"Affirmative, Captain," the Vulcan replied directly. He sounded remarkably calm for someone who had nearly been splattered against the space doors or taken aboard a Klingon warship. *"I can report that only my ego has been damaged by my recent misadventures."*

"Good to hear it, Mister Spock," Pike said curtly. "We'll talk more of this later. Pike out."

Colt anticipated Pike's next command. "Restoring shields, sir."

He gave her an approving nod, grateful for her prompt action. Sick as he was, he needed everyone else at the top of their game. The stomach cramps increased, signaling that he was descending into the third and final circle of Rigelian hell. He wheezed audibly as the fever overcame Boyce's temporary remedy. A fresh cough scraped at his lungs, which cried out for more oxygen. The air on the bridge felt as thin as Vulcan's. Chills, alternating with hot sweats, racked his body. His vision blurred, and he had to blink to clear it. He glanced down at the back of his hand; discolored veins bulged beneath the skin, spreading out to the capillaries.

Stage three, he thought. *Septic shock.*

On-screen, the stolen shuttle accelerated toward the *Fek'lhr.* Pike watched tensely as a Klingon tractor beam latched onto *Climber One* and guided it aboard the larger vessel. It seemed that Yamata and his partner had extracted Spock from the shuttle just in time.

"Now what?" Number One asked aloud.

Good question, Pike thought. Would Krunn still command the battle cruisers against the *Enterprise,* with intent to destroy or capture the Federation spaceship, or was it enough that he had finally gotten his daughter back? And what was Merata saying to her father now? Did she still want revenge against the *Enterprise* or merely to be reunited with her father?

Long seconds ticked by as it occurred to Pike that, with Merata now safely aboard the *Fek'lhr,* Krunn no longer had any reason to go easy on the *Enterprise.* What if he remained intent on that "reckoning" he warned of before? The threat of a full-scale war with the Federation might not be enough to deter him. To the contrary, there were many in Starfleet who believed that the Empire was itching to take on the Federation and that war was all but inevitable. He'd seen strategic analyses that predicted all-out hostilities within a decade at most.

Was today the day that war began? Was this the spark that set off a galactic conflagration?

"Shields, Yeoman?"

"Fifty percent, Captain," she reported, "but holding."

Pike braced himself for another salvo, even as he realized that he was in no shape to direct a defense against three battle cruisers. To be honest, he doubted that he could even make it to sickbay under his own power; he felt like he already had one foot in the grave. He exchanged a meaningful look with Number One, who began to rise from her seat at the helm. Klingons or no Klingons, he needed to turn over command to her. He was very near the end of his rope.

"Number One," he began, "I'm afraid—"

"The Klingons!" Colt blurted. "They're breaking away!"

Pike glanced at the screen, where, in fact, the *Fek'lhr* had turned about and was speeding away from the *Enterprise*, followed promptly by the other two battle cruisers. He watched with relief as they shrunk rapidly into the distance.

"Sensors confirm that they are exiting the system," Weisz reported, "and not wasting any time about it."

"Whew!" Colt wiped her brow in relief. "I got

to say, I thought we were goners for few moments there."

You and me both, Pike thought, but apparently Krunn was in no hurry to start a war now that he had his daughter back. If and when the Federation and the Empire finally came to blows, it would not be over Merata. Pike considered that a victory, of sorts, although he doubted that the Cyprians would agree. *Guess we're on our own, and no closer to finding a cure for this damn fever*

He rose from his chair, ready at last to turn it over to Number One, only to have his legs give out beneath him. Dizziness assailed him, and his vision dimmed. Gasping for breath, he crashed onto the deck. A darkness as black as space replaced the bright lights of the bridge, even as he heard Number One crying out from what sounded like light-years away.

"Captain!"

Twenty-six

"We're ready on our end, Number One," Garrison reported from the bridge. "Enterprise *is tapped into Cypria III's global media network. All we need is the go-ahead from the authorities down on the planet.*"

"Thank you, Mister Garrison," she replied. "Stand by for the green light."

She and Rosha Mursh had the briefing room to themselves. Rosha sat at the head of the conference table, facing the viewscreen, while Number One was a few seats to her right, operating the viewer controls. She had contemplated delegating this task to Spock, so that she could remain on the bridge while the captain was fighting the fever in sickbay, but had ultimately felt that she understood the players and politics down on Cypria III better than Spock. He was certainly capable of looking after the bridge in her absence, even if he had somehow allowed Merata to get the drop on him before.

Funny that, she thought. It was unlike Spock to be so careless. Far be it from her to question his account of the incident, but she couldn't help but wonder . . .

"*This had better work,*" Atron Flescu grumbled upon the viewscreen. His ruddy face lacked its usual professional smile. Dark circles under his eyes suggested that he had not been sleeping well. "*I can't believe you talked me into this.*"

"I believe it is the only option left to us, Prime Minister. We are all set here. Just say the word and we'll commence."

"*I don't know,*" he said, balking at the last minute. He tugged nervously on his collar. "*I'm still not sure . . .*"

"We've already discussed this," she reminded him patiently. "It is in your best interests, as well as ours. Rumors of Merata's return to the Klingons are already provoking unrest on your planet, as we both know too well. It's imperative that we put a positive spin on this latest development in order to calm your people and put this controversy behind us."

The facts were indisputable. News reports from Cypria III, monitored by the *Enterprise*, made it clear that the violent disturbances she had witnessed on the planet were escalating as word spread that Little Elzy had been "stolen" again by the Klingons. Demonstrations, marches, and even riots had been reported all over the planet, with angry crowds besieging even the prime minister's mansion in Sapprus, shouting and chanting and clashing with Flescu's own security forces. Government vehicles had been torched, campaign posters and holograms vandalized. There was even wild talk of declaring war on the Klingons, even though the Cyprian military had no real warships at its disposal, a fact that Number One regarded as extremely fortunate. If all else failed, it was better that the unrest be confined to the planet, although that still left Flescu in a highly uncomfortable position, particularly with an election coming up.

"I suppose I do have a civic duty to quiet any disorder and restore calm," he said, coming around. "I have to think of what's best for Cypria."

Not to mention keeping Elzura from being used against him by his political opponents.

"Trust me, Prime Minister," Number One assured him. "This is our best chance to achieve a peaceful resolution to all our problems."

"I hope you're right," Flescu said, after mulling it over for a moment. "And it's not like I have any better ideas. We have to try something . . . or my career is mulched."

Number took that as a yes. "Is everything prepared on your end?"

"The media have been informed to expect a statement regarding Elzura and are standing by to broadcast. Give me a few moments to introduce Madam Mursh."

"Understood." She muted the audio to check on Rosha. "Are you also ready to proceed?"

"I think so," the Cyprian said hesitantly. She

caught herself wringing her hands and placed them quietly on her lap below the table. She took a deep breath to steady her nerves. "Let us get on with this."

Number One inspected the older woman. She could only imagine how hard the last few days had been on her. At least Soleste and Junah were both said to be recovering from their respective injuries, although Junah was presently confined to the brig, locked up in the same cell his sister had recently occupied. Given his alleged attack on Spock, this seemed a prudent course of action. Stunning a Starfleet officer with his own laser pistol pretty much guaranteed a one-way ticket to the brig.

Maybe Junah should have been raised as Klingon too, she thought. *Sounds like he'd fit right in.*

A blinking light on the console indicated that she was linked into the ship's main communications array, so that she could control the transmission directly from her seat in the briefing room. She listened closely as Flescu wrapped up his opening remarks.

"—*ultimately, this distressing affair is first and foremost about family, so it is only fitting and proper that we hear from the one most intimately affected by recent events, Elzura's own loving mother*—"

Number One signaled Rosha and routed the signal to the planet's waiting media.

You're on, she mouthed silently.

Rosha's face appeared on the viewer, just as, in theory, it was appearing on screens and billboards all over Cypria III. Number One imagined it looming over the mob crowding the plaza outside Envoy House and before the irate citizens surrounding the prime minister's mansion. She muted the audio from her own screen to avoid an echo effect in the briefing room as Rosha bravely addressed her entire planet.

"My name is Rosha Mursh. Most of you already know who I am, thanks to your constant support for my family during this difficult time. Speaking on behalf of my entire family, we will be forever grateful for your thoughts, prayers, and concern. That all of Cypria has rallied to try to help us bring Elzura home is deeply moving and proves beyond a doubt what I have always known, that we are a deeply caring and generous people."

So far, so good, Number One thought, impressed by Rosha's quiet dignity and presence. *Here's where it gets tricky.*

"I know that many of you have come to think of Elzura as family, as a daughter of all of Cypria, and that you are understandably disappointed and angry that she will not be returning to our beautiful world after all. Certainly, no one was looking forward to that long-awaited homecoming more than my family and I. We have spent many long, painful years waiting and hoping and praying to be reunited with our lost little Elzy at long last . . . which is why it is so very hard to tell you all that, despite our most fervent wishes, that precious little girl is gone forever."

On cue, Number One inserted a microtape into the console. Her finger hovered above a blinking button.

"You have all seen the holos of our dear little Elzy, the beautiful child who has captured all our hearts, but what you have *not* seen is this . . ."

Number One pressed the button. Shocking images and audio, downloaded from the holographic recorder in Soleste's prosthetic eye, replaced Rosha on the screen as they were broadcast to every corner of the planet.

Merata, in unbridled Klingon ferocity, snarled like a feral beast, all wild eyes, ridged brow, and pointed teeth. Number One understood that this recording came from Merata's aborted escape attempt in sickbay. She dialed up the volume so that Merata's savage fury came across even more emphatically. Looking far more Klingon than Cyprian, the intimidating young warrior bared her teeth and glared murderously from the screen.

"*My name is Merata!*" she roared. "*A daughter of the Empire—and I care nothing for your pitiful world.*"

Number One cut off the recording, returning

the screen to Rosha, who dabbed her eyes before continuing.

"That was hard to watch, I know. I didn't want to believe it either. I fooled myself into thinking that there was still some trace of our Elzura inside the bloodthirsty monster you just saw, that perhaps there could still be a place for her on Cypria . . . until I watched her nearly beat my son to death with her bare hands."

Number One pressed another button and an image of Junah Mursh, his face battered and bruised, took over the screen. Blackened eyes, a busted nose, broken teeth, and split lips testified to the severity of Merata's attack. She held the ugly image on screen for a count of five before switching back to Rosha once more.

"If not for the heroic response of Captain Pike and his brave crew, my son and elder daughter and I might not have survived the bestial wrath of . . . that Klingon who calls herself Merata." Rosha choked back a sob. "That's when I was forced to recognize the dreadful truth, that Elzura—our little Elzy— truly died ten years ago, in every way that matters. What remains is *not* my daughter, *not* Cyprian, and *not* anyone who can ever live among us peacefully. *Merata* is Klingon, and she belongs with Klingons, where we can only hope that she will live out her life as she sees fit, in a way she never could on Cypria."

Well said, Number One thought, finding herself touched by the woman's obvious emotion and sincerity. She briefly considered replaying the sickbay recording, just to drive home what Rosha was saying, but decided that was unnecessary. Chances were, the Cyprian media would be replaying the damning images for days and nights to come. With any luck, the fearsome Merata would displace Little Elzy in the public's consciousness, making it easier for them to let go of the latter.

At least that was the aim.

"Elzura is lost to us," Rosha said, "and always has been. All we can do now is mourn her loss and comfort each other, treasuring the loved ones who are still with us, as we sadly move on with our lives. And we must not hold this tragic inevitability against the selfless crew of the Federation ship *Enterprise*, who has shown nothing but kindness and compassion to my family. We cannot blame them for seeing the truth about Merata before our own hearts could face it. They are visitors, guests to our planet, who simply found themselves in the middle of a torturous situation that was never of their making. And they need our help."

Here it comes, Number One thought. *Our last hope of beating the fever.*

"I said before that we Cyprians are a deeply caring and generous people, and I truly believe that. Let us prove that once and for all by putting aside our own sorrow to come to the aid of innocent travelers in distress." Her eyes grew wetter, but her voice did not falter. "I know that's what Elzura would have wanted."

And perhaps Merata as well, Number One wondered, *or am I being too generous there?*

"May the Seasons bless Cypria," Rosha concluded, "and all our families."

Number One shut off the transmission, surrendering the screen to the broadcasters on the planet. No longer before the eyes of her world, Rosha allowed herself to weep quietly in her seat. Number One looked away, granting the other woman privacy and time to compose herself. Rosha had done an admirable job as far as Number One was concerned. All that remained was to see if a mother's heartfelt words were enough to sway public opinion on Cypria III, and if there was still time enough to stop the fever from taking a deadly toll upon the crew—and the captain.

"Cypria to Enterprise." A chime heralded the return of Flescu to the screen. He looked perhaps a tad more optimistic than he had before. A pearly white smile tempted Number One to dial down the brightness on the screen. *"Well, that went better than I expected. It's too soon to tell, of course, but I can't imagine anyone really wants that vicious Klingon hellion coming home anymore."*

"Let us hope that is the case," Number One said,

"so we can resume discussion of the ryetalyn without further delay."

Flescu turned his attention to Rosha, who wiped her eyes as she looked up at the viewer. She appeared calm and controlled.

"*An excellent oration, Madam Mursh,*" the prime minster said. "*You missed your calling. You would make a fine politician.*"

Rosha frowned. "There is no need to be insulting, sir."

Number One repressed a smirk.

Twenty-seven

"So," Pike said weakly, "about that business with Merata . . ."

Doctor Boyce's best efforts had done little to slow the fever's relentless progress. Confined to a biobed in sickbay, while Number One attended to the bridge, the captain looked worse than Spock had ever seen him. His skin was pale and clammy in appearance, his lips dry and cracked. Discolored veins pulsed across his brow and along his throat. His eyes were sunken and bloodshot, the tiny red streaks testifying to his essential humanity. Pike's voice, usually so firm and commanding, was little more than a hoarse whisper. He shivered despite the insulated blankets and sucked on a hand respirator as he spoke, pausing between sentences to feed oxygen to his lungs.

"With all due respect, Captain, now is not the time." Spock stood stiffly at the foot of the bed, while a nurse counted out small purple tablets into a plastic cup. The life-signs monitor above the captain's head charted a precipitous decline in Pike's vitals. His blood oxygen levels were sinking, as were his pulse, metabolism, and neural activity. "You need your rest."

Pike managed to shake his head, to an almost imperceptible degree. "Indulge me."

"The facts are simple, if somewhat embarrassing." Spock felt uncomfortable lying to the captain, but, politically, it was better that the official record held that Merata escaped back to the Klingons on her own, without the assistance of any Starfleet personnel. "Following the altercation with her brother, I felt it best to transfer Merata to the brig. Unfortunately, I underestimated her resourcefulness, and she succeeded in turning the tables on me. I apologize sincerely for my carelessness in this instance."

Pike gazed thoughtfully at Spock. A hint of skepticism showed in his eyes.

"Apology accepted, Mister Spock." A knowing smile lifted the corners of Pike's cracked lips. "Everything seems to have worked out for the best. No need to beat yourself up about it. You're only human."

Spock wondered how much the captain truly suspected. "I beg to differ, sir."

A brutal coughing fit cut off whatever retort the captain might have offered. Flecks of blood stained the inner face of the respirator. He gasped into the device until he could manage to speak again.

"What's keeping the doctor?" Pike muttered. "I don't have all day."

Spock feared that might literally be the case, unless the promised cure materialized. The *Kepler* had returned to the *Enterprise* three hours ago, bearing a sizable quantity of processed ryetalyn. Spock gathered that they had Rosha Mursh to thank for the Cyprians' change of heart concerning the precious mineral. Although this was a welcome development for the crew, benefiting the ship, he could not help being taken aback by the fickleness of humanoid emotions; it was as though the Cyprian people had been gripped by a passionate, emotional hurricane that had ultimately blown over almost as fast as it had arisen. The sheer volatility of their reactions was unnerving, to say the least, and served to demonstrate why his own people had wisely chosen the path of logic instead. Emotional responses were too . . . explosive.

"Hold your horses." Boyce emerged from his lab, gripping a hypospray. "It's not like this formula was going to mix itself."

"That my cocktail, Doctor?" Pike asked. "I think you forgot the olive."

"Very funny." Boyce sounded less than amused. He glanced up at the diagnostic monitor, and the worry lines on his face deepened. His rumpled blue jumpsuit looked like it hadn't been changed in days. "Leave the comedy to me. It doesn't suit you."

Spock eyed the hypospray in Boyce's hand. "Is that the cure, Doctor?"

"I sorely hope so," he replied. "I prepared the formula along the lines suggested by the latest medical literature, tailoring it specifically to humanoids of Terran descent, but we're in uncharted waters here. It *should* work, in theory, but I have to stress that this treatment is highly experimental. At the very least, I ought to conduct further tests and run a few more computer simulations."

"No time for that, Doctor," Pike said. "Consider me your guinea pig."

Spock could not keep silent. "Captain, I must protest again. It is folly to volunteer yourself as the first test subject. You are too valuable."

"As opposed to some poor expendable ensign?" Pike's resolve showed through the illness sapping his vitality. "No, Spock. I am not about to subject any member of my crew to a risk I'm not willing to face myself." Running out of breath, he took another hit of oxygen from the respirator. Even his whispers rasped. "Think of it as one of the perks of command."

"But logically—"

"This isn't about logic, Spock. It's about responsibility . . . and trusting you and Number One to carry on if things go south."

Spock could tell that Pike's mind was made up. "Are all Starfleet captains so stubbornly illogical?"

Pike chuckled, despite his physical distress. "Stick around long enough, and you may find out."

"I am no hurry, sir, to serve under another captain."

"The future will get here regardless, Mister Spock." Pike turned his gaze toward Boyce. "And speaking of time passing . . ."

Boyce hesitated. "I'm serious, Chris. This is a pretty potent concoction. There's no telling what effect it could have on your nervous system. In your weakened state, it could kill you . . . or put you in a wheelchair for life."

"That's a chance I'm willing to take, Doctor. Get on with it."

Poisoned veins pulsed like a countdown. Pike grimaced and clutched his stomach. Severe abdominal pains, Spock recalled, were among the penultimate symptoms of the fever, preceding violent seizures and death. That the captain was evidently suffering such pains, despite the various analgesics available to Boyce, indicated a definite need for haste. There was no stage four.

"All right," Boyce conceded. Spock stepped aside to let the doctor approach his patient. "Heaven help us if this doesn't work . . ."

He pressed the hypospray against Pike's jugular. After all the tension and debate, the quiet hiss of the device felt oddly anticlimactic. Boyce stepped back to await the results of the treatment, joining Spock a short distance from the bed. Pike winced and rubbed his neck.

"Is that it?" he asked. "How soon before—"

Convulsions rocked his body as the drug took effect. Pike began to thrash atop the bed, his back arching grotesquely. His eyes rolled upward until only the whites could be seen. Swollen veins pulsed like those of a Talosian. Froth bubbled up from between his clenched jaws.

"Spock!" Boyce raced back to his patient. "Help me hold him down!"

Spock hurried to assist the doctor. Pike's flailing limbs fought him with surprising vitality, but they were no match for his Vulcan strength. Following the doctor's lead, Spock rolled Pike onto his side to keep him from choking on his own saliva. Up on the monitor, Pike's life-signs fluctuated wildly.

"Can you give him something, Doctor," Spock asked, "to halt the seizure?"

"Not without risking a dangerous drug interaction. We're taking enough chances here already." Boyce gripped Pike's jaw and tilted his head back to clear the airway. "The last thing we need is another question mark!"

Spock saw the logic in the doctor's restraint. It seemed that there was nothing to do but wait to see if Captain Pike survived the serum's considerable impact on his body. He restrained the captain until the convulsions gradually subsided and Pike's thrashing limbs quieted. The captain's eyes closed and he sank limply back against the bed. Spock could not immediately determine if this was a positive sign or not.

Had the cure proved worse than the disease?

Along with the doctor, he gazed up at the monitor. To his slight surprise, Pike's vital signs, although weak, had stabilized. Spock's keen ears heard Pike breathing softly.

"Well, I'll be damned," Boyce said.

He ran a handheld medical scanner up and down the length of Pike's unconscious body, then examined the readings. "The drug appears to be fighting the infection. The inflammation is going down, and his immune system is responding positively. Respiratory and cardiovascular indicators are looking better too." He placed his palm across Pike's forehead; this struck Spock as a distinctly primitive way to measure a patient's temperature, but Boyce seemed pleased by the results. "His fever is ebbing."

"Then it's working, Doctor?" Spock asked. Boyce's previous statements had definitely indicated as much, but Spock felt a need to hear him say it. It was irrational, but undeniable.

"You bet your pointed ears it is!" Boyce turned exuberantly toward the nurse. "Start producing this serum in mass quantities. We're going to need all we can get."

She ran briskly toward the lab. "Yes, Doctor!"

A great deal of tension seemed to evaporate from Boyce's weary body. He dropped heavily into a nearby chair and sighed in relief. Clearly, his concerns about the serum had run deep. Spock sympathized; he too had experienced an uncomfortable degree of apprehension, which was now abating.

"I don't know about you, Mister Spock, but I could use a stiff drink." Boyce slumped against the back of the chair. "Don't suppose I could interest you in a dry martini?"

"Thank you, Doctor, but I will abstain."

"Suit yourself." He smiled wryly at Spock. "Guess you're not getting bumped up to first officer today."

Spock realized that he needed to alert Number One of the positive outcome of the test. He began to make his way out of sickbay.

"That is satisfactory to me, Doctor. As I informed the captain earlier, I am in no hurry."

The bridge awaited him.

"The captain regrets that he cannot be here in person to bid you farewell," Spock said. "Along with much of the crew, he is still recovering from his recent illness."

Rosha and Soleste Mursh were on the hangar deck, waiting for the *Kepler* to transport them and Junah back to Cypria III. As *Climber One* had been lost to the Klingons, who were unlikely to return it, the Starfleet shuttlecraft had been drafted for the task. Junah was already aboard the shuttle, under restraint, which was fine with Spock, who did not miss his presence. Although Spock understood, on an intellectual level, that the hostile Cyprian youth had been under extraordinary pressures in his own right, Junah had hardly coped with those stresses well; one could only hope that time and maturity would grant him greater control over his turbulent emotions.

In the meantime, Spock was content to deal with Rosha and Soleste instead.

"Tell the captain we understand," Rosha said. "I trust that he and the others are doing well?"

"Doctor Boyce assures me that the afflicted crew members are expected to make a full recovery, for which we have you and your fellow Cyprians to thank." His voice grew more somber as he acknowledged Rosha's trials and disappointments. "I am sorry that your own visit to the *Enterprise* did not bring you the outcome you hoped for. My condolences on losing your daughter a second time."

"Thank you, Mister Spock," Rosha said, sighing. "At least I know now that she is alive and healthy and has found a new home elsewhere in the galaxy. It's not the life I would have chosen for her, but I suspect that I'm not the only parent whose child took a different path than the one you planned for them."

Spock thought of his own father, who had yet to forgive Spock for choosing Starfleet over the Vulcan Science Academy. "In that respect, I believe you are correct."

Rosha gazed fondly at Soleste, who was letting her mother assist her to the shuttle. Doctor Boyce had wanted Soleste to avail herself of a motorized wheelchair while she was still recovering from her injuries, but Soleste had insisted on leaving sickbay on her own two feet. She leaned against her mother for support.

"At least I have one daughter back," Rosha said. "For good, I hope."

"You don't have to worry about me anymore." Soleste squeezed her mother's hand. "My tracking days are over." A rueful expression came over her face, as though she was contemplating all the years she had wasted searching for her lost little sister. "It's hard to let go, I can't deny that, but Elzura—I mean, Merata—is where she wants to be. I guess I'll just have to learn to live with that."

"And live for yourself," her mother counseled. "At last."

Spock wished them well.

Twenty-eight

"Can I help you, Mister Spock?"

Pike sat at his desk in his private quarters, reviewing a stack of reports and requisitions. Cypria III was now days behind them, and Doctor Boyce had grudgingly cleared the captain to return to work, provided he eased back into his duties gradually and did not overexert himself. Spock suspected that Pike and the doctor had very different definitions of "gradually."

"I wished to get back to you, sir, regarding that opening on the *Intrepid*."

Pike looked up from his paperwork. "And what have you decided, Lieutenant?"

"While the prospect of joining an all-Vulcan crew does indeed offer certain advantages, I believe that the *Enterprise* is where I can best serve Starfleet as well as further my own career. This ship is, in its diversity, a more intellectually stimulating environment than the *Intrepid* and, I like to think, in greater need of a qualified Vulcan science officer."

If he had truly desired to live among Vulcans,

Spock reflected, he would have stayed on Vulcan. *Like Merata, I too must choose my own destiny—and right now the* Enterprise *is where I belong.*

"All right," Pike said. "If that's your decision." He looked as though he approved. "Even though it means putting up with a shipload of embarrassingly emotional humans?"

"I believe I can manage, sir."

Acknowledgments

Like many fans, I first encountered Captain Christopher Pike in the two-part *Star Trek* episode "The Menagerie," featuring flashback footage of Pike's grueling visit to Talos IV. I'm not sure when I became aware of the fact that the Pike scenes were lifted from the original *Star Trek* television pilot, "The Cage," but it was many years before I finally got to see that original adventure in its entirety.

With the fiftieth anniversary of *The Original Series* coming around, it seemed high time to revisit Pike and his crew, including the young Lieutenant Spock, although I'm hardly the first *Trek* writer to do so. In preparation for this book, I devoured as many Pike-era novels and comic books as I could get my hands on, including memorable stories by such authors as D. C. Fontana, Peter David, Michael Jan Friedman, Margaret Wander Bonanno, Jerry Oltion, David Stern, Dan Abnett, Ian Edginton, and others. Needless to say, this wasn't exactly a hardship, and I borrowed shamelessly from those earlier works as needed. (Thanks in particular to Fontana, for inventing Chief Engineer Caitlin Barry, whom I got a lot of mileage out of.)

Every *Star Trek* novel is a team mission, so I want to thank my editors, Margaret Clark and Ed Schlesinger, for encouraging me to visit Pike's *Enterprise,* and the good folks at CBS for giving me the green light to proceed. Thanks also to my agent, Russ Galen, for closing the deal as he has so many times before.

Finally, as ever, I have to thank my girlfriend, Karen, and our four-footed housemates, Sophie and Lyla, for keeping the house warm even though it's snowing outside as I type this.

About the Author

Greg Cox is the *New York Times* bestselling author of numerous *Star Trek* novels and stories, including *Foul Deeds Will Rise*, *No Time Like the Past*, *The Weight of Worlds*, *The Rings of Time*, *To Reign in Hell*, *The Eugenics Wars* (*Volumes One* and *Two*), *The Q Continuum*, *Assignment: Eternity*, and *The Black Shore*. He has also written the official movie novelizations of *Godzilla*, *Man of Steel*, *The Dark Knight Rises*, *Ghost Rider*, *Daredevil*, *Death Defying Acts*, and the first three *Underworld* movies, as well as books and stories based on such popular series as *Alias*, *Buffy the Vampire Slayer*, *CSI: Crime Scene Investigation*, *Farscape*, *The 4400*, *Leverage*, *Riese: Kingdom Falling*, *Roswell*, *Terminator*, *Warehouse 13*, and *Xena: Warrior Princess*.

He has received three Scribe Awards from the International Association of Media Tie-In Writers and lives in Oxford, Pennsylvania.

Visit him at www.gregcox-author.com.